I0819015

ROBERT B. PARKER'S

BOOKED

The Sunny Randall Novels

Robert B. Parker's Booked
(by Alison Gaylin)

Robert B. Parker's Buzz Kill
(by Alison Gaylin)

Robert B. Parker's Bad Influence
(by Alison Gaylin)

Robert B. Parker's Revenge Tour
(by Mike Lupica)

Robert B. Parker's Payback
(by Mike Lupica)

Robert B. Parker's Grudge Match
(by Mike Lupica)

Robert B. Parker's Blood Feud
(by Mike Lupica)

Spare Change

Blue Screen

Melancholy Baby

Shrink Rap

Perish Twice

Family Honor

For a comprehensive title list and a preview of upcoming books, visit PRH.com/RobertBParker or Facebook.com/RobertBParkerAuthor.

ROBERT B. PARKER'S

BOOKED

A SUNNY RANDALL NOVEL

ALISON GAYLIN

G. P. PUTNAM'S SONS
New York

PUTNAM
— EST. 1838 —

G. P. Putnam's Sons
Publishers Since 1838
An imprint of Penguin Random House LLC
1745 Broadway, New York, NY 10019
penguinrandomhouse.com

LIBRARY OF CONGRESS CATALOGING-IN-PUBLICATION DATA

Names: Gaylin, Alison, author.
Title: Robert B. Parker's Booked / Alison Gaylin.
Other titles: Booked
Description: New York : G. P. Putnam's Sons, 2026. |
Series: A Sunny Randall novel; 13
Identifiers: LCCN 2025040825 (print) | LCCN 2025040826 (ebook) |
ISBN 9780593854402 (hardcover) | ISBN 9780593854426 (ebook)
Subjects: LCGFT: Fiction. | Detective and mystery fiction. | Novels.
Classification: LCC PS3607.A9858 R6325 2025 (print) |
LCC PS3607.A9858 (ebook)
LC record available at https://lccn.loc.gov/2025040825
LC ebook record available at https://lccn.loc.gov/2025040826

Printed in the United States of America
1st Printing

The authorized representative in the EU for product safety and compliance is Penguin Random House Ireland, Morrison Chambers, 32 Nassau Street, Dublin D02 YH68, Ireland, https://eu-contact.penguin.ie.

ROBERT B. PARKER'S

BOOKED

I've given my memoirs far more thought than any of my marriages.

—GLORIA SWANSON

ONE

I know what you're going to ask me," Spike said. "And the answer is yes."

We were at his restaurant, Spike's. We were sitting at our favorite table on a steamy July afternoon, enjoying the air-conditioning and each other's company. It was our first weekday lunch together in months.

Our food had just arrived—small Caesar salad for me, a massive portion of spaghetti Bolognese for my best friend. Emphasis on *massive.* Maybe it was the fact that I hadn't dined with him much over the winter and spring—I'd been spending most of the time at Richie's place on the Jersey Shore—but when the server brought his plate, I did a double take. A carb assault like that in the middle of the day would have put me right to sleep. But who was I to judge? Even at our (slowly, mind you) advancing age, Spike could still bench-press any member of his staff. That included his chef, Jorgen, a seven-foot-tall mountain of a man who probably weighed as much as my car. I'd seen Spike do it at the restaurant's Christmas party. Jorgen had dared him. The big guy had been as shocked as anyone when he'd gone airborne.

"What am I going to ask you?" I said.

"No need to be coy," Spike said.

"I have no idea what you're talking about."

Spike put down his fork and sighed heavily. "Yes, Sunny. I'll be your best man."

I nearly choked on my salad.

"What?" Spike said. "We both know I'm too butch for maid of honor."

I gulped some water and took a breath. "Spike," I said, "I'm not planning a wedding."

"Why not?" he said.

"I'm engaged to be engaged," I said. "End of story."

"You got engaged to be engaged on New Year's Eve. It's July now."

"Wow," I said. "Who needs a calendar when I've got you?"

Spike went to work on his spaghetti, cutting it into bite-sized morsels. He was a spaghetti cutter, not a twirler, which struck me as odd for a restauranteur/gourmand—or, for that matter, a grown-up. It was nothing new. He'd always eaten his spaghetti like a ten-year-old. But all this time apart, I supposed, had made me start observing things more closely. Not just Spike and the way he consumed pasta, but my other friends, my hometown, my parents, who somehow seemed to have aged more in my absence than they had in the past ten years. I loved them all. I'd missed them all. So had my miniature bull terrier, Rosie, who was curled up on the curved banquette between Spike and me, munching a crust of bread Spike had slipped her, while staring up at him with such blatant adoration, it made me a little jealous.

"I'm assuming this delay is about you, not Richie," Spike said.

"Why would you assume that?"

"You're big on delays," he said. "Richie isn't."

"Astute," I said.

"I try."

Spike took a bite of his chopped-up pasta. He broke off another piece of bread and passed it down to Rosie. She barked appreciatively. The two older women at the next table gaped at us, as though they'd never heard a dog barking in a restaurant before. "Move along," I told them. "Nothing to see here."

One of them clicked her tongue at me. I can't stand it when people click their tongues at me. I thought of several wiseass remarks, but refrained from saying any of them. Who said I hadn't matured?

Instead, I addressed Spike. "No more treats after this. Rosie's watching her figure."

Rosie devoured the piece of bread and rested her chin on Spike's knee. If she were a cat, she would have purred. Not for the first time, I envied my dog—her ability to find contentment in the simplest of things.

The truth was, Spike was right. The delay in wedding planning was about me. But it wasn't for the reasons he was probably imagining. It had nothing to do with my feelings for Richie. Throughout the winter, he and I had been more in sync than we'd ever been, even at the happiest points of our marriage. It wasn't because of my job, which I'd been able to handle quite well from my rented office space in Asbury Park, with my assistant, Blake James, holding down the fort in Boston most of the time. It wasn't even my two biggest fears, change and commitment. I'd made peace with both of those monsters back on January 1, when I'd accepted the key to Richie's apartment.

Something else was holding me back. Something that I hadn't put into words until now.

"Peak Season," I said.

"Pardon?"

I shoved a forkful of salad into my mouth. I could feel Rosie shifting under the table, her chin moving from Spike's knee to mine—an emotional support animal if there ever was one. I slipped her a crouton. It was the least I could do.

"Peak Season down the Shore," I said. "That's what's keeping me from planning a wedding."

"Because . . ."

"Because I hate it."

Spike put down his glass of iced tea.

"*Hate* might be a strong word," I said. "But it's a different place during the summer."

He nodded. "Go on," he said. Like a psychiatrist.

"I mean, there are so many people," I said. "It's noisy. You can't get a dinner reservation . . ."

"To be fair, you could say the same things about Boston all year round."

"Yeah, but it doesn't stink of coconut oil."

Spike nodded again. "Good point."

"Thank you."

"On the other hand—"

"Always with the other hand."

"You aren't marrying the Jersey Shore. You're marrying Richie."

I looked at Spike. He was right. I could imagine my therapist, Susan Silverman, using his exact words, if I'd ever been able to broach the topic during one of our sessions. But the thing was, it wasn't just my own aversion to the Jersey Shore during Peak Season that was making me leery of taking the proverbial Next Big Step. It was that Richie loved the Jersey Shore during Peak Season. He adored the bustle of the restaurant/bar he managed, Candy's Room. He didn't mind waiting in line for movies or coffee, because it meant business was booming—not just at The Room, as the locals called it, but everywhere. He stopped and tipped even the least talented buskers on the boardwalk and he was unbothered by the beach traffic, and even though I hadn't asked him about it, he probably loved the smell of coconut oil, too. And while all of that combined wasn't even close to a red flag, it did give me pause. Maybe Richie and I were more fundamentally unalike than I'd thought. Or maybe we were just at different places in our lives.

"I just want to make sure that this time around, it sticks," I said.

"Is Richie coming to Boston anytime soon?"

"I asked him to come tonight," I said.

"That's soon."

"Yeah, well. My parents invited us to dinner," I said. "He has to make sure he's got coverage at The Room, because they've got a band playing, and it's going to be busy, busy, busy." I sighed. "As per fucking usual."

"Wait. Parents? In the plural?"

"Yep. Elizabeth is coming, too."

"Hmm."

"I hope he can make it," I said. "I don't want to deal with my mother and sister alone."

Spike took another bite of his pasta. "Sauce needs more basil. Gotta talk to Jorgen."

"Spike?" I said.

"Yeah?"

"Does Flynn like anything that you find . . . ah . . . hard to take?"

He shrugged. "Well, yeah," Spike said. "He's British."

"But you're still with him."

"Sure I am."

"You might marry him someday."

"Hey, let's not get ahead of ourselves. I've only known the guy for a few months."

I laughed.

"What's funny?" he asked.

"It's been a year," I said.

Spike raised an eyebrow at me. "Wow," he said. "Who needs calendars?"

I smiled. Spike smiled back. Rosie put a paw on my knee, and I felt the way I always did when I was with the two of them—like everything was going to be all right. "Maybe I just need to get used to the smell of coconut oil," I said.

"Yep."

"And if not, there's no reason why Richie and I can't remarry and maintain two residences."

"That's right," Spike said. "Just do me a favor. Let me know as soon as you get officially engaged."

"Why?"

"Takes a long time to have a tux made properly," he said. "When you're a man of my proportions."

I grinned. "Deal."

As soon as I went back to my salad, my phone rang. Blake's name was on my screen. "What now?" I whispered. It had been an especially busy morning, with two client meetings, plus a very lengthy Zoom call with a potential client, a Beacon Hill attorney who loved to phrase and rephrase questions, as though I were a hostile witness. Reluctantly, I answered the phone.

"Sunny?" Blake's voice had a strange tone to it. Like someone was holding a gun to his head.

"Is everything all right?" I asked.

"I don't know," he said.

"What do you mean?"

"A lady came in to see you about ten minutes ago," he said. "I told her you were out and couldn't be disturbed, but she wouldn't listen and . . . I don't know . . . She was pretty unhinged and I . . . I may have said something about Spike's."

I was about to ask Blake if this unhinged lady had told him her name, when an audiobook-ready voice bellowed, *"Sunny."* I realized I didn't need to.

"She's here," I told Blake.

"Oh, man," he said. "That was fast. I'm sorry."

"It's okay. I know her."

She was making a beeline for our table. I said goodbye to Blake and ended the call so I could give my complete attention to the woman who demanded it.

Melanie Joan Hall. Bestselling author. Longtime friend of mine. World-class diva. She wore a black linen pantsuit, a broad-brimmed black hat, enormous Prada sunglasses, and the general attitude of an incoming missile.

Spike stood up and gave her a smile. "Melanie Jo—"

"Don't say my name." She leaned in close. "I need to talk with you both. In private."

TWO

Melanie Joan asked Spike if there was a computer in his office. He said yes. She said, "Take me there. Now."

Spike did as he was told.

One of the dog-averse women at the next table said, "Excuse me, are you Melanie Joan Hall?"

"You're my favorite author," said the other.

Melanie Joan ignored them. This was shocking to me. I'd known her for more than a decade, and no matter how distracted or busy or in danger she was, Melanie Joan Hall always made time for her fans. Not now, though, apparently. Without so much as a glance at the women, she followed Spike, her shoulders squared, Louboutins clacking. "Come along, Sunny."

I barely had time to attach Rosie's leash.

Once we were in Spike's office with the door closed and locked, Melanie Joan took off her hat, but not her sunglasses. She collapsed onto his leather desk chair. "I'm doomed," she said.

"How so?" I said.

She emitted a sound—a bloodcurdling mash-up of sigh, groan, and scream.

Rosie growled. I picked her up and shushed her.

"*Doomed* is a serious word," Spike said.

She made the sound again. I held Rosie close. Spike and I stood there, on the other side of his desk, waiting for her to elaborate.

Yes, Melanie Joan Hall was a drama queen—a condition that had become a good deal worse as she'd grown older and more catered to. But when the woman said she was doomed, I knew enough to take her seriously. Our paths had first crossed when she hired me to protect her from her ex-husband, John Melvin, a psychiatrist who made Hannibal Lecter look like Dr. Ruth. More recently, she'd retained my services to track down yet another stalker, whose threats to derail her career and her life made both of us yearn for Melvin.

"What's wrong, MJ?" Spike said.

Just as I was about to call 911, Melanie Joan snapped out of her paralysis. "This," she said.

She turned on Spike's computer and clicked away at the

keyboard. When she found what she was searching for, she made that awful sound yet again.

Rosie squirmed in my arms. Spike kept a dog bed in the corner of his office, just for her. I put Rosie down on the floor and she scurried over to it, hopped inside, and curled up like a giant pill bug. I couldn't say that I blamed her.

"Look at this," Melanie Joan said. "Just *look at it.*"

Spike and I moved around his desk and focused our attention on the screen.

"Hmmph," Spike said.

It was a one-star reader review of Melanie Joan's upcoming book, *Stronger Alone.* I skimmed it. I'd seen a lot of press about the book, which was set to come out in late fall—her very first memoir. In an interview with *The Globe*, Melanie Joan had described it as *the most difficult and important project I've ever undertaken.* But the reviewer had used language that was, shall we say, not as flattering.

I looked at Melanie Joan. This was what she'd interrupted my lunch over? A one-star review by some rando on a site called . . . I looked at the name again. "What is ReadAnon?"

Melanie Joan let out a massive sigh. "ReadAnon is the most important website in the publishing business."

I glanced at Spike.

"It's a book review site, like Goodreads, only it's all anonymous," Spike said. "Think 4chan, but for people who are able to read."

"How do you know about this?" I asked. "You hate the Internet almost as much as I do."

"Flynn loves ReadAnon," Spike said. "He can post cookbook reviews and be as honest as he wants without anyone coming for him on his Instagram."

"What's his screen name?"

"If I told you, he'd have to kill me," Spike said.

I chuckled.

"Excuse me," Melanie Joan said.

I turned to her. "Okay, look," I said. "I'm sorry you got a bad review, Melanie Joan. But come on. You're a successful author. Doesn't that kind of thing come with the territory?"

"This is different," she said.

"How?" Spike said.

Melanie Joan took off her sunglasses. Her eyes were puffy and bloodshot, dark circles visible beneath layers of concealer. I'd never seen her look this unphotogenic. "Book Babe has more followers than anyone on ReadAnon," Melanie Joan said. "That's power. Real power."

"You're tougher than this, MJ," Spike said. "It's just a review."

"A horrible review," she said. "Did you read it?"

"People are assholes," I said. "Especially when they can be anonymous about it."

"Did you *read* the *review*, though? It doesn't just trash my writing. God knows I'm used to that. It trashes *me*, Sunny. It brutalizes Melanie Joan Hall, the human being. It took a lot of courage for me to write a memoir. You put something personal out there, you expect a little common decency from someone who calls themselves a critic, but *no* . . ." She went on for a while. A long while. I waited for her to take a breath.

"Pardon my ignorance, Melanie Joan," I said. "But what does all of this have to do with Spike and me?"

She stood up and took one of my hands in both of hers. Her grip was viselike. "I need you to track down the person behind the Book Babe account," she said.

I blinked at her.

"I have to talk to her. Him. Whatever. I must get Book Babe to listen to reason. Say something nice about me. Or my life as an author will be over. I won't be able to show my face anywhere."

At long last, she let my hand go. She grasped her knees, deep-breathing as though she'd just finished a marathon. I stared at her. A million thoughts ran through my mind, the top one being *My God, she's finally lost it.* "Melanie Joan," I said, as gently as I could. "Don't you think you might be overreacting?"

"You don't understand," she said.

"Sure I do," I said.

"You don't," she said. "You're a Luddite. Your dog has a more active social media presence than you."

I was starting to get annoyed. "Look, your book isn't coming out for months. People have short attention spans. One bad ReadAnon review can't tank your entire career, no matter how important you think this Book Babe person is."

"You don't get it at all," Melanie Joan said.

"Maybe not," I said. "But there are things I do get, and

they're called the right to privacy and freedom of speech. I'm not going to dox a private citizen for you, just because they've typed some mean things about your book."

Melanie Joan looked at Spike imploringly.

"Sorry, MJ, but I agree with Sunny," Spike said.

She started to make the sound again. I asked her to stop. She did. It was a small victory.

"If you don't dox Book Babe," Melanie Joan said, "my career is over."

"Oh, come on."

"I'm telling you the truth. Bookstores are already canceling their orders."

"Seriously?" Spike said.

"*Why?*" I said. "It makes no sense."

Melanie Joan put her sunglasses back on and collapsed onto Spike's chair again. Spike and I sat down on the couch against the wall and waited for her to answer. For several seconds, the room was silent, save the gentle sound of Rosie's snoring.

"I did something stupid, you guys," Melanie Joan said finally. "Really, really stupid."

THREE

Melanie Joan was correct. She had done something really, really stupid. After reading Book Babe's scathing review the previous night, she'd downed a few glasses of wine to numb the hurt. Then she'd tossed back a few more. Then she'd hit the tequila bottle. All told, Melanie Joan—a rather petite woman—had consumed enough alcohol to make Jorgen flunk a Breathalyzer test.

But that wasn't the stupid part.

Once she'd fortified herself with all that booze, Melanie Joan had returned to her computer. She'd given Book Babe's review one more perusal. And at that very low point, she'd posted a comment.

"What was the comment?" Spike said.

"Get fucked, you worthless piece of shit."

Spike's eyes widened. "Pardon?"

"That was it," she said. "That was the comment."

"Oh," Spike said.

"I also told Book Babe to do the world a favor and drink bleach," she said.

"Oh," I said.

"And eat a bag of dicks."

"Oh," Spike said.

"Anything else you suggested they ingest?" I asked.

"No," she said.

"Well, that's something."

Melanie Joan leaned back in Spike's chair. She took off her sunglasses and rubbed her eyes. She looked different, somehow. Smaller.

When I'd first met her, she told me that she thought of herself as two different people, Melanie Joan the famous scribe and Joanie. Joanie was the name she'd gone by as a young girl, before she published her first blockbuster romance novel, *A Girl and Not a God*. Joanie was quiet and bookish and a little insecure. As the years had gone by, I'd seen Joanie less and less. It seemed that as a result of all the trauma she'd endured, her survival instincts had kicked in and her true self had been subsumed by the glamorous, thick-skinned celeb. Now, though, it felt as if Joanie was reemerging.

"It was the dumbest thing I've ever done," she said. "And you know, Sunny, I've done some really dumb things."

I moved next to her. I leaned over the computer and scrolled through Book Babe's many comments. **Thanks for warning me off**

this one, one commenter said. **This doorstop is going into my "never to be read" pile,** quipped another. **I've always thought Melanie Joan Hall was a privileged bitch,** said another. **Thanks for confirming my suspicions.** I was starting to get why Melanie Joan was so upset about this review. But I didn't see her own comment. I told her so.

"I got rid of it," she said. "About a minute after I posted."

"Whew," I said.

"You guys don't understand," she said. "I don't even understand it. I guess I'd forgotten what happens to my brain chemistry when I mix alcohol with my water pill."

"What do you mean?" I said.

"I mean that I remember posting that comment. I remember deleting it. And then, at some point, I fell asleep in front of the computer."

"Well, thank God you deleted it," I said.

"That's right," said Spike. "No harm, no foul."

Melanie Joan shook her head. "Plenty of harm," she said quietly. "And completely foul."

As quick as she was to delete the comment, she hadn't been fast enough. When she woke up in her home office the following morning, Melanie Joan discovered that someone had screen-grabbed it, she said, and posted it all over social media.

"It'll be okay," Spike said.

"No, it won't," Melanie Joan said.

"So the classy romance lady used a few curse words." I gave her a little punch on the arm. "Your fans aren't going to abandon you for that."

"She's right," Spike said. "Lay low for a few days, everyone will have forgotten about it."

"No, no, no," Melanie Joan said.

"What's wrong?" I said. "What are we not getting?"

She twisted one of her rings around, a large, impressive emerald. "There was a lot more to the comment than I remembered writing," she said.

Spike looked at her. "What do you mean by 'a lot more'?"

She cleared her throat. "I . . . apparently shared some observations about Book Babe's sex life."

"You slut-shamed her?" Spike said.

"To the extreme," Melanie Joan said. "This is stuff I could never imagine *thinking*, let alone typing."

"Did you use the c-word?" I said.

"Repeatedly," she said.

"Oh," I said.

"As both an epithet and a body part," she said.

"Oh," Spike said.

"I never use that word. I've never . . . put together sentences like those. I don't know what's happened to me."

"I'm sorry, Melanie Joan," I said.

"I'm getting trashed by all the reader accounts on TikTok. My name is mud on both X and Bluesky. It's something both sides can agree on. I'm . . . I'm canceled."

"There must be something you can do," I said.

"I posted an apology," she said. "But the responses were so . . . well, it obviously didn't do any good, so I took it down."

"Have you talked to your editor?"

Melanie Joan cringed visibly. "He wants to meet with me today. In his office," she said. "Do you know the last time my editor asked to meet with me anywhere that wasn't a Michelin-star restaurant, with him footing the bill?"

I winced. "I'm sorry."

"Don't be," she said. "I brought this on myself."

Melanie Joan stood up. "You're right, Sunny. I'm asking too much of you," she said. "If I'm canceled, I'm canceled." She put on her hat and started toward the door. Rosie woke up, skittered toward her, and nuzzled her leg. Melanie Joan knelt down. She patted Rosie on the head. "I do wish human beings were as forgiving as dogs."

I'm not going to lie. It pained me.

I tried to imagine Melanie Joan Hall without the cheering audiences at her appearances, without the book-signing lines that went on for blocks. I tried to picture her without her fans. It was surprisingly sad—like imagining someone losing her life partner, her children, her best friend. After all the disastrous relationships she'd endured, Melanie Joan's readers were her one constant—and as far as I could tell, her only real source of love.

Melanie Joan opened Spike's office door and closed it softly behind her. I could feel a knot in my stomach. *Melanie Joan Hall, without her fans.* Spike and I looked at each other.

"Better hurry if you're going to catch her," he said. "You know how fast that woman moves."

FOUR

I caught up with Melanie Joan half a block away from Spike's. She was just about to get into a Mercedes limo. I knew her driver, Charles. I asked him to wait. She told him not to listen to me. "She pities me, Charles," Melanie Joan said. "Can you imagine? *Moi.* MJH. A charity case."

She slid into the backseat and closed the door. She opened the window, though. That gave me hope. I pleaded with Charles not to start it up. "You know what I charge, Melanie Joan," I said. "No one in their right mind would call that charity."

After a little back-and-forth and a lot of cajoling on my part, she agreed to let me work for her. I wondered if that hadn't been her aim all along—getting me to beg for the job I'd just turned down. If so, chalk one up to Melanie Joan Hall and her gold-medal-worthy manipulation skills.

She exited the limo. Together, we walked back into the restaurant, around the perimeter of the bar, and into Spike's office, where he was sitting at his desk, hands folded, waiting for us.

She took off her hat and glasses and collapsed onto Spike's couch. I sat next to her. Rosie hopped up and settled in between us. She rested her chin on Melanie Joan's knee. In a less fragile state, Melanie Joan might have complained about dog hair on her St. John slacks. (I recognized them. Spring collection.) But now she gave Rosie a sad smile and patted her head.

We hammered out the specifics of this particular hire. As I'd already hinted, money wasn't an issue. Melanie Joan always paid above and beyond what I charged. The thing that concerned me was what might happen if I were to successfully unearth this anonymous critic. I asked her what she was planning to do with the information.

"I just want to appeal to Book Babe's sense of decency," she said.

"How do you figure you'll do that?" I said.

"You're asking . . . what? Am I going to bribe Book Babe? Or threaten her?"

"Do you plan on breaking the law?"

"Come on, Sunny. You know me."

"Yes," I said. "Yes, I do."

She gave me wide eyes. I said nothing. She turned to Spike. "Can you believe this?"

"It's a fair question," he said.

"I don't know whether to be outraged or hurt or terribly

disappointed in you both," she said. Tears sprung into her eyes. Spike handed her a Kleenex. She spent some time deep-breathing. Composing herself. Emotional as she was, Melanie Joan made it a rule not to cry. She was doing everything she could not to break that rule.

After what felt like about an hour, she was able to speak. "Do you think you can find this person quickly, Sunny?"

"I don't know," I said.

Melanie Joan explained that if I was unable to identify Book Babe within the next day or so, there wasn't much point in going further. "When you're talking about the situation I'm in, which is snowballing on the Internet as we speak," she said, "even a few hours is a long time."

"I'll try my best," I said.

"That's all I can ask for," she said. She put her hat and sunglasses back on. She stood up. So did Spike and I.

Melanie Joan gave us both quick, tight hugs. Then she smoothed her jacket and straightened her spine, like a soldier, readying for battle.

"You haven't let me down yet, Sunny," she said.

After Melanie Joan left, Spike and I watched the door for a while, as though we both expected her to come bursting back in.

"She's right about the time frame," he said. "A friend of Flynn's had a few too many sakes one night and went online, just like Melanie Joan. He got into it with a commenter. Went to bed. By morning, there were death threats in his DMs. By afternoon, he'd lost twenty thousand followers."

"Wow."

"Right?"

"What was the fight about? Politics?"

"Nope," he said.

"What, then?"

"Broccoli rabe."

"Seriously?"

Spike shrugged. "People online love getting pissed off," he said. "Politics, vegetables . . . Doesn't matter. It all comes down to the adrenaline rush."

"Like a bar brawl," I said. "Only with keyboards."

"Don't insult bar brawls," he said. "Every one I've been in has been completely justifiable."

I smiled. "Sorry." I reattached Rosie's leash. She skipped toward the office door. And then, as though Spike and I had wished it on ourselves, Melanie Joan did, in fact, come bursting back in. "I forgot to ask you something, Sunny," she said. "Would you mind accompanying me to that meeting with my editor?"

FIVE

Melanie Joan gave me a ride back to my office in her limo. While she and Charles waited outside, I dropped Rosie off with my assistant. Blake tried to engage her in a game of fetch—which, as usual, consisted of Blake throwing a stuffy toy across the room and Rosie taking it to a quiet corner and ripping it to shreds.

Meanwhile, I filled him in on our latest case.

Like me, Blake hadn't heard of ReadAnon. But it wasn't because he was a Luddite. Before tragedy struck and he'd begun a new life working for me, Blake James had been an Instagram influencer with more than five hundred thousand followers and his own YouTube channel. The reason he didn't know ReadAnon was that he wasn't a fan of books—or of any form of entertainment he couldn't watch on a screen while working out.

He had, however, heard of Melanie Joan Hall. "My aunt loves her stories," he said. "Loved, I mean." Blake cleared his throat. He always got choked up when the topic of his aunt came up, and so I waited for it to pass.

"If Ms. Hall had told me who she was when she came here, I wouldn't have been so freaked out," he said.

"Yeah, well, she's got reason to be anonymous." I told him about Melanie Joan's drunken decision to torpedo her own career.

"Yikes," he said.

"She blamed it on her water pill," I said.

"Doesn't she have an assistant or a manager or someone to keep her from doing stupid things?"

"She tends to keep her entourage at a minimum," I said. Though it did make me think. Melanie Joan had been through at least four literary agents since I'd known her—the most recent amid highly unsavory circumstances. And don't even get me started on her significant others. Outside of Spike and me, Melanie Joan seemed to have real difficulty finding people she could trust.

It made me remember her film agent, Tony Gault. I was pretty sure she still had him on retainer. Tony was equal parts sleazy and sexy, an alchemy that I'd once found irresistible. Long before I'd recommitted to Richie—before my on-and-off relationship with Jesse Stone, even—I'd had something with Tony that could be described as an addiction.

I hadn't seen or spoken to Tony in years, but Melanie Joan

had never said anything about firing him. And as far as I knew, he'd never tried to kill her. So maybe she trusted him, too.

Outside the office, a car horn blared. Blake raised his eyebrows at me.

"Melanie Joan's limo," I said.

"Jeez," Blake said. "Patient, much?"

"I know," I said.

I told Blake to get acquainted with ReadAnon while I was gone, and to go through as many of Book Babe's reviews as he could. "Flag anything that looks like it might reveal something personal," I said.

"You got it," he said.

Rosie yelped. She was sitting amid the remnants of her stuffy toy, tail thumping. Blake opened his desk drawer, grabbed a treat, and tossed it to her.

"I don't know if she should be rewarded for that type of behavior," I said.

"Rosie should be rewarded for everything," Blake said.

"True," I said.

Rosie trotted over to Blake. He picked her up and told her what a good girl she was. I left the office thinking about Rosie and how, unlike Melanie Joan, she was always in good hands.

SIX

The Boston branch of Melanie Joan's New York–based publisher, Scepter Books, was situated on the top floor of a six-story Federal-style building on Farnsworth Street. I'd never been there. Neither had Melanie Joan. She'd visited the New York offices, she'd told me in the car, usually to sign books. "A month before my pub date, I sign hundreds of first editions," she'd explained. "In turn, they serve me potato chips and beluga caviar, and mimosas, made with Dom, of course."

On Farnsworth Street, however, the only thing getting served was attitude.

The receptionist was a guy in his mid- to late twenties with delicate features, cultivated stubble, and purposefully mussed brown hair. He wore horn-rimmed glasses, a white oxford with an open collar, and a Harris Tweed jacket that likely had elbow patches. He could have stepped out of a Ralph Lauren catalog were it not for the expression on his face—like he smelled something decomposing. "Oh," he said to Melanie Joan. "Hello."

"Melanie Joan Hall and Sunny Randall," Melanie Joan said. "Here to see Evan Woodrow."

The receptionist nodded. Grudgingly, he stood up. "Follow me," he said.

"Do we have to?" I smiled at him.

He didn't smile back.

The hallway was dotted with framed bestselling book covers—most all of which had been written by Melanie Joan. The receptionist completely ignored them—and us. It made me angry. Here she was, essentially signing this kid's paychecks, yet he was treating Melanie Joan with the cordiality of a prison guard. All because she'd tied one on and typed the c-word into an amateur critic's comments section.

That was what got a world-famous author canceled these days? I was no expert on the publishing industry, but it seemed to me that if Melanie Joan had been a man, she might have gotten a little more sympathy from Elbow Patches here.

Once we got to the end of the hall, he turned to the door on the right and knocked softly. "Yes?" a man's voice called out.

"Melanie Joan Hall is here." Elbow Patches said my friend's name as though it left a bad taste in his mouth. I was so offended on her behalf that I barely noticed the fact that he hadn't mentioned me at all.

"Come on in, Melanie Joan," said the voice, which I presumed was that of her editor, Evan Woodrow. Compared to the receptionist, he sounded downright friendly.

Melanie Joan moved past Elbow Patches and opened the door. I followed, knocking into him in a way that could have passed for an accident. Maybe.

Evan Woodrow's office was very clean and bright, with a nice view of the street outside and a few plaques on the walls—awards of some sort. His desk was exceptionally tidy. Not a pen out of place. Next to his computer sat a short stack of bound manuscripts that looked untouched. No framed pictures. Nothing personal of any sort. It made me wonder how much time Woodrow actually spent in here.

"Sunny Randall," he said, once we were seated across from his desk. "Haven't I seen that name in the news?"

Woodrow was a wan, sallow-faced man with a sparse combover. He wore a rumpled shirt with coffee stains on the front and thick glasses that made his eyes look like fried eggs. He may have been Melanie Joan's longtime editor, but, sartorially speaking, he couldn't have been less compatible.

"Sunny's been in the news a lot," Melanie Joan said. "She's one of Boston's premier private detectives."

"That's nice," Woodrow said.

"Thanks," I said.

He looked at Melanie Joan. "Is Sunny acting as your lawyer?"

"What? No. Why would I need a lawyer?"

“Well, then,” he said, “you brought a private detective to my office because . . .”

“Sunny has graciously agreed to track down Book Babe so we can jump into damage control before publication,” she said. “I’ve got a plan, Evan. A good one.” She started to elaborate, but Woodrow cut her off.

“Listen, I’m not going to waste your time, Melanie Joan.”

“What?” Melanie Joan said.

“You know what a fan I am of your work, and you’ve done very well for Scepter. But . . .”

“But?” Melanie Joan said.

“Have you been online at all?” he said. “Since this morning?”

“I mean—”

“Have you read the news?”

She shook her head.

He turned his computer screen so that we could see what was on it: an article from the *New York Post*, headlined THE FALL OF HALL.

“Oh . . .” Melanie Joan said.

“It’s just one article,” I said.

He tapped his keyboard, and another article popped up, this one from *Time* magazine online: MELANIE JOAN HALL SHOWS THE WORLD HER UGLY SIDE.

I cleared my throat. “Must be a slow news day,” I said.

Evan Woodrow said nothing. Melanie Joan stared at the screen as though she’d forgotten how to blink.

“I respect you too much to lie to you,” Evan Woodrow said.

"The powers that be aren't sure your memoir can survive this scandal."

"Oh, God," Melanie Joan said.

"You're kidding, right?" I said.

"I wish I was, but the truth is, Melanie Joan's sales aren't what they used to be. And now that she's trashed a highly influential critic—"

"Oh, come on," Melanie Joan said. "My sales are excellent. Do you have any idea how much fan mail I get?"

Woodrow sighed. "It's not your fault," he said. "It's just that your fans are aging out. There's a new generation of romance readers, and they'd rather spend their cash on Colleen Hoover or Leila Donnelly."

"Fuck Leila Donnelly," Melanie Joan said.

"Melanie Joan," Woodrow said.

"Who is Leila Donnelly?" I said.

"She has seven books on the *New York Times* Bestseller List," Woodrow said. "Three of them have been on there for more than a year." He raised his eyebrows and dropped his jaw, as though he was in awe of my ignorance.

"I read mostly nonfiction," I said. "Except for Melanie Joan. I've read all her books."

"Leila Donnelly is terrible," Melanie Joan said. "Her characters are simps. Her romances are degrading. Her books are an insult to women. To all people who can read, quite frankly."

"Well, Greg feels differently."

"Who's Greg?" I said.

"Greg Scepter," Melanie Joan said.

"As in Scepter Books?"

Woodrow nodded.

"Unusual last name," I said.

"A fitting one, though."

"His mother, Gloria, was the true Scepter of Scepter Books, rest in peace," Melanie Joan said. "I doubt little Greggie has read anything longer than a spreadsheet."

"We're publishing Leila Donnelly now," Woodrow said.

"What?" Melanie Joan said.

"She just signed a five-book deal with Scepter. It hasn't been announced."

"Un. Fucking. Believable," Melanie Joan said.

"My point is, Book Babe was one of her first champions," Woodrow said. "Donnelly was self-published. Reclusive as can be. No social media presence whatsoever. But then Book Babe posted a five-star review of a book of hers called *The Heartbeat Chronicles* and it became an instant bestseller. Like it or not, that's power."

"I've still never heard of her," I said.

"Look, there isn't any way to soften this," Woodrow said. "Barring some type of miracle, we're pulling your memoir."

Melanie Joan gasped audibly.

"What does that mean?" I said.

Again with the awestruck face. "We're pausing publication," he said.

"Really?" I said.

"For now," he said.

Melanie Joan gaped at Woodrow. "How can you do this to me?" she said. "After all I've done for you?"

"I'm truly sorry," Woodrow said. "But it isn't my decision."

Melanie Joan's lip trembled. "You were . . . You were an editorial assistant when I met you. A child. I . . . I made your entire career."

"A child?" I said. *"Him?"*

"You'd never know it to look at the two of us today," Evan Woodrow said.

"No," I said. "You definitely wouldn't."

"Yeah, well. I work at my appearance," Melanie Joan said. "Evan doesn't have to because he isn't a public figure."

"You work at everything," I said. "It's one of the things that makes you one of the truly great writers." I glanced at Woodrow. If what I'd said had registered at all, those sunny-side-up eyes didn't show it.

Full disclosure: That thing I'd said about reading all of Melanie Joan's books had been a lie. Years ago, I'd dipped into *A Girl and Not a God*, but I hadn't been able to make it through the first chapter. That didn't matter, though. What had always impressed me about Melanie Joan Hall—what I stood in awe of—was that she didn't care whether people like me read her books or not. She knew her audience. She respected them. And every day she worked hard to reach them, entertain them, satisfy them.

"Who knows?" Woodrow said. "Maybe when BookBabeGate dies down, we can reconsider . . ."

"Oh, shut up, Evan," Melanie Joan said. She stood up. She picked up her hat and opened the door.

Melanie Joan left Evan Woodrow's office. I followed her out.

"I wish it didn't have to be this way," Woodrow called out as I closed the door, "but this new breed of critics. The TikTokers and the online reviewers, Book Babe especially. They wield the sword."

"Wield this," I said. I was pretty sure he didn't hear me.

Melanie Joan didn't say a word until we were in the elevator and the doors had closed. "I guess you're off the hook," she said.

"No, I'm not," I said. "I'm going to find Book Babe for you."

"But it doesn't matter," she said. "Evan said—"

"Evan can fuck right off," I said.

Melanie Joan turned to me, a smile on her face that could melt hearts, change minds, and sell books by the millions. "That's my girl," she said.

SEVEN

Book Babe had posted more than five hundred reviews on the ReadAnon site. And when I returned to the office, I learned that my assistant, Blake, had already familiarized himself with them—not only tallying up the number of one-, two-, three-, four-, and five-star reviews the account had doled out, but paying close attention to Book Babe's preferred genres, favorite books, and personal details disclosed in the reviews, including frequently used turns of phrase.

All this, plus he'd updated my website and walked Rosie, who, after greeting me briefly, was now sleeping peacefully under Blake's desk, in the dog bed he'd bought her for Christmas. Even for the enthusiastic twenty-two-year-old I'd come to know and appreciate, that was a lot. When he presented me with a five-page printed document he described as "the profile of Book Babe I worked up," I nearly asked him if he'd fallen off the energy drink wagon again. Instead, I said, "You think you can summarize this for me?"

"Sure." Blake sat back down at his desk. "First of all," he said, "I'm pretty sure Book Babe is a woman."

"How do you know that?"

"She's read a lot of books about pregnancy and she has very strong opinions about them," he said. "She'll complain about the books written by men, even if they're doctors. She'll say things like, 'Obviously this dude's never had to deal with swollen ankles.' Which, you know, is a pretty good point, but also—"

"Connotes personal experience."

"Yeah."

"Okay," I said. "When were these pregnancy reviews posted?"

"About three years ago."

"So it's possible she's got a two- to three-year-old kid."

"Exactly. Or she was just really into pregnancy books three years ago, for some other reason."

"Right," I said. "We never assume."

"You taught me that."

"Yes, I did," I said.

He smiled.

I smiled back. "What else?" I said.

"Well, let's see," he said. "Book Babe likes inspirational stuff, self-help. She reviewed a holistic diet book I promoted on my Instagram account last year. She gave it three stars."

"Was it a fair review?"

"I never read the book."

"You just promoted it."

He shrugged. "It had a nice cover."

"What are her other reading preferences?"

"She loves books about Hollywood," he said. "Autobiographies by old-time movie stars like Cary Grant and Cher. They usually get four or five stars, and a lot of times she uses the same words to describe them." He squinted, as if the words were printed in a tiny font on the wall behind me. "Brave, revelatory, and aspirational."

I tried to figure out if I'd ever heard someone lump Cary Grant and Cher into the same category. "This is all good, Blake," I said. "Very thorough."

"I worked really hard, Sunny."

"I can tell."

He beamed at me.

Blake was a constant surprise. When I'd hired him, I'd been wary of adding anyone to my staff, which consisted of Rosie and me (with Spike volunteering on a regular basis). But Blake needed a job. And to be honest, I'd felt sorry for him. He'd been through so much. I figured he'd work for me just long enough to get back on his feet again and find his true calling—maybe as a personal trainer or a hair model. But no. Beneath those luxuriant locks lurked a keen investigative mind.

"I'm guessing Book Babe is a romance reader," I said.

"Major," he said. "I think there's like a hundred romances she's reviewed, just within the past year. She has strong opinions on them. Her newer reviews are a lot more critical than her older ones—with, like, a few exceptions. She has faves who she says nothing but good things about."

"Maybe that's her beef with Melanie Joan," I said. "She's mad at her for writing a memoir instead of a romance."

"Actually, no."

"No?"

Blake shook his head. "The only Melanie Joan Hall book she's posted about is *Stronger Alone*."

"Weird."

"You want to know something weirder?"

I nodded.

"Of all the reviews she's written—and we're talking all five hundred and thirty of them—*Stronger Alone* is the only book she gave one star."

Rosie woke up from her nap. She stretched out her paws and yawned, then capped it off with a snort. Blake beamed, as though she'd just performed some incredible feat. "Good girl," he said.

I beamed, too. "Isn't she beautiful?"

"Flawless," Blake said.

I lifted Rosie from the floor. She snuggled against me. "As I see it, there're two possibilities," I said. "Either Book Babe is a celebrity memoir buff who doesn't think *Stronger Alone* is as good as the others she's read. Or she's someone who personally hates Melanie Joan."

"I think it's the second thing," Blake said.

"Why?"

"The way the review is written."

I nodded, as though I knew what he was talking about. Like I said, I'd only skimmed it.

"Oh, I almost forgot," he said. "Richie called."

"He did?" I pulled my phone out of my pocket. It had been on Do Not Disturb since the meeting with Woodrow, so I set it back to normal.

"He said he's still trying to get coverage for tonight."

"Oh, right." I'd forgotten all about dinner at my parents'. It had felt so important this morning, when I'd FaceTimed Richie and asked him to come. *Will he leave the Jersey Shore for me,* I'd thought, *even for a night?*

I rolled my eyes. I'd actually been serious when I'd thought that. *Who's the drama queen now?* I carried Rosie into my office and set her on my lap. Once she was comfortable, I pulled up ReadAnon and read the review carefully.

EIGHT

"*Stronger Alone* is, without a doubt, the worst book I've ever read."

That's how Book Babe's review of Melanie Joan's memoir started. It went downhill from there. Besides calling Melanie Joan a "tone-deaf, hyperprivileged narcissist who plays the victim in order to exploit the sympathy of her fans," Book Babe singled out specific incidents from *Stronger Alone* to back up this thesis—from Melanie Joan's "obvious exaggeration" of John Melvin's abuse of her ("Nobody would be dumb enough to stay in the marriage she describes") to her "villainization" of an unnamed actress Melanie Joan had wound up firing from the Netflix adaptation of *A Girl and Not a God* ("Of course Hall tries to make herself into the wronged one, just like she always does in this grim piece of garbage," Book Babe wrote.

"But IMHO, that actress—more talented, intelligent, and good-hearted than this so-called author, I'm sure—has grounds for a lawsuit"). Perhaps worst of all, Book Babe quoted *Stronger Alone* at length for laughs—which Blake said she didn't do in any of her other reviews. "Melanie Joan Hall can't write—we all know that about her," Book Babe concluded. "But far worse than that is her complete lack of self-awareness. At least most hacks know what they are."

I skimmed a few more of Book Babe's reviews. Blake was right. Some were positive. Some were negative. But I couldn't find a single one that was this deeply personal. Book Babe was someone who knew Melanie Joan. She was someone who'd been hurt by her, or by this book. Most likely both.

I called Melanie Joan. "I'm sorry," I said.

"Oh, God, what now?" she said.

"I read the review," I said. "In full."

"Oh," she said.

"I probably would have written a worse comment than you did," I said. "In fact, I feel like writing one now."

"Don't," Melanie Joan said. "I'm in enough trouble as it is."

"I was just kidding," I said. "Kind of." I asked if she could email me the *Stronger Alone* manuscript.

Melanie Joan let out a mirthless laugh. "At least somebody will read it," she said.

A few seconds after we hung up, I received an email from Melanie Joan with a PDF of the manuscript attached. I opened it and started to read. It was better written than her romance novels, but still a little over-the-top for my taste. I decided to write down all the names of the people she mentioned negatively, then try to figure out if any of them could be Book Babe.

One candidate jumped out right away—the unnamed actress, whom Melanie Joan referred to in the book as Tallulah Airhead. (If her readership was, as Woodrow had said, "aging out," he might have tried suggesting a pop-culture reference that was less than a hundred years old.)

In any case, her final standoff with "Tallulah" was described in the book's prologue:

> As I approached her trailer, my heart pounded. I'd already been through so much in my life—terror, trauma, debasement no woman should be forced to endure, most of it at the hands of people I thought I loved and trusted. But none of it had prepared me for this moment—when I would come face-to-face with the person who was actively destroying my greatest creation, Cassandra Demeter—of *A Girl and Not a God*. I had just watched the dailies. Not only was her acting an embarrassment (drinking and diet pills were rumored to have been involved), but she had rewritten blocks of dialogue without permission, turning my heroine into a simpering fool. The ingratitude! I knocked on Tallulah's door, though I hated showing her that courtesy. If her trailer hadn't been leased by my own production company, I'd have broken it down.
>
> "Go away!" she called out. "I'm meditating."

It was as if my entire life had prepared me for this moment—the burn of each indignity making me stronger. I was a sword forged in fire, ready to do battle. "You're a disgrace," I told her through the trailer door. "You're destroying my life's work. And you are fired."

By the time she'd gotten off her meditation pillow and opened the door, I'd called security.

"Ouch," I said.

A Girl and Not a God had been released on Netflix four years ago. It had been quite a hit. The actress who'd apparently replaced Tallulah Airhead—a then-unknown by the name of Meredith Tanner—had won an Emmy. I remembered calling Melanie Joan and congratulating her. She'd never mentioned the fact that Meredith had been a pinch hitter, and why should she? Melanie Joan Hall had won the game. Until, perhaps, now.

I called Melanie Joan.

"Who is Tallulah Airhead?" I said.

She made that sound again. Rosie jumped off my lap and scurried out of my office.

NINE

Once my dog was safely ensconced in her bed under Blake's desk, I got back to Melanie Joan. It took a lot of cajoling on my part, but eventually she breathed out the name of the despised actress: Natalie Blythe.

"Never heard of her," I said.

"Of course you haven't," Melanie Joan said. "I made sure of that."

"How?"

"Let's just say I very discreetly spread the word about her lack of professionalism."

"Ah."

"Listen, Sunny, I don't need your moralizing."

"'Ah' is moralizing?"

Melanie Joan let out a heavy sigh. "Did you know that she

managed to steal several designer dresses from the wardrobe department on her way out?" she said. "She's lucky I didn't have her arrested."

"You said in the book that she rewrote 'blocks of dialogue' in *A Girl and Not a God*."

"That's right."

"Do you remember her writing style?"

She snorted. "What writing style?"

"Her phrasing. The words she used," I said. "Any of it remind you of Book Babe?"

Melanie Joan laughed for a full thirty seconds.

"I'm serious," I said, once she caught her breath. "Did she ever use words like *brave*, *revelatory*, *aspirational*?"

"You think Natalie Blythe is Book Babe."

"I think it's possible," I said.

"She can't even read a script in its entirety."

I shrugged elaborately, as though she could see me through the phone. "Book Babe's review of *Stronger Alone* specifically mentions the actress you talk about in the prologue. It says that she is more talented, intelligent, and good-hearted than you."

"I'm familiar with the review, Sunny."

"It also says the actress has grounds for a lawsuit."

"So what?"

"So," I said, "did Natalie Blythe ever try to sue?"

Rosie woke up from her nap, slithered out from under Blake's desk, and trotted back into my office. Her nails clacked on the hardwood floors. I reminded myself to trim them. "She did try to sue," Melanie Joan said.

"What happened with it?"

"It went nowhere. A few days after I fired her, I heard from her lawyer. Her lawyer heard from my legal team. End of story."

"One more question," I said. "Does Natalie Blythe have a young child? A three-year-old?"

"Sunny, I haven't even said her name out loud in the past four years," Melanie Joan said. "How the hell would I know anything about her personal life?" She started trashing Natalie Blythe—telling me how her unprofessionalism nearly torpedoed the Netflix series, and how, up until that final conversation in Natalie's trailer, Melanie Joan had been speaking to the actress only through intermediaries. "Do you have any idea how difficult that was?" she said. "I was the executive producer. The big kahuna, Sunny. Yet I had to rely on others to communicate with my lead actress. Oh, and did I mention she stole clothing from wardrobe?"

"You did."

"Yeah, well. She stole shoes, too."

"Horrible," I said. "But it all points to something that Natalie Blythe does have going for her."

"Kleptomania?"

"Motive."

"Oh."

"Think about it," I said. "Book Babe is a romance reader. She doesn't review any of your fiction, but she does praise your competitors—Julia Quinn, Colleen Hoover, Leila Donnelly in particular. She's given all her books five stars."

“Ugh.”

“Then she gets her hands on a galley of your book. A memoir that trashes Natalie Blythe in the first chapter. She gives it her only one-star review.”

Melanie Joan went quiet again. I checked my phone to make sure we were still connected. “That was Book Babe’s only one-star review?”

“Yep.”

“Wow.”

“Her most personal one, too.”

Melanie Joan exhaled. “You know what?”

“What?”

“You’re making some sort of sense.”

“I try.”

“Natalie Blythe is also idiotic enough to think Leila Donnelly is a good writer.”

“She’s reviewed a lot of movie actors’ memoirs, which seems on brand, right?”

“It does.”

“And wellness books. Was she into wellness?”

“Always late to the set because she was doing yoga or meditating,” she said. “She also drank a lot of smoothies. But who doesn’t?”

“Still, you put it all together . . .”

Melanie Joan exhaled. “I’ll tell you something, Sunny. If she is Book Babe, I’ll send her flowers. I’ll tell her anything she wants to hear. I’m desperate enough to apologize to her. For everything.”

“That’s saying a lot.”

“I just want my career back,” she said. “This morning. With Evan . . . I guess it didn’t really sink in until now.”

“We still have time,” I said.

“We do, right? It isn’t like I signed anything in there.”

“That’s right,” I said. “You can get your career back. Scepter can still publish your memoir.”

I told Melanie Joan to call me if she remembered anything about Natalie that might help me track her down. She told me she would.

After we hung up, I looked up Natalie Blythe on IMDb. In the past four years, her only credit was “Dead Girl” in a low-budget horror movie called *Summer of Murder*.

The woman definitely had grounds for a lawsuit.

I googled images of Natalie. She resembled a young Melanie Joan Hall, which I’m sure neither one of them was happy about. There were a lot of pictures of her pre-firing—in a sparkling gown at the Emmys, showing off a backless dress at a premiere, posing for a women’s magazine in a comfy sweater and jeans. Post-firing, though, the images were scarce. Just a handful of ads for actors’ showcases, a cheesy-looking shot of Natalie playing the title role in a dinner-theater production of *Evita*, a group shot of women in workout wear and matching T-shirts, Natalie at the center. There was one image, though, that made me stop scrolling. It was the profile pic from Natalie’s Instagram. I clicked on it. The account was private. But the shot was clear enough—a beaming Natalie

Blythe, holding a small boy. He looked to be just about three years old.

"Oh, ho!" I said.

My phone chimed. I looked at the screen. Melanie Joan again. I started to tell her about my new discovery, but I was drowned out by sobs.

TEN

I asked Melanie Joan if she was all right. She choked out a "no" and asked me to come to her town house. I asked if she was in physical danger and she said "no" again, but added, "My life is over."

Her sobs grew louder. I knew she wasn't willing or able to tell me what was wrong, believing instead that I should witness the horror in person. I told her I'd be there right away, and she recited the address—a strange thing to do, considering I'd rented her town house for more than a year and it was only about six blocks away from where I worked.

"Do you want me to bring Spike?" I said.

"He's on his way," she said.

I hung up the phone, grabbed my purse, and headed out of my office, with Rosie scurrying after me. I was neither insulted nor surprised that Melanie Joan had called Spike before me. Rosie was my emotional support animal. Spike was hers.

I attached Rosie's leash and told Blake that if I wasn't back at the office by five p.m., he should lock up and leave.

Melanie Joan's butler, Harold, greeted me at the door. I knew him well. He'd worked for the author for years, in all five of her residences. He was about my dad's age, but he had perfect posture, a nearly line-free face, and thick salt-and-pepper hair that seemed to be his own. I'd often thought that Melanie Joan spiked his coffee with whatever youth drugs she was popping, just so he could keep up with her.

"Mr. Spike is in the drawing room with Ms. Hall, her editor, and her literary agent," Harold said.

I wasn't sure what he meant by "the drawing room." Harold must have seen me trying to make calculations, and so he made a subtle gesture with his head at a closed door just past the foyer. When I lived here, I'd always thought of that space as the TV room, but to each his own.

"Thanks, Harold," I said. "Who is Melanie Joan's literary agent these days?"

"Mr. Gault," he said. "He just arrived from L.A."

Oh, really, now? "Tony Gault?" I said.

"Yes."

"He's her film agent."

"He handles it all now," Harold said. "After that . . . series of unfortunate events, Ms. Hart decided to streamline her representation."

I gave him a look. Calling what happened with Melanie Joan's previous agent a "series of unfortunate events" was like calling the *Titanic* a delayed boat trip.

He said it again. "Mr. Gault handles it all."

I didn't relish the idea of being in the same room with Tony Gault. I was relatively sure that the last time I'd seen him, he'd been in the process of putting his clothes back on. And the memory was not an unpleasant one. (I was engaged to be engaged—not dead.) That aside, I didn't want to go into the so-called drawing room blind. I was annoyed at Spike for not psychically sensing I was at the door.

Harold's jacket pocket dinged. He plucked out the phone and switched it to vibrate. I eyed the case—crystal-studded, with the Gucci logo at the center.

"This is Ms. Hart's phone," Harold said. "She asked me to keep it for the moment." He dropped it back into his pocket. It vibrated, as if in protest.

"Harold?" I said.

"Yes?"

"Can you please tell me what the hell is going on in the drawing room?"

He nodded sagely. "Ms. Hart's editor brought over papers to terminate her contract."

"Oh . . . man."

"Act surprised when she tells you."

"I will."

Harold leaned down and scratched Rosie behind the ears. "Good girl," he said.

I wondered which one of us he was talking to.

"I blame the new regime, you know," Harold said.

"Pardon?"

"Mr. Scepter," he said. "The son. He's not like his mother was."

"That's what Melanie Joan says."

"We've known him since he was a boy, Ms. Hall and me. And by 'known,' I mean tolerated. Barely tolerated, in my case."

"I think she's with you on that," I said.

"My assessment of him is this: He has always adored computers more than books. More than writers." He stopped petting Rosie and stood up straight. "And he's always been a little shit."

I raised my eyebrows.

"I'm sorry for the offensive language," he said.

"No offense taken," I said.

The door to the drawing room opened. Spike exited and closed it quickly behind him. I could hear Melanie Joan bellowing from within. "This cannot be happening! I will not allow it!"

"What took you so long?" Spike said. "It's bad in there. I had to physically hold her back from strangling her editor."

I nodded. "I can't really say I blame her."

"He was a true advocate for Ms. Hall when Mrs. Scepter was alive," Harold said. "His opinions seem to have changed with the regime."

"When they change that easily, they aren't worth much to begin with," I said.

"Indeed," Harold said.

Rosie reared back onto her hind legs and placed her front paws on Spike's shin. He scooped her into his arms. I was beginning to think he was Rosie's emotional support animal, too.

I followed Spike back in. Melanie Joan had redone the TV room since I lived there. There was emerald-green silk wallpaper, an antique chandelier. No TV. At the center of the room was a large polished mahogany table. It was all very Founding Fathers, save the miserable woman at the far end of the table in head-to-toe St. John, her forehead affixed to the mahogany. Evan Woodrow was on one side of her, Tony Gault on the other. Both seemed to be trying, in vain, to keep her from exploding into tiny pieces. "This can't happen," Melanie Joan kept saying, over and over. "This can't happen. It can't happen. It cannot."

"Melanie Joan?" Spike said. "Sunny's here."

She looked up at both of us. Her eyes glistened. "This can't happen," she said.

"I'm afraid it can," Evan Woodrow said. He looked at me. "Help me out here, Sunny."

"Are you kidding me?" I said.

I moved toward Melanie Joan and put my hand on her back, purposefully avoiding eye contact with Tony. I glanced at Spike. If he remembered my extended fling with Melanie Joan's agent, it wasn't registering at the moment. He was too busy staring at Evan Woodrow like he wanted to kill him.

"Evan," Tony was saying. "I think there's a very real chance we can fix this, especially with Sunny on board."

"Fix it how?"

"Melanie Joan publicly apologizes, Book Babe publicly forgives Melanie Joan. We do a press conference. You resume publication—and sell even more copies of *Stronger Alone*."

"None of that sounds likely," Evan said. "No one knows who Book Babe is. And beyond that, I don't make the rules."

"Why not?" I said. "Why not make the rules, just this once?"

"Sunny can find Book Babe," Spike said.

Evan looked up at him. He started to say something, then stopped. Probably out of fear.

"Evan, Sunny was the one who put John Melvin behind bars," Tony said. "If she can do that with a psychopath, imagine what she can do with some . . . random librarian."

"We don't know that she's a librarian." Melanie Joan said it into her hands. "She might be a failed actress."

Tony looked up at me. Unfortunately, he'd aged very well. "Is that true, Sunny?"

"There's a strong possibility," I said.

"See?" Tony said. "She's already got a lead."

Evan let out a heavy, whistling sigh, like a balloon deflating. "I'll try and buy a few more days off Greg," he said.

Melanie Joan stopped sobbing. Her spine straightened. She plucked a Kleenex out of the box in front of her and dabbed delicately at her eyes.

"Thank you." She said it to me, not to Evan Woodrow.

ELEVEN

Evan stuck around for a few minutes, kicking back in his chair and smiling pleasantly at Melanie Joan, as though he expected her to serve him tea and cookies.

Melanie Joan glared at him. "Nice seeing you." She said it pointedly. But either he didn't notice or he didn't care.

Spike walked up to where Evan was sitting and loomed over him, his arms crossed over his chest. I had to say, Spike was a damned good loomer. When Evan turned around, a type of fear crept into his eyes—basic and primordial, like a mouse coming face-to-face with a woolly mammoth. He slipped the legal papers back into the tired-looking satchel he had looped over the back of his chair. "I'll be going, then," he said.

"Yes," Spike said. "Yes, you will."

Evan picked up the satchel and headed toward the door.

"Goodbye, Evan," Melanie Joan called out.

"Good riddance, Evan," I said.

After Woodrow left, I turned to Melanie Joan. "Harold said that he used to be different before Greg Scepter took over."

"He was," Melanie Joan said.

"I find that hard to believe," Spike said.

"No, no, Harold's right," she said. "He had a real passion for books. We'd talk for hours about some of the treasures he'd find in the slush pile. He seemed to love his job. He even dressed better for work."

"No way," I said.

"Well, he was never Idris Elba, but at least his suits were pressed," she said. "Greggie took over, and now the only thing Evan seems to care about is not making waves. Not getting fired. He's a sniveling yes-man. He may as well be in the movie business." She glanced at Tony. "No offense, Antoine," she said.

"None taken," he said. "But I will say we're all pretty well dressed."

"Antoine?" I said.

"That's right, Sonya," Tony said.

I suppressed a smile. "Good memory."

"Just because I haven't seen you in a while doesn't mean I've forgotten you." Tony wore an immaculately tailored charcoal suit—probably a Zegna—with a pale blue silk tie that brought out his eyes. "You're pretty unforgettable, you know."

I glanced at Spike. He raised an eyebrow in a way that said, *Oh, yeah. Now I remember who this guy is.*

"How's Jesse?" Tony asked.

"We're broken up."

He grinned. "Playing the field, then?"

"God, how old are you?"

"Hey," he said. "It's a timeless expression."

"Actually, I'm with Richie now."

The grin dissolved. "Your ex-husband."

"Ex and now future," I said.

"I'm the maid of honor," Spike said.

Tony took a moment, digesting the information. "Richie's a lucky guy," he said.

"I'll make sure and let him know," I said.

"I have no doubt you will," Tony said.

I felt my cheeks flush. I hated them for that. "Tell me what you know about Natalie Blythe, Tony," I said.

"What?"

"Sunny thinks she might be Book Babe," Melanie Joan said.

Tony stared at her. "Seriously?"

"I know," she said. "That was my response, too, but Sunny made a convincing case."

He turned to me.

"I can make it again, if you want," I said. "The case, I mean."

"Who is Natalie Blythe?" Spike said.

Before I could answer, there was a soft knock on the door. Spike opened it, and Harold walked in. "I'm sorry to disturb you, Ms. Hart," he said. "But I thought you might like your phone back. It's been very active."

"Who's been calling?"

"Texting," Harold said.

"Texting?" Melanie Joan said.

Harold removed the phone from his pocket delicately, as though it were a ticking bomb. He handed it to Melanie Joan face down. During this process, which took about five seconds, the phone vibrated at least ten times.

Melanie Joan turned it over. The color drained from her face. "My God," she whispered.

"What is it, MJ?" Spike said.

Melanie Joan's gaze shifted from his face to Tony's before resting on mine. "I think I've been doxed," she said.

TWELVE

Melanie Joan placed her phone back on the mahogany table face up, presumably so that she didn't have to touch it. Spike, Tony, and I stood next to her, reading the texts as they came in.

HACK

TALENTLESS BITCH

DRUNK OLD P.O.S.

DIE

"Lame bunch of insults," Tony said.

"Very," Spike said.

Melanie Joan said nothing. I knew how she felt. It wasn't the texts themselves. It was the sheer volume of them. And they kept coming, seconds apart, most of them in all caps, many of them from blocked numbers. There were pictures, too—photoshopped depictions of Melanie Joan in grotesque situations. Those were a lot worse than the texts. She stared at her screen. "Why is this happening?" she said. "People like me. They've always liked me."

I understood. Melanie Joan Hall thrived on the love of strangers. She had worked for decades to earn it. But now she was seeing them turn on her, in real time. On her own phone. It seemed almost like a coordinated attack. "Turn your phone off," I said.

"I can't. What if . . . What if Evan calls . . . Or . . ."

"He can call me," I said.

"Or me," Tony said. "I'm your agent. Come on, MJ."

Another picture text arrived. Melanie Joan reached out to enlarge it, but I got there first. I took the phone and handed it back to Harold and told him to keep it in a safe place. Obligingly, he slipped it back into his jacket pocket.

"You should go to a hotel, Melanie Joan," I said.

"Why?" she asked.

"Because," I said, "if they have your number, they might also have this address."

"Oh . . ." she said.

"Sunny's right," Tony said.

"I'm sorry to have distressed you, ma'am," Harold said. "I

hadn't read any of the texts. I thought it might be something urgent."

"It is urgent," Melanie Joan said. "It's my entire life falling to pieces."

Tony told Melanie Joan that he'd book a room for her at the Four Seasons under an assumed name. He asked if she wanted to use the one she usually did.

She shook her head. "Make it for Joanie Chandler," she said.

"Okay." Tony walked to the corner of the room and put his back to us.

"Joanie Chandler?" Spike said.

Melanie Joan crossed her arms over her chest, a faraway look in her eyes. "When I was in eighth grade, I had a crush on a boy named Eric Chandler," she said. "I must have written Joanie Chandler in my notebook a thousand times. Joanie Chandler, Joanie Chandler, Joanie Chandler . . ."

Spike cast a worried glance at me. I returned it.

"The Spring Revels happened at the end of the year. The last song was 'Stairway to Heaven.' Eric asked me to dance. I felt like I was dreaming. We kept slow-dancing, even after the song got fast."

"We'll fix this, Melanie Joan," I said.

She kept talking, as though she were alone in the room. "Eric owns a diner now, back in Utica. A couple years ago, I did a signing there at the library. First time I'd been home in probably thirty years. Eric showed up with his wife and five kids. The place was packed. But I recognized him instantly . . ." She looked at me finally. "Five kids, could you imagine?"

"No," I said. "I couldn't."

"It's interesting, isn't it? Thinking about what your life might be like if you'd been more open to the roads not taken?"

"Melanie Joan, I promise I will make you glad you don't have five kids and a diner in Utica."

"That's a tough promise to keep."

Melanie Joan's phone vibrated in Harold's pocket, again and again and again. He plucked it out and turned it off. "My apologies," he said.

I told Melanie Joan and Spike that I was going to head back to my office and do what I could as far as finding Natalie Blythe.

"Can you stay with me, Spike?" Melanie Joan said.

"Of course," Spike said. He put Rosie on the floor. I reattached her leash. I called out a quick "See ya!" to Tony while he was still making the reservation. That was the best way to say goodbye to Tony Gault—no fuss, no awkwardness. No conversation. Talk about the road not taken . . . Though, to be fair, Tony had always been more of a pit stop.

Rosie and I had just about reached my office when I heard someone shouting my name. I turned around. Tony Gault was jogging toward me in that perfect suit of his. "Oh, for God's sakes," I whispered.

"Man, you walk fast," he said, once he reached me. "You and that little stubby-legged dog. What do you do, take her on the treadmill?"

"Rosie is naturally athletic," I said. "What do you want, Tony?"

Rosie strained at the leash. I pulled a non-rawhide bone out of my purse and gave it to her. I figured that would occupy her for about two minutes, which was all I needed to spend with Tony Gault. He was still catching his breath. I wasn't winded at all, which I found strangely satisfying. He ran a hand across his forehead. His Rolex gleamed.

"Back at Melanie Joan's place," he said, "you asked me what I know about Natalie Blythe."

Now he had my attention. "Yes? What is it?"

He took a step closer to me. Instinctively, I took a step back. "Promise me first," he said, "that you won't tell Melanie Joan."

THIRTEEN

Tony and I went into my building and took the elevator up to my floor. I handed Rosie off to Blake, who gladly took her. Once we were in my office, I said, "Okay. Out with it. I don't have a lot of time." Tony took a breath. For at least fifteen seconds, I waited for him to speak.

"Tell me why you think Natalie Blythe might be Book Babe," he said.

You're so exasperating, I thought. But I didn't say it. The fact was, Tony wasn't trying to be exasperating. He was just being Tony—always striking a deal, engineering a quid pro quo, getting the other player to show her hand first. He couldn't help himself. It was imprinted in his Hollywood agent DNA.

So I told Tony everything—from the "grounds for a lawsuit" line in the one-star *Stronger Alone* review, to the distinct lack of Melanie Joan Hall's work among the romances she'd touted, to the timing of the pregnancy book reviews. My most recent search was still on my computer screen, so I turned my monitor to him and showed him Natalie Blythe's Instagram profile pic. "Do you know about this kid?" I said.

Tony shook his head.

"If that's her son," I said, "she was expecting him at the same time Book Babe was reading up on pregnancy."

We were both silent for a few moments. In the other room, I could hear Blake telling Rosie she was the best girl in the world. I knew he was feeding her treats, and I wanted to tell him to stop. At least half of Rosie's recent weight gain could be blamed on my softie of an assistant. But I didn't say anything. I could tell Tony was thinking about Natalie, and I didn't want to break his concentration.

"You make a pretty convincing case," he said.

"Right?" I said. "She's at least worth investigating."

"I guess I didn't think she could be that stupid."

"What do you mean?"

He exhaled. "After Natalie got fired, she signed an NDA. It included a clause that says she can't say or do anything to harm MJ's career, and in exchange it included a pretty massive payout," he said.

"Oh . . ."

"I'd say that review would fall into the category of career-ruiner, wouldn't you?"

I looked at him. "Melanie Joan never told me about a payout."

"She doesn't exactly know about it," he said.

“What does ‘doesn’t exactly’ mean?”

“I told Melanie Joan that we took care of the problem, and it involves a small portion of her quarterly royalties,” he said. “She asked no further questions.”

“So you told no lies.”

He smiled. “One of the many things I like about you, Sunny,” he said, “is that you get things without my having to explain them.”

I smiled back. “That’s possibly the most patronizing compliment I’ve ever received.”

“Hey, it’s from the heart.”

“So,” I said, “where are you depositing these checks?”

“Meaning, where can you find Natalie Blythe?”

“One of the many things I like about you, Tony . . .”

“Touché,” he said. “It’s a small bank in Gloucester.”

My eyes widened. “Gloucester, Massachusetts?”

“Yep,” he said. “She’s from around here. I don’t know if MJ already told you.”

“She did not.”

“She may have erased that from her memory,” Tony said. “But that was the main thing Melanie Joan liked about Natalie Blythe—you know, before everything went pear-shaped. ‘A Boston girl,’ MJ said.” He gave me a picture-perfect grin. “Claimed Natalie reminded her of you.”

“Great.”

“Before things went pear-shaped. Don’t forget I said that.”

I took a breath. Thought. “It makes sense she’d come back home to lick her wounds.”

"And, trust me, she could afford a nice place in Gloucester on what we've been paying her." He rubbed his chin and gazed up at the ceiling, giving me a view of a strong jaw, a cultivated five-o'clock shadow. He wore a thick gold ring with a red stone in it. His college ring—Stanford. I didn't know many men my age who still wore their college rings. I was sure my shrink would have plenty to say about it.

"Gloucester's drivable," I said. "I mean, if she really does live near her bank."

He nodded. "Too bad I don't have a home address for her."

A thought came to me. I sat down at my desk and pulled up my recent image search. I clicked on the picture of the women in matching T-shirts, Natalie Blythe at the center.

"You know what Natalie does for a living these days?" I asked Tony. "I mean, besides not ruining Melanie Joan's career?"

"No idea," he said.

I stared at the picture on my screen. The women's shirts were pale pink, one word across the front in glittery cursive: *Infinity*. It was sourced from one of the women's Substacks—not Natalie's—called *My Health Journey*. And when I skimmed the entry, I saw that it was about joining a yoga class. The author didn't say where.

"Find something?" Tony said.

"Maybe," I said.

I remembered what Melanie Joan had told me—how Natalie was always late to the set because she'd been meditating or doing yoga. I googled "Infinity Yoga, Gloucester, Mass.," and within seconds, I found a website. It was actually called Infinity Wellness Center, but I knew it was the right place. At the top of the home page was a quote:

> "In today's high-pressure world, we all must take time to recharge. Find peace within, and the possibilities are 'infinite.'"
>
> —*Natalie Blythe, Owner*

I turned the screen around so that Tony could see. "Found her," I said.

"Man," he said. "You're good."

I made myself not recall the last time he'd told me something similar. I called Blake into the office. "I'm going to Gloucester," I said.

"Now?" Blake said.

"We'd better hurry," Tony said. "That spa may close soon."

I looked at him. "*We?*"

"Sunny," he said. "If Natalie is Book Babe, you're going to have to convince her that it's essential to publicly make peace with Melanie Joan, ASAP."

"I'm aware of that."

"Who better to do that than the guy who proverbially signs her checks?"

I thought about it.

"I have no idea what he's talking about," Blake said. "But he kinda makes sense."

"He does," I said. "Unfortunately."

“Goody,” Tony said. “Let’s go to the beach.” He gazed at me in a way that I remembered. It made me slightly uncomfortable.

“You want me to watch Rosie until you get back?” Blake asked. “If it gets late, I can always bring her to my place.”

I thought about it for five seconds, then told him it was okay. I’d bring Rosie with me. Blake said it wasn’t any trouble, but I said, “No, thank you, Blake.” I reattached Rosie’s leash. “Rosie loves the beach,” I added. It was not true. She wasn’t a swimmer, and digging in the sand tired her out. Plus, she had no learning curve when it came to drinking ocean water, which was frustrating for both the dog and myself.

The real truth was this: I wanted a chaperone.

FOURTEEN

"Alone at last," Tony said, once we were in my car and buckled up.

"Not really," I said. "Rosie's here."

Rosie left her spot on the backseat and crawled into Tony's Zegna-clad lap. My chaperone. I realized that before today, Tony had never laid eyes on Rosie. Our hook-ups had all taken place when I was in New York or L.A. on business. And even though I may have shown him pictures of my dog (I showed everybody pictures of my dog), it would have been the previous Rosie he'd seen. I'd barely been in contact with him since Rosie I had passed.

"I hope your dog doesn't shed," Tony said.

I took my hand from the ignition key. "That's all you're going to say about her?"

"What else is there to say?"

"Well, starting with the obvious," I said. "She's the most adorable creature on the planet."

"Next to her owner." Tony smiled. He had a killer smile, which no doubt helped him close many a deal back in Hollywood.

He wasn't going to close this one, though.

"Thanks, Antoine." I started up the car and pulled out into traffic. My GPS told me I had two miles before I-93 N. I could feel Tony's gaze on me. For the tiniest moment, I remembered what it felt like when that gaze was a type of prelude.

"So, what's your timetable?" Tony asked.

"You mean, as far as finding Book Babe?"

"No," he said. "As far as marrying Richie."

I turned to him. "We don't have a date set," I said.

"That's interesting."

"Why?"

Tony shrugged. "You were married to him before."

"And?"

"Well, it's not like you need to get to know him better," he said. "I mean, a second engagement is usually more of a technicality."

I exhaled. "Richie lives in Asbury Park now," I said.

"New Jersey?"

"One and the same."

"What's he doing out there?"

"He's general manager at a place called Candy's Room."

"Home to the world's greatest Springsteen tribute bands."

My eyes widened. "You know it?"

"Of course I do. I'm not chained to Hollywood."

"Still."

"I get around, Sunny," he said.

"Clearly."

"I love that place," he said. "The giant Exxon sign over the bar. 'Who's The Boss' trivia nights. The names of the drinks. The Pink Cadillac. Rosalita's Margarita . . ."

"Born to Rum."

"Right." He chuckled. "What a great place to work."

"Richie thinks so," I said. "Anyway, that's why we haven't set a date. We're still trying to figure out what our living situation is going to be like."

"You like the Shore?"

"Very much," I said. "Most of the time."

"So, what's the problem? You've got the type of job you can do from anywhere. You love to drive. Live in Asbury Park."

"But Spike's in Boston. So is my dad. My loft . . ."

"You can probably keep the loft, right?" he said. "And it's driving distance . . . Man, I can't believe I'm telling you to speed up your wedding plans."

"You're not the only one."

"I'm sure, but I, uh . . . have a vested interest against it."

I smiled. I couldn't help it. Though I did add an eye roll for good measure.

"I mean it, Sunny," he said. "When Melanie Joan told me what had happened with ReadAnon, I was upset, of course. Her publisher's insane overreaction. It wasn't fair. But then she told me she was hiring you to find Book Babe, and I thought . . . well, that is definitely a silver lining."

"That's flattering," I said.

"I'm just being honest," he said. "I've missed you. A lot."

"Again, that's—"

"Flattering. I know. I promise I'll stop. I respect you and your choices," he said. "I just wanted to get it all out in the open. I'm not a big fan of subtext."

I turned and looked at him. "We had fun, Tony."

"I know."

"It was a long time ago."

"I know."

"So, what do you say we change conversation topics?"

"Fair enough," he said. "Or we could just listen to the radio."

"Fair enough."

My radio was set to the Bruce Springsteen station—it had been ever since I'd driven back to Boston from the Jersey Shore. I turned it on. "I'm on Fire" was playing. Speaking of preludes . . . I shut it off quickly and checked the GPS. We had about forty minutes to Gloucester, and I wanted them to be as subtext-free as possible. "Let's talk about Natalie Blythe," I said.

FIFTEEN

By the time Tony and I arrived in Gloucester, I'd learned a lot about Natalie Blythe. I'd learned that, like me, Natalie had gone to Boston U. I'd learned that she'd come from a "large and welcoming" Irish family in West Roxbury and that she'd fallen in love with acting after playing the Virgin Mary in her third-grade Christmas pageant. I'd heard that her mother's untimely passing from cancer had broken her heart, but that she had found solace in self-help books by Louise Hay and Eckhart Tolle—and by the romances her mother had loved. "She claimed she's read all of Melanie Joan's books," Tony had said. "A few of them more than once."

But as he also pointed out, the word *claimed* was doing a lot of heavy lifting. "I only know all of this because it's what Natalie told Melanie Joan and the other producers during the casting process," Tony said now, as I pulled into a public parking lot overlooking Wingaersheek Beach. "So it's not exactly sworn testimony."

"The motive was obvious," I said.

"Right," he said. "And actors tend to be great liars. It's part of their skill set."

I refrained from telling him that I'd also heard that said of Hollywood agents. "You ever see her reading?" I asked. "Or listening to an audiobook? Did she talk about books with you or with anybody?"

"I didn't see much of her at all," he said. "She started pissing off Melanie Joan one day into shooting. She was gone, I think, within the first week."

I turned off the car. "Melanie Joan's memoir makes it sound like a much longer time."

"I was as surprised as anybody when I read that prologue," he said. "I barely even remembered that there had been another Cassandra before Meredith took over, and out of left field, Melanie Joan's talking about how Natalie retraumatized her."

"By rewriting her character."

"Yep," Tony said. "You do not fuck with Cassandra."

"Clearly."

"Hey, what should I do about this dog?"

Rosie knew the word *dog*. It woke her up. She shook her head vigorously. Tony lifted her off his lap and handed her to me. Rosie was small, but very dense—more so lately, thanks to Blake's bottomless treat drawer. I found the weight of her reassuring.

"Great," Tony said. "She sheds."

"If Rosie stays long enough to shed on you, it means you've earned her trust."

We both got out of the car. I reattached Rosie's leash and set her down beside me.

Tony swatted at his jacket and pants. "She must really trust me," he said.

"That makes one of us," I said.

"Hey," Tony said. "I'll earn your trust." He winked at me. Winking at me had never been the way to earn my trust.

He left to feed the meter. I stood next to the car, waiting for him, gazing out at the beach.

Wingaersheek Beach was, for lack of a less irritating word, dreamy. Smooth white sand that was distinctly non–New England–like, and some of the clearest, calmest water I'd seen outside of the Caribbean. I inhaled deeply. It made me remember how much I loved the smell of the ocean when it wasn't laced with coconut oil.

My phone vibrated, breaking my reverie. I slipped it out of my purse and looked at the screen. Richie.

I put it up to my ear. "You'll never guess where I am right now," I said.

"No idea," he said.

"I'm in Gloucester," I said. "And I'm thinking of you."

Richie knew Gloucester. When he and I were married, we used to escape here over the summer, booking a room at one of the many seaside hotels just to jump into the ocean, dry off, and go to the Seaport Grille for lobster and martinis. Then it was back to the hotel . . .

"Nice memories," Richie said. Reading my mind. "Why are you in Gloucester?"

"I'm working for Melanie Joan Hall."

"Again?" Back when he was less averse to my taking dangerous cases, Richie had helped me on my first Melanie Joan Hall assignment. It was a successful collaboration, if not the safest one. We wound up putting John Melvin in jail. "What is it this time?"

"Don't worry," I said. "I'm here to talk to a spa owner to see if she gave Melanie Joan's book one star on ReadAnon."

"She hired you for that?"

"It's more serious than it sounds," I said. Then I recounted the day's events.

"That's a lot," he said.

"Right?"

He cleared his throat. "Not that I'm condoning this, but my dad might be able to help."

I winced. I wasn't above asking Desmond Burke for help. I'd done it plenty of times. But my job was to unearth a snarky book nerd. And life-and-death as it may have felt to Melanie Joan, I wasn't sure it warranted getting the Mob involved.

"Dad's been branching out into tech," Richie said.

"Ah."

"I know, I know," he said. "But if you're feeling desperate . . ."

"Speaking of feeling desperate," I said. "How close are you to Boston?"

I expected a sly laugh, but I didn't get one. Instead, I heard background noise—people talking much louder than they needed to. A harmonica riff I immediately recognized as the beginning of "Thunder Road." My heart sank. "I take it you couldn't find coverage for tonight," I said.

Richie exhaled. "I'm sorry, Sunny."

I stared out at the beach, at a young couple walking along the water's edge, holding hands. It was a lovely image. Maybe I'd paint it tonight, after dinner, when I'd be back at my loft. Alone. "Assistant manager went home with a stomach bug," Richie was saying. "She was going to cover for me. And we've got one server taking PTO, two others down with the same bug as the assistant manager . . ."

"Jeez. Don't tell the health inspector."

"Summer down the Shore," he said. "It's so crowded, there's always something going around. You know how it is."

"Yeah," I said. "I do." I hated the way my voice sounded. Like I was pouting or something. I cleared my throat and told him I understood. Of course I did. My job had taken me away from Richie many times, and he always understood. Well, he *said* he did. He could've been thinking any number of thoughts that showed a distinct lack of understanding. But like me, he knew enough not to voice them. "I can stand anything for three hours." I forced out a laugh. "Even my mother."

"Even Elizabeth."

"Let's not get carried away."

Richie laughed. "I'll make it up to you," he said.

A seagull landed on top of my car. Rosie strained at her leash. "Stop." I said it a little too harshly.

Richie asked if I was okay, and I said, "I'm fine. Rosie is just being annoying."

Richie said he missed Rosie, and I said, "She misses you, too."

"Call my dad about your case," he said. "He really might be able to help."

I told him I had to go. After we hung up, I picked up Rosie and hugged her tightly.

"You okay?" said Tony. The second man to have asked me that within the past minute.

I turned around. I had no idea how long he'd been standing behind me or how much he'd heard, but I sure as hell wasn't going to ask him. "Let's go to Infinity," I said. "Before we run out the meter."

SIXTEEN

The Infinity Wellness Center was located across the street from the lot where we'd parked, in an unassuming one-story building that had once housed a veterinarian's office. I remembered the vet from one of my trips to Gloucester with Richie. We'd rushed Rosie I here after she'd eaten a big bag of Mallomars. Not the greatest memory—in fact, I'd blocked a lot of it—but everything had worked out in the end. I hoped the same for this particular expedition. I also wanted to stop remembering Richie for a few minutes.

From the outside, only the sign was different. The waiting area had changed, though. The walls had been painted a pale violet, and there was soft sitar music playing, comfortable chairs, cubbyholes for patrons' shoes, and potted bamboo plants. A small Zen garden was perched on a slate table at the center of the room, and the magazine rack, stocked with old issues of *Cat Fancy*, was long gone. But something about the place still exuded vet energy. Rosie even whined when she came in.

The woman behind the front desk looked like she'd walked right out of wellness community central casting—from her long silver hair, to her Indian print blouse, to the clusters of multicolored stones and crystals adorning her ears, wrists, and neck. But it was only when she looked up at us and did a full-on double take that I realized how out of our element Tony and I were. Him in his Zegna suit and his expensive haircut. Me in my black Jil Sander shift and my equally expensive haircut. I wished we'd had time to change. This woman probably thought we were here to serve her a summons.

"Can I help you?" She wore a name tag that read LARCH. Was it pronounced like the tree? Or was it an odd spelling of Lark? I had no clue.

"I hope so, Larch." I pronounced it like the tree. She didn't correct me. I gave her what I hoped was a disarming smile and asked if I could speak to Natalie Blythe.

Rosie barked.

"Is that an emotional support dog?" Larch said. "I ask because we usually don't allow animals."

"That's funny," I said.

"Why?"

"Because this place used to be a vet's office."

Larch didn't even crack a smile.

"Anyway," I said. "Yes. She is. And she doesn't bite."

"I should hope not." She gave Rosie one of those wary looks I found hard to tolerate, given how obviously sweet my dog is.

I scooped Rosie into my arms and refrained from saying something sarcastic. "She won't bother you," I said. "I promise."

Larch kept her wary gaze on me. She picked up a phone and told Natalie she had visitors. When she asked for our names, I told her mine, and then Tony took a step forward. "Tony Gault," he said. "She'll know who I am."

Larch repeated Tony's name into the phone. After a few moments of listening, she spun away from us and spoke to her boss in a voice so low, I couldn't even make out consonants.

"Natalie will be right with you," Larch said. "I have to check on one of the Reiki tables."

Larch left, and then Natalie Blythe walked in. She was disarmingly tall—nearly Tony's height, and he was well over six feet. She was dressed very expensively, in pale pink yoga pants I recognized from the Lululemon catalog ($200), an embroidered Dior "Dioramour" T-shirt (around $1,500), and a diamond tennis bracelet and earrings that could have easily set her back half a million. I no longer felt intimidating in Jil Sander. I started to introduce myself, but Natalie had eyes only for Tony. Her benefactor. She didn't seem very happy to see him. "I'm hoping you just happened to be in the neighborhood," she said, "and that you'll be leaving soon."

"Nice to see you, too, Natalie," Tony said.

"It isn't personal," she said. "I just know who you work for."

"Understood," Tony said.

"He isn't delivering bad news," I said.

"Not necessarily," Tony said.

"What are you talking about?" She looked at me as if she was just noticing me for the first time. "Who is she?"

"Sunny Randall," I said. "I'm a private investigator."

Her gaze shifted from Tony's face to mine and back again. "Is Melanie Joan missing?"

"No," I said.

"Well, then, what the hell are you doing here?"

"Are you Book Babe?" I just blurted it out. Like ripping off a bandage. Tony gaped at me. He probably didn't think it was the best approach, but I didn't care. If we kept dancing around like this, we weren't going to get anything other than thrown out of Natalie's spa.

Natalie blinked at me. Her earrings glittered. "What?" Her expression was as noncommittal as it could possibly be.

"Melanie Joan just wants to talk to you," I said. "Make peace. She's not interested in the fact that you may have broken your NDA."

"What? I didn't break my NDA."

"Look at this logically," Tony said. "If Melanie Joan gets fully canceled, she won't sell any more books. If she doesn't sell any more books, there will be no quarterly earnings. Your business will suffer."

"Think of your son," I said. "His future."

She stared at me. "How do you know I have a son?"

I started to reply, but Tony kept talking. "My guess is, if you were to take down the review, Melanie Joan would give you anything you want," he said. "She'd pull the entire prologue, I bet."

Natalie frowned at him, then turned her gaze on me, then back to Tony again. She shifted her weight and crossed her arms over her chest and looked him up and down, as though she was trying to figure out if he was wearing a wire. "Get out of here, Tony," she said.

"Natalie, we need to talk about this. It can be a real opportunity for you, if—"

"Get out of here," she said again. "Go play in traffic."

"But—"

"I'll talk to the private detective," she said. "Cute dog, by the way."

"Thank you," I said.

Tony cleared his throat. His cheeks flushed slightly. "Fine," he said. "I'll meet you back at the car, Sunny."

Natalie stood next to me, watching Tony leave. Neither one of us said a word. Once we were alone, she closed her eyes and took a deep breath through her nose, then let it out slowly. Yogic breathing. I'd learned it from a meditation app. It was said to be calming, and sometimes I found it to be. *In with the positive energy, out with the negative.* Natalie yogic-breathed again, two more times. It seemed to have worked. When she opened her eyes and trained them on me, they were tranquil blue pools.

"What prologue?" she said.

SEVENTEEN

Natalie Blythe and I sat on two of the plush chairs surrounding the Zen garden table. Rosie curled up in my lap. Infinity Wellness Center was about to close for the day, and Larch had the good sense not to return from her Reiki table inspection, so we were alone in the waiting room. I explained the basics of what had happened between Melanie Joan, her publisher, and Book Babe. Natalie seemed genuinely surprised.

"Melanie Joan wrote a memoir?" she said.

"Yes."

"And the prologue is about firing me?"

"Yes," I said.

She shook her head. "I can't believe this."

"She didn't name you," I said. "She used a pseudonym. Nobody would know, and even if they did—"

"It isn't that," Natalie said. "I don't care about that. What shocks me is, considering the type of life that Melanie Joan Hall has lived—the abuse, the stalking . . . hell, all her exes getting killed off—that she'd remember me rewriting a few lines of dialogue and treat it like the worst thing that ever happened to her."

I looked at her. "Well, she said you did more than that."

"If she did," she said, "she's lying."

I didn't say anything. I knew Melanie Joan Hall. She wasn't a liar. Not intentionally. But she was a natural-born storyteller. It was possible that she'd exaggerated events in her mind, and on the page.

Regardless, Natalie was right about one thing: Melanie Joan had been through hell. She was a control freak who had been unable to control anything in her life other than the characters she'd created. And that was why rewriting those characters was the worst sin anyone could commit against her. In Melanie Joan's mind, Natalie had robbed her of what little power she had.

I didn't bother explaining that to her, though. I wasn't here to psychoanalyze her former employer. And anyway, I doubted she'd understand.

Natalie asked me exactly what Book Babe had written about *Stronger Alone*, and I told her, as best as I could remember. "She singled you out—well, your pseudonym. She said you had grounds to sue," I said.

She smirked. "I guess maybe I still have one fan."

"I'm sorry about what happened," I said. "To your career."

"You know what? I'm not."

"Really?"

"I mean, the truth is, I wasn't all that happy being an actor. Even when I was fairly successful at it, I was always stressed out, always worrying about my next role. What I had to look like to get that role. What I had to *be* like. If I wasn't cast, I took it personally. And even if I did get the part, I'd be on edge for the entire shoot, worrying about living up to whatever wrong-headed image of me I'd put out there in order to impress the director."

"Sounds like a nightmare."

"It was," she said. "And don't even get me started on reporters and critics. Social media . . . I was a mess."

"I would be, too."

"Right?" she said. "So . . . I tried to relax any way I could. I drank too much, and it made me feel worse. I tried Xanax, but I hated being dependent on pills. Then I discovered meditation. It worked. I found it not just helpful in easing my stress, but it opened up a whole new world for me—and I wanted to show the world to everyone. I started thinking maybe acting wasn't my calling. Maybe the *cure* for it was."

"Interesting."

"So, weirdly, the whole thing with Melanie Joan was a blessing in disguise. It forced me to realize how much I hated acting. Plus, the NDA money made it so I could pursue my real dream." She raised her hands and spread out her fingers. "Owning this place."

"So, you aren't bitter."

She shook her head. "I'm grateful," she said. "But please don't tell Tony Gault."

I laughed. "Knowing Tony, he'd probably talk you into a new deal where you're the one paying Melanie Joan."

"And I wouldn't know what hit me until I was signing the check."

"Talk about finding your true calling," I said.

"Yep."

Rosie stretched and yawned and rolled over onto her back. Natalie rubbed her belly and asked what kind of dog she was. I told her, and she asked if all miniature bull terriers were as "darling" as Rosie. Against all odds, I was starting to like this woman. "So you don't miss Hollywood," I said.

"Not even a little bit," she said. "I'm happy here. I've got lots of family nearby, so I'm able to raise my little boy on my own."

"His dad's not around?"

She shook her head. "Donor. I did IVF." She smiled at me. "Melanie Joan paid for that, too."

"Nice," I said.

"It is," she said. "You have kids?"

"No," I said. "Just Rosie. And my boyfriend has a son in junior high."

"You've got your hands full, then," she said. Natalie petted Rosie some more. Rosie obligingly moved from my lap to hers.

It hit me that I'd called Richie my boyfriend, not my fiancé. And that brought to mind my conversation with him in the parking lot. The unpleasant fact that he couldn't make it to Boston and my equally unpleasant reaction. I quickly closed the door on that. *Save it for your next therapist visit,* I told myself. But then I remembered that Susan Silverman was on vacation for the next two weeks—in Crete, I was pretty sure. She wasn't even in an amenable time zone. Not that I'd have been inclined to interrupt her if she was, but it would have been nice to have that option.

Rosie was licking Natalie's chin. "Sorry," I said. "She does that when she really likes someone."

I told Rosie to stop, but Natalie said she didn't mind. "Between this good girl and Book Babe," she said, "I'm feeling very seen today."

I watched her, thinking. "Natalie?"

"Yeah?" she said.

"Was there anyone on the set of *A Girl and Not a God* who was especially upset when you got fired?"

"I don't remember," she said. "I mean, I've blocked so much of that week out of my mind."

"Understandable," I said.

"Why do you ask?"

"Book Babe wrote that you have grounds for a lawsuit. As though she knows the truth of what happened." I looked at her. "As though she was there."

"Ah." Natalie nodded slowly. "Come to think of it, there was someone," she said. "A friend."

"Who?"

"Kim Lash," she said. "Head of wardrobe."

"Really? Wardrobe?"

"We'd go out for drinks sometimes, trash Melanie Joan . . ."

"She didn't like Melanie Joan, either?"

"Kim didn't have anything against her personally," she said. "But she liked me. We'd worked together previously, on a Hallmark movie. She said I wasn't being treated fairly. She felt sorry for me."

"That's . . . strange."

She laughed. "What? Someone liking me?"

"No," I said. "It's just that Melanie Joan told me that after she fired you, you stole a bunch of designer clothes and shoes from the wardrobe department."

"First of all, it was just one dress and one pair of shoes."

"Okay."

"And I didn't steal them. Kim gave them to me."

"She did?"

"It wasn't like the new actress was going to wear them. I'm a foot taller than her," she said. "And Kim paid for the clothes herself." She exhaled hard. "Melanie Joan said I stole them?"

"She wrote it in the book."

Natalie raised an eyebrow at me. "That would be grounds for a lawsuit," she said.

"Exactly."

Natalie pulled out her phone. She found Kim Lash in her contacts and texted me the information. "You can tell her I gave you her number," she said. "Kim and I still talk every once in a while."

"Thanks, Natalie." I stood up. "This is really helpful." Rosie jumped off her lap, and I reattached her leash.

"Kim's a big reader," she said. "I hope she is Book Babe and you can put this thing to rest."

"Me, too," I said. "And Tony wasn't lying about taking that story out of the prologue. I really do think we can convince Melanie Joan that it would be in everyone's best interest."

Natalie shrugged. "Whatever." She looked downright serene.

I decided I should get back into meditation. It obviously had done wonders for Natalie's outlook on life.

"Just out of curiosity," she said as I started to leave. "What was the pseudonym she used for me?"

"Tallulah Airhead."

She snorted. "And you're telling me this woman couldn't use a rewrite?"

EIGHTEEN

When I got back to my car, Tony was leaning against it, staring intently at his phone. I felt bad for not having thought to give him the keys. But it was a good ten degrees cooler in Gloucester than it had been in Boston, what with that ocean breeze. He seemed comfortable enough.

"Natalie Blythe isn't Book Babe," I said as I approached.

Tony didn't look up from his phone. "How do you know?"

"I trust her," I said. "And she has no reason to lie about it."

He sighed heavily. "That sucks."

"It is what it is. Anyway, I may have another lead."

He still didn't look at me. "That sucks, Greg," he said, and it was only then that I noticed he had his earbuds in. "That really, really sucks. Kicking MJ when she's down. Doesn't she have better things to do?"

I moved into his line of vision and mouthed the words *What is going on?*

Tony glanced up at me. He mouthed *Greg Scepter* and pointed at his phone. He looked more serious than I'd ever seen him. It changed his whole face. "You can't do that," he said.

I asked what was going on again. He held up his index finger and turned away. "This is no way to treat your biggest-selling . . . No, of course not. I'd have heard from her if she'd seen . . . Please . . . Give her a cha— Two days. Okay? Hello?"

Tony yanked out his earbuds.

"What happened?" I said.

"I hate doing business with that guy," he said.

I asked for a third time. "What happened?"

"He's about to cut MJ loose," he said. "I just begged him for two more days, but . . . well, you just heard it."

"He didn't say no."

"That's true," he said. "Because he hung up on me."

"I thought Evan said he could buy us some time."

"Well, it's different now."

"Why?"

"Because of Leila fucking Donnelly."

I frowned at him. "The author?"

"Scepter says she posted something." He motioned me over and began tapping on his phone. "A video."

I moved next to him. "I thought she wasn't online."

"She's not on social media," he said. "She's reclusive. It's part of her brand. But apparently she does have a website."

How did someone go about branding herself as reclusive? I peered at the website on Tony's screen—pale gray, with Leila Donnelly's name at the top and two buttons: `the books` and `the author`. Typewriter font. I supposed that was how one did it.

He tapped the "author" button. At the top of the page was a headshot of Leila Donnelly. She looked exactly the way I'd expected her to. Young, waifish, and unsmiling. Long, dark, wavy hair parted in the middle. Enormous sad eyes. No makeup. She wore a black tank top, and there was a small tattoo on her right shoulder. A pink-and-white flower. She had a disgusted air about her—as though the very act of posing for a picture violated her personally. Beneath the photo was her author bio. One sentence. No capital letters: **leila donnelly lives on the east coast of the united states.**

"Where's the video?" I said.

"Good question."

But then Tony tapped the back arrow and we both saw it, at the bottom of the main page. A link that read: **leila speaks.**

It connected us to a YouTube video—a still of Leila staring down the camera in that same black tank top. "Jesus," I said. The video had been posted at four p.m. today, and already it had more than five hundred thousand views. Tony's finger hovered over the PLAY arrow. "Are you ready?" he said.

"I don't think so," I said.

"Me neither," Tony said. But he hit play anyway.

NINETEEN

After the video ended, Tony and I said nothing for a long while. It was hard to look on the bright side of what we'd just seen—especially considering that the video had gained thousands more views in the past minute we'd spent watching it.

I cleared my throat. Forced a smile. "Look, maybe Melanie Joan might have to pause the memoir for a little while," I said. "But it's not that big a deal. People have short attention spans, and she's . . . like . . . the Madonna of romance writers. Who is Leila Donnelly in this world?"

Tony stared straight out at the ocean, the sky pink from the setting sun. "The Taylor Swift of romance writers."

"Oh."

We both went quiet again. He gazed back down at his screen. I tried one of those yogic breaths. It didn't work very well.

Tony groaned.

I looked at him.

"I just thought of something even worse," he said.

"What?" I said.

"The video now has five hundred fifteen thousand views."

"Yeah? And?"

"What if Melanie Joan is one of them?"

"Oh, no . . ." I plucked my phone out of my bag and called Spike.

He answered immediately. "Please tell me you've found Book Babe," he said.

"I wish," I said.

"Shit," he said.

I cleared my throat. "Has Melanie Joan, uh, seen the latest?"

"What's the latest?" Spike said.

I exhaled. "I'm hoping and praying I should take that as a no."

"She's sleeping," he said. "She was spiraling, so I convinced her to take an Ambien and lie down."

"Thank God." I told Spike about the video in which Leila Donnelly offered a whispery condemnation of Melanie Joan, whom she called an "out-of-touch, elderly pick-me girl who weaponized her privilege against one of the most generous members of the romance community, Book Babe." The final thirty seconds of the video consisted of a screenshot of Melanie Joan's notorious ReadAnon comment. It had been the first time I'd ever seen it in full, and I had to say, it was an eye-popper. I considered myself pretty worldly, yet there were sex acts described in the comment that made me yearn for a whiskey and one of Melanie Joan's water pills—just to erase the images from my memory.

"I've never seen the comment," Spike said.

"Consider yourself lucky," I said.

Spike was silent for a few seconds, taking in all I had told him. "Donnelly really called MJ elderly?" he said.

"Yep."

"How can we keep her from seeing it?"

"I don't think we can. But we can at least prolong the inevitable so Tony can be there to deal with her reaction," I said.

"Thanks a lot," Tony said.

"You're the one getting the regular commission," I said. "Spike, are you in the hotel room with her?"

"Same suite. I'm in the living room."

"When did she go to sleep?"

"Probably half an hour ago."

"Anyone else there with you?"

"Harold."

"Does he still have her phone?"

"I'm pretty sure. Harold, do you have her phone? He does. He just showed it to me."

"Does she have anything in the room with her? Laptop or tablet?"

"Fuck. We didn't check."

I told him we were on the way. Tony and I got into my car. Rosie hopped into the backseat. Spike stayed on the line, his voice shifting over to Bluetooth as I pulled out of the parking lot. “She’s got a tablet in there with her,” he said. “Harold just told me.”

“Can you sneak it out without waking her?”

“I’m going to try.”

I glanced at Tony. His jaw was tight. Both of his hands were balled into fists, that college ring of his glimmering. I’d never seen him this tense. Come to think of it, I wasn’t sure I’d ever seen him tense at all.

“I woke up in L.A. this morning, and everything was fine,” Tony said. “Beautiful sunrise. Perfect weather to go jogging . . .”

“I hear you,” I said. “Right up until lunch, the most stressful thing on my agenda was dinner at my parents’.”

“Was that what you were talking about on the phone earlier?” Tony asked. “Did Richie have to cancel on dinner?”

I gazed out the window. “To be fair, I gave him very short notice.”

I could feel him watching me. “You want to know the best thing about not being in a relationship?” he said.

“No,” I said. “But I bet you’re going to tell me anyway.”

“You never get disappointed,” he said. “That’s the best thing.”

I turned and looked at him. He had a point, I supposed. But it wasn’t one I wanted to openly agree with. I went back to the window.

Over the Bluetooth, I heard muffled conversation—Spike and Harold. Neither of us had ended the call. “Everything okay over there?” I said.

“Harold just said he heard something in the bedroom,” Spike said.

"Something?"

"A stirring," Spike said.

"A stirring?" Tony said.

"Harold's words, not mine." Spike told us he was going in. "Harold, if you can distract her, I'll try and sneak the tablet out," he said. But the end of his sentence was drowned out by a scream so ear-piercing, I nearly swerved into the next lane.

Rosie yelped.

Tony and I looked at each other.

"Guess she saw the video," Tony said.

TWENTY

By the time we got back to Boston, I was already late for dinner at my parents' house. I called my dad and let him know I'd be there, hopefully within the hour, as I turned onto Avery Street, where the Ritz-Carlton was located.

"I'm sorry. It's work stuff," I told Dad.

"Anything I can help with?"

"Not unless you've developed an expertise in anonymous online activity."

"Is your client getting threats?"

"Nope," I said. "Just a one-star review."

"Hmph."

"I'll explain tonight," I said. "Oh, and Richie can't make it."

"I know," Dad said. "He called to apologize. I'd just reschedule the whole thing. But your mother insists. She's made her signature scrod."

Mom's scrod. It keeps getting better and better. I told Dad I'd be there as soon as I could. We hung up.

"You sure you don't want to switch places?" Tony said.

"Don't tempt me," I said.

"How bad can dinner with your parents be?"

"With my dad, it's a joy. With my mother added to the mix, and my sister, Elizabeth . . . well, let's just say I'd rather forcibly keep Melanie Joan from further destroying her own life."

"Wow."

Rosie was on Tony's lap. She'd plopped there halfway through the drive home, but Tony hadn't pushed her away. And when I'd tried to shoo her into the backseat, he'd told me not to worry about it. *Getting shed on is the least of my troubles,* he'd said, that preternatural calm of his slipping away.

As it turned out, Tony's business had been on a downturn for a while, and the process had accelerated in the aftermath of the most recent writers' strike. Several of his clients' projects had fallen through. Some of them had left the movie business for good. At this point, Melanie Joan's career was Tony Gault's one reliable asset. And now that was in serious danger. This confession had thrown me for a loop. I hadn't known how to respond. *I'm sorry,* I'd tried. *I had no idea . . .*

It is what it is, he'd replied. *Forget I ever said anything.*

For the rest of the ride, he'd been quiet.

I glanced over at him now, staring out the window and petting Rosie as though she were a worry stone.

"We'll fix this," I said.

He gave me a tight smile. "I have faith in you." I didn't like seeing him like this—thoughtful, concerned. Unbothered by dog fur. Much as I'd lost touch with Tony, his shallowness was one of the few things I could depend on—proof that some things in the world never changed.

I pulled up in front of the Ritz just as Spike was exiting through the revolving doors. Tony lifted Rosie from his lap. "This pooch is very comforting," he said.

"Thanks," I said.

"Maybe I should get one of my own."

I gave him a long, appraising glance. "You sure you can handle the commitment?"

"Hmm . . ." His face relaxed, and he winked at me, the old Tony returning. "No," he said. "No, I'm not."

"I didn't think so."

Spike jogged up to my car. He looked exhausted and on edge at the same time.

"How is it up there?" Tony asked.

"Harold managed to get her tablet into the safe and lock it," Spike said. "He also talked her into an in-room IV drip therapy session."

"So she's temporarily incapacitated," Tony said.

Spike nodded.

"Good man, Harold."

"The guy knows how to strategize."

Tony said a quick goodbye and headed into the hotel. Spike took his place in the front seat. Rosie bounded into his lap, and we headed toward his restaurant, where I knew the evening rush was just beginning.

I briefed him on the trip to Gloucester, telling him all about Natalie Blythe and how Melanie Joan had inadvertently helped her to find her true calling.

"So she's obviously not Book Babe," he said.

"No, but she did give me a lead," I said. "The head of wardrobe on *A Girl and Not a God.* I'm going to call her on my way to my parents'."

Spike nodded slowly. "Speaking of dinner at your parents' . . . "

"Yeah?"

"When we were on the phone earlier, I heard you telling Tony that Richie can't make it."

I sighed. "It's no big deal."

"But your mother is involved," he said. "And Elizabeth."

"I'm a grown woman," I said. "I've been in therapy for years. This will be a good test of it."

"Okay, fair enough," he said. "But is your mother making that scrod?"

"Yes. In fact, she is."

"I know that scrod. I wouldn't wish it on my worst enemy."

I smiled at Spike. "I'll grab a slice from Regina Pizzeria on my way home."

I made a left turn and hit a mass of rush-hour traffic. Fortunately, Spike's restaurant wasn't that far.

Spike let out a huge sigh. "Okay, fine. I'll go to your folks' house with you."

"You have a job," I said. "Just like Richie. And unlike Richie, you've spent a large part of your day helping me with *my* job."

"Who cares?"

"I mean it," I said. And I did. I was lucky enough to have friends in my life like Spike, who routinely dropped everything to help me out—whether that meant beating the crap out of some thug who tried to kill me, scaring a reluctant informant into submission, or, in this most recent case, babysitting a diva author with muscles of steel and a voice that could shatter glass. But I took advantage of that privilege too often. Spike had his own troubles. Richie had his, as did my father and my shrink, Susan Silverman, and every other friend and colleague I assumed had nothing truly crucial going on in their lives compared to mine.

I was worried I might have a touch of main character syndrome, and that if I didn't stop believing that my problems were bigger and deeper and more important than everyone else's, I was never going to be able to make a successful go at a second marriage to Richie.

I stared out the window. Traffic had barely moved. Even at the end of the day, the steam-heat was floating off the asphalt in visible waves. Spike was right. At this time of year, Boston was just as unpleasant as Asbury Park was. And unlike Asbury Park, half these people probably didn't even want to be here.

"Busy night at the restaurant?" I asked.

He nodded. "We've had big crowds lately."

"What's Flynn doing?"

“He’s got a Zoom interview,” he said. “Then he was going to come by and work some magic in the kitchen.”

“Yeah?”

“I’ve got shepherd’s pie on the menu, and Flynn’s is a lot better than Jorgen’s.”

“Why don’t you get out of the car?” I said. “We’re only about a block away, right? It would be faster if you walked.”

“You sure you don’t want me to come to dinner with you?” he said. “Flynn won’t mind. He’s friends with everybody at the restaurant. And there’s nothing at work that my manager can’t handle.”

“You love your job,” I said. “Your man’s going to be in the kitchen. You should be there.”

He looked surprised, which made me wince.

“Thanks, Sunny.”

Traffic was at such a standstill, I didn’t need to put my hazards on. Spike simply lifted Rosie from his lap and set her down on the seat, slipped out of the car, and closed the door behind him. Nobody even bothered to honk.

After Spike left, Rosie put her paws up on the passenger-side window and stared out after him. She began to whine. “I know, sweetheart,” I said. “But we’re both going to have to stop being so selfish.”

TWENTY-ONE

I called Kim Lash from my car. It went straight to voicemail, so I left a message. I kept it vague, mentioning Natalie's name and asking if I could talk to her about Melanie Joan. I figured vague was best. When it came to returning a stranger's phone call, curiosity could be a powerful motivator.

Before heading to my parents', I picked up a bottle of my mom's favorite Chablis, walked and fed Rosie—and left her at my loft. I didn't like doing this. Rosie and my dad adored each other, and my mom didn't mind her, either. But Elizabeth loved to complain about my dog so much that it was practically a passion, and I wasn't about to indulge her.

I was around ten minutes away from my parents' place in Newton when my phone rang. It was Kim Lash. *Curiosity strikes again.* "Thanks for calling me back," I said.

"Sure, hon." She had a gravelly voice. From what, I didn't know. Cigarettes, age, years of screaming, all of the above . . . Over the phone, who could tell? "Are you a friend of Natalie's?" she asked. "I haven't seen her since she left showbiz."

"Actually, I just met her today," I said. "But I've known Melanie Joan for years."

Kim chuckled. "Melanie Joan Hall. She's something."

"She sure is."

"You work for her?"

"Sometimes."

"What's your job?"

"I'm a private investigator," I said. "But right now, I'm kind of . . . helping her out with damage control."

She chuckled again. "Man, oh, man. You've got your work cut out for you."

"You've heard about what happened?"

"Who hasn't?" she said.

"Natalie," I said. "I mean, not when I spoke to her this afternoon."

"That was probably before Leila Donnelly, right?"

I cringed. "Yeah."

"It's been all over the news," she said.

"It has?"

"Leila Donnelly's like Garbo," Kim said. "She never speaks, so when she does, it makes headlines."

"Garbo . . ."

"Before your time?"

"No, no. I know who she was. It's just an interesting analogy," I said. I was thinking about Blake. The profile he'd come up with on Book Babe. "Do you like books about old Hollywood? Like . . . movie star memoirs?"

"Sure," she said.

"How about self-help books?"

"Some of them."

"You have any young kids?"

She didn't answer for a few seconds.

"Like two, three years old?"

"If you don't mind my saying, Sunny, these are some weird-ass questions."

I exhaled. "I know." I was five minutes away from my folks' house, and this wasn't going anywhere. I decided to cut to the chase. "Look. I talked to Natalie because I thought she could have posted that one-star review of Melanie Joan on ReadAnon."

Kim snorted. "Natalie's a doll," she said, "but she's not the book-critique-writing type."

"Are you?"

"What?"

"Are you Book Babe?" I said. "Natalie seemed to think it was possible."

Kim inhaled sharply, then blew into the phone. Smoking a cigarette. "That's what Melanie Joan hired you for?" she said. "She's paying you to find out who shit on her memoir?"

I cleared my throat. "She wants to personally apologize for her inappropriate response to the review."

"Oh, boy."

"Are you Book Babe?"

"No."

"And I should believe you because . . ."

"I am a big reader, and I have a ReadAnon account. But I just look at other people's reviews. I don't post them."

"Nobody will know, if that's what you're concerned about," I said. "Melanie Joan feels awful about what she said. She wants to apologize. And that apology can be as private as you want. If you're Book Babe, you can keep posting and be as anonymous as ever."

"Look," Kim said. "I like Melanie Joan's books."

"You do?"

"A lot. And yes, she can be a nightmare. But I think that comes from perfectionism. She's probably harder on herself than she is on anybody else, Natalie included."

I thought for a moment. "That's interesting."

"You should have seen her on set. She'd spend all night re-writing her own pages, bring them in early, when nobody was there but the crew, try the new lines out herself in front of the camera . . ."

"I didn't know she did that," I said. "But it doesn't surprise me."

Kim took another long drag off her cigarette. I could practically smell the smoke in my car. "I've worked with a lot of authors turned executive producers and I've never seen anyone as committed as Melanie Joan," she said. "So even though I like Natalie and I felt bad for Natalie, I understood where the lady was coming from. She doesn't want anybody messing with all that hard work."

I stopped at a red light. I looked out the window. It was nearly eight p.m. and the sky was a lush violet, shot through with vestiges of the sunset, porch lights glowing. I thought about the young couple I'd seen earlier on the beach. Maybe I'd paint them on this street instead. It would be a good way to escape this case—which was turning out to be so much more frustrating than I'd imagined it would be. "So, obviously, you understand Melanie Joan," I said.

"Maybe not completely," Kim said. "But I do respect her. And I'd never trash her work."

I swallowed hard. "I believe you." It was the truth, unfortunately.

"We had some good times on that set, man," Kim was saying. "Best wrap party I've ever been to. Kobe steaks, caviar bar, top-shelf tequila . . . Her publisher sprung for it. She even came."

"Gloria Scepter."

"Lovely woman. She said nothing was too good for Melanie Joan."

"She passed away."

"I heard. I also heard her son took over."

"Yeah," I said. "He doesn't share his mother's enthusiasm."

"I'm sorry."

"He just dumped Melanie Joan over this mess. We're trying to get him to change his mind."

"Hey, I don't know how hard it is on an anonymous site,"

she said. "But maybe you should find someone who can hack Book Babe's account."

I started to explain my ethical issues, but cut myself off midsentence. With Melanie Joan in danger of losing both her livelihood and Tony's, I didn't feel quite the same conviction that I'd had at lunchtime.

"You said it yourself," Kim said. "The apology could be done in private. If Book Babe wants to stay anonymous, you guys could honor that."

I didn't say anything. But I did find myself nodding.

"Just something to think about," Kim said.

"I will." We said goodbye and I ended the call. I thought about it. The light turned green. I pressed the gas pedal, still thinking about what Kim had said. Then I remembered what Richie had told me about his dad, how Desmond was branching out into tech.

I spotted my parents' house. Elizabeth's rose-gold Mercedes was parked out front like a high school graduation present. I wondered whether she'd brought her latest boyfriend—a twenty-eight-year-old content creator named Cody—and if her Spotify was still permanently set to the soundtrack from *Wicked*. When we were kids, Elizabeth had been fourteen going on forty—serious and judgmental beyond her years. But these days, she seemed to be aging in reverse. She was still judgmental as hell, though. I had to give her that.

I pulled up to the curb behind Elizabeth's midlife-crisis coupe. I grabbed my bag and the wine for my mom, but I wasn't ready to get out of the car. I kept thinking about the case. About

Melanie Joan and what might happen to her if I wasn't able to find Book Babe quickly. I started to call Richie, but I decided not to. He was at work and understaffed on a night that promised to be crushingly busy.

I called his father instead.

TWENTY-TWO

"Tell Sonya about your pod, Cody," Elizabeth said.

My sister's content creator boyfriend didn't reply. He was completely absorbed in his phone. He had been all evening. We were nearly done with dinner, and he'd maybe said three sentences, all of which started with "Pass the . . ."

"Babe?" said Elizabeth.

Cody looked up. "Huh?"

"The new podcast, babe. Tell Sonya."

He turned to me and smirked. "Three words. Serial killers' last meals."

"That's four words," I said. "But go on."

We were nearly done with dinner. I'd been measuring the evening in bites of scrod, and I was about four bites away from sweet release. I hadn't mentioned Melanie Joan or the case, because no one had asked me about it. Dad had tried, only to be interrupted by Mother, who preferred talking about Richie's job and why he had "chosen it over his future family" tonight.

"So, like, for each episode I spotlight a different killer," Cody was saying. "I talk for maybe ten minutes about what they did to get on death row. Murders, trial, bla, bla, bla . . . But then we get to the meat."

"The meat?" my father said.

"Their court-sanctioned last meal," Elizabeth said.

"Ah." Dad said it genially. Dad was always genial.

"Every episode, I describe what the murderer ordered before his execution. And then . . ." Cody peered around the table, a gleam in his eyes. "I eat it."

"Spoiler alert," I said.

"I also critique it from a culinary and societal perspective," Cody said.

"The meal," Dad said.

"The whole, entire meal. Unless the serial killer didn't finish it. I only eat as much as he did, for accuracy's sake."

"It's got something for everyone," Elizabeth said. "True-crime fans. Foodies."

"That's not everyone," I said. "But go on."

"It's a significant portion of the podcast-listening population, Sonya," Elizabeth said.

"How many of these recordings have you made, Cody?" my mother said.

"A dozen," Cody said.

"How industrious," Mom said.

"And filling," I said.

"You're telling me," Cody said. "John Wayne Gacy ordered a whole bucket of KFC original recipe, twelve fried prawns, an extra-large order of fries, and a pound of strawberries. Oh, and a Diet Coke. Irony. Anyways, he ate the whole thing, so I did, too. It was a lot. But, you know. The pod wants what the pod wants."

Elizabeth beamed at him.

"Such devotion to craft," my mother said. "You creative people never cease to amaze me."

"I can't do anything half-assed," Cody said. "It would be an insult to the Cody Culture."

"Cody Culture?" Dad asked.

"That's his fandom," Elizabeth said.

I managed to keep from gagging.

My dad said "ah" again, without a hint of sarcasm. It didn't faze me. It was our family dynamic, and I knew it well. My dad humored my mom and they both humored Elizabeth (and anyone she happened to be involved with, whose egos tended to be even more fragile than hers). Nobody humored Dad or me, which was fine. But get-togethers like this one exhausted me. I wished Richie was here, so that at least I could have somebody to roll my eyes at.

"So, Sunny," my father said. "This case of yours—"

"I imagine it must be going quite well," my mother said, "seeing how it made you an hour late for dinner." She polished off her glass of Chablis and poured herself another.

I exhaled. Took another bite. "Great scrod, Mom."

"Gerald James Bordelon ate fried sacalait fish as part of his last meal," Cody said.

"I don't know that I'm familiar with sacalait," my mother said. "Is that a white fish?"

"I want to hear about our daughter's case, Emma," my father said.

My mother sighed dramatically. She drank more wine and started clearing the table. I told my dad about the case. I covered everything—except for my Hail Mary phone call to Desmond Burke back in the car, when I'd asked if he could set me up with a good hacker. Former police captain Phil Randall would not have approved of uncovering someone's identity without a warrant, or, for that matter, a crime. At any rate, Desmond had said he might know of a guy. Barring miracles (which had been known to happen, but not very often), that guy was Melanie Joan's and my only hope.

When I was through talking, Elizabeth piped up first. "I love Book Babe," she said.

This surprised me. Elizabeth had always been an avid reader, but not of the genres favored by Book Babe. I'd known her as something of a literary snob.

"Really?" I said.

"Don't look so surprised," she said. "I'm actually in a book club, where we read nothing but Book Babe's five-star books. Right, Cody?"

Cody said nothing. He was back on his phone.

"It's a lot of fun," Elizabeth said. "I've discovered so many good authors I'd never heard of before."

"Like who?"

"Leila Donnelly. She's fantastic."

"Seriously?"

"Why does that shock you?"

"Because," I said, "you don't read romances."

Elizabeth stood up. She collected her place setting, as well as Cody's. "Yes, I do."

"Since when? You always said they were silly and childish."

"People change, Sonya," she said. "I know that's hard for you to believe. But you should try it sometime. Expand your horizons. Stop doing the same old tired, boring things everyone expects you to do."

Like dating someone born in the same century as me? I wanted to say that, but she swept into the kitchen before I could get a word in.

"Are you sure the actress was telling you the truth?" Dad said once I was through. "Actors can be very convincing liars."

"Natalie Blythe?" I shrugged. "I feel like if she was that talented an actress, Melanie Joan wouldn't have been able to derail her career."

"Good point," he said.

"Any other ideas?" I said. "What would you have done back in the day, hypothetically, if Book Babe was at large and suspected of an actual crime?"

Behind me, I heard the kitchen doors swing open, the clack

of my mother's heels. "Sonya, you know that I don't like you getting your father involved in your cases," she said.

"Your hearing is excellent, Mom."

"I'm serious," she said. "You know it's bad for his health. His blood pressure. His stress levels. Yet you keep persisting. If I didn't know better, I'd think you were a terribly insensitive and selfish person."

My cheeks heated up. On one hand, my mother calling me insensitive and selfish was a pot-meet-kettle kind of thing. But on the other, she had a point. My dad did have high blood pressure. He'd been shot a couple years ago and still walked with a cane. He wasn't getting any younger or healthier, and here I was indulging the very thing that had sapped so much of his energy: his drive to investigate. Was this another symptom of main character syndrome?

"That isn't fair, Emma," Dad said. "It isn't insensitive or selfish to treat an old guy like me like he's got something worthwhile to say."

"No, no. Mom's right," I said.

My mom nearly dropped the glasses she was carrying. "Really?" she said.

"Yes, and I'm sorry."

I picked up the two serving trays and brought them into the kitchen, following my mother. My dad started to get up, too, but I told him to stay where he was. "You've got to rest that leg," I said.

"That's a load of bull." He struggled to get up, his body

trembling. Slowly, he eased back into his chair. He gave me a sad smile. "Hey, who am I to argue with the smartest detective I know?" It broke my heart a little.

"Be right back," I said.

Cody stayed where he was, his entire being absorbed in his iPhone screen. Bombs could have gone off, he wouldn't have budged. I grabbed the remaining glasses from the table, set them on top of the two trays, and brought them into the kitchen. Elizabeth was sitting on a counter stool, reapplying her makeup. My mother was supervising the housekeeper, Donna, as she loaded the dishwasher.

When I placed the trays and glasses on the counter, my mother stopped and turned to me. "I'm sorry I was harsh with you, Sunny, but I worry about your father," she said. "He's so good at taking care of everyone but himself."

"I get it, Mom."

She gave my arm a quick squeeze. It wasn't lost on me that she'd called me Sunny, a nickname I knew she personally loathed. Just like my father, she was changing with age. There was a softness to her now, an awareness and vulnerability that I didn't want to think too hard about.

When I left the kitchen, my dad was on his feet.

"Dad. You should be resting."

He ignored the comment. "You know what we would have done," he said. "We'd have talked to the family of the fugitive. Or maybe the significant other. Someone they cared about. Put them on the five o'clock news."

I looked at him. "Get them to make a direct appeal."

"That's right," he said. "Thinking about what the equivalent of that would be now, if you got Melanie Joan to make a video and post it on YouTube. Just like that other author did."

"Leila Donnelly."

"Yep," he said, "only it would be an apology. If she wants Book Babe to come forward, Melanie Joan would really have to humble herself."

I snorted. "That's a tall order."

"I know. I've met her."

"She was rather sweet on you, if I recall."

Dad laughed. I laughed, too. When it came to women who were handfuls, Phil Randall was catnip and he knew it. He leaned on his cane and winced. I told him again that he should sit down.

"You wanna do me a favor?" he said.

"Anything."

"Don't worry about me."

"That's an impossible request."

"Like asking Melanie Joan to humble herself?"

"Just like that."

Elizabeth left the kitchen and made her way over to Cody. She sat in his lap. He didn't look up from his phone. "Isn't he wonderful, Sonya?" she said.

And then my phone rang. I'd never been so happy to take a call. I didn't check the screen. For all I cared, it could have been a scammer or a heavy breather. (Did people heavy-breathe into phones anymore?) But when I heard Desmond Burke's Irish lilt, I was doubly glad to have answered.

“My technological expert will meet you,” he said. “Midnight at Icon. He’ll be in the VIP lounge.”

I cast a quick glance at my dad and spoke very quietly. “Name?” I said. “Description?”

“The hostess will bring you to him,” Desmond said. “Ask for Swinging Dick.”

TWENTY-THREE

Icon was known as one of the hottest nightclubs in Boston, but that didn't impress me. I'd never been much of a nightclub person, even in my youth. The flashing lights, the noise, the loud music, the overpriced, watered-down drinks . . . Give me a healthy pour of twelve-year-old scotch in a discreet hotel bar with good acoustics—one where you didn't have to scream out your drink order—and I was content. Desmond's hacker seemed to prefer a different type of ambience. But what would you expect from a guy who called himself Swinging Dick?

After hanging up with Desmond, I'd made up a quick excuse involving Melanie Joan and headed home to walk Rosie, shower, and change. It had taken me a little while to pull together an outfit that struck the right balance between club-appropriate and age-appropriate. I'd settled on jeans, Jimmy

Choo kitten heels, and a sleeveless Courtney Zheng blouse in beige silk that felt expensive without being flashy. I'd shifted my wallet, phone, and .38 into a smaller shoulder bag, kissed Rosie goodbye, and hurried out the door, arriving at my destination with minutes to spare.

As nightclubs went, Icon was impressive. Two big rooms packed with gorgeous people, a different DJ in each room, and enough multicolored strobes and disco balls to necessitate a seizure warning. It was just after midnight. I'd bypassed a round-the-block line and even the bag search to get in, explaining to the bouncer, and then to the hostess, that I was here to see Swinging Dick. Miraculously, I'd been able to keep a straight face both times.

The thing was, his real name was perfectly normal. Desmond—who'd only just started collaborating with Mr. Dick—had given it to me, adding that the hacker had spent some of his youth in our city, "but that's not necessarily reason to trust him."

You mind if I ask around about him? I'd said.

I'd consider it a favor, Desmond had said.

Far be it from me to deny my once and future father-in-law a favor. On my way home from my parents', I'd called Gina Delvecchio, an old friend from my days on the force. She was semiretired now, but had spent twenty-five years with the BPD as a juvenile officer. She'd told me that Swinging Dick's real name sounded familiar, and that she was more than happy to make a few calls. I'd thanked her, adding that I didn't normally associate with criminals, and she'd replied, *That reminds me, how's Richie's family?*

Gina had always been kind of a smart-ass.

I was thinking about Gina now—her smart mouth and her excellent memory—as the hostess led me through the second of the two enormous rooms, bobbing and weaving her way around patrons.

She raised a tattooed arm above the fray and pointed to the VIP section, situated at the edge of the dance floor and up a small flight of stairs. It was a lot quieter there. I followed her to a corner banquette, where a man sat with his back to us. He wore a dark, shiny suit. It strained against his body, which was roughly the size of a vending machine.

He seemed to be alone at the table. But when I got closer, I saw a boy sitting beside him. He wore a backward baseball cap and his head was down. He may have been asleep. I told myself not to make any snarky "father of the year" comments.

On the table, there was a bottle of champagne on ice. I waited for the hostess to leave, then walked up to the human vending machine. "Swinging Dick?" I said.

The little boy lifted his head. "Sunny Randall." His voice was deeper than I'd expected. Looking at his face, now illuminated by the glow of the sleek tablet on the table in front of him, I saw that he was an adult. Barely. He had big doe eyes and freckles across his nose and a sweet little peach fuzz mustache.

"You're Swinging Dick?" I asked him.

He nodded. "This is Ralph."

"Hi, Ralph," I said.

The vending machine said nothing.

"Ralph doesn't talk," said Swinging Dick. He scooched a little closer to his enormous pal. "Join us," he said.

I perched at the edge of the banquette, across from Ralph. I hugged my bag close to my side. My phone vibrated with a text.

Swinging Dick poured out a glass of champagne and slid it in front of me. "Cristal. 2015." He said it like he expected me to swoon.

"Maybe later," I said. "If I feel like we have anything to toast."

"I got something for you to toast," Swinging Dick said with a painstaking wink.

"I highly doubt it," I said.

"Hey, be nice," he said. "I'm a delightful person, once you get to know me."

I was getting tired of this conversation. "I'm assuming Mr. Burke told you what I need."

"Yeah."

"How fast can you do it for me?"

"Depends," he said.

"On what?"

"Whether I decide to take the job."

I blinked at him. "You work for Desmond Burke. And he asked you to do it."

"Actually, I'm a contractor, not a full-time employee," he

said. "And I only accept work that I find interesting. And well-paying. Am I right, Ralph?"

Ralph nodded slowly, his meaty hands folded in front of him on the table like a stack of catcher's mitts.

"Ralph, on the other hand, works for me."

"Full-time," Ralph said.

"I thought you told me he doesn't talk," I said.

"I do occasionally," Ralph said.

I glanced down at the glowing tablet, which Dick had placed on the table. My name was on the screen, followed by my driver's license photo and a chunk of computer code.

"What's that?" I asked him.

"Research." Swinging Dick smirked at me. I was really starting to hate this kid.

"Ah." I unzipped my shoulder bag. Just enough for him to see my .38. I left it open until I could sense him looking down at it.

"What's that?" he said.

"Insurance."

The smirk grew broader. "Ooh. Color me scared."

"Are quips like that part of your delightful personality?"

He continued, undeterred. "I know you're a good shot," Dick said. "I know you've worked some high-profile cases and you've got a reputation as a tough guy. Well, for a girl."

I leveled my eyes at him. "Color me impressed."

"But I'm burying the lede here," he said. "I also know your social, your address, and your FICO score." He grinned. "I can get you in some serious trouble if you don't play ball."

"What do you mean, 'play ball'?"

"Thirty K ought to do it," he said. "I prefer cash, but no sweat if you don't do paper. I've got Venmo."

I stared at him.

"Consider it a gratuity," he said.

"What if I were to tell Mr. Burke about this gratuity?"

"Well, I guess our deal would be off," he said. "And, um . . . so would your credit score. Am I right, Ralph?"

Ralph let out a tired "Ha." A part of me felt sorry for him, having to listen to this little prick full-time.

"The thing is, Sunny, I can, like, fully destroy your life if I want to."

I said nothing. I slipped my phone out of my bag and checked the screen. The text was from Gina Delvecchio. The first line: *I knew the name sounded familiar.* I read it. "Oh, ho," I said.

"What are you doing?" Dick said.

I held up an index finger and texted Gina back: *What's your favorite wine?* I intended to buy her a case.

"Didn't your mom ever tell you it's not polite to play with your phone in the middle of an important conversation?" Swinging Dick said.

I put the phone down and smiled sweetly at him. "Interesting choice of words, Terrence."

"What did you call me?"

"That's your real name, right? Terrence Fitzpatrick? Or do you prefer Terry?"

"Uh . . ."

I leaned back in the seat and crossed my legs. I wanted to be comfortable for this. “Anyhoo, Terry,” I said, “I heard you really put Louise through the ringer back in the day.”

“Louise?”

“Your mom.”

“How do you . . . Why do you know her name?”

I turned to Ralph. “Did he swear you to secrecy?”

Ralph shrugged.

“Oh, well. I’m going to tell you something about your boss, and you can either keep it to yourself or use it to get a raise. My guess is he doesn’t pay you enough.”

Ralph lifted an eyebrow.

“You’re pissing me off, Sunny,” Swinging Dick said, his finger hovering above the tablet. “You don’t want to piss me off.”

I kept talking to Ralph. “Back when Terry here was a freshman in high school, he hacked into school records to change his D on the chemistry final to a B.” I leaned closer to Ralph and stage-whispered, “Didn’t want to get grounded. Not that he had that much of a social life.”

I glanced at Swinging Dick, aka Terry Fitzpatrick, former C student at East Boston High.

His mouth dropped open, but he didn’t say a word.

I went back to Ralph. “Problem was, Terry wasn’t such a good hacker back then, so he left a trail that was real easy to follow, even for a high school principal.” I winked at him. “The principal was Louise Fitzpatrick, aka Terry’s mom.”

“That’s . . . That’s not true.”

“And his mom reported him to the police.”

Ralph’s eyes went big. “His own mom?”

"Yep," I said. "Wanted to teach him a lesson, apparently. But that isn't the worst part."

"She's lying," Swinging Dick said.

"What's the worst part?" Ralph said.

"After the two officers cuffed him and put him in the squad car, *Swinging Dick* here was so freaked out, he peed himself. All over the backseat. Poor Louise had to post bail and bring an extra pair of pants."

"She's lying. I swear."

Ralph looked at me, then at his boss.

I shrugged. "You want to call my bluff?" I said. "I have the arrest papers, plus an eyewitness account from one of the officers who took him in. Right here on my phone."

Swinging Dick bit his lip. He gulped so hard I could see his T-shirt collar moving. "Those are . . . Those records aren't supposed to be public."

"Yeah? Neither is my Social Security number, asshole."

He switched off his tablet. "What do you want me to do?" he said.

"Nothing you don't want to do yourself," I said. "I'd hate to see you take on work that you find uninteresting."

"I'll do the job," he said.

"That's a start."

"You don't have to give me any money."

"Better."

"And I'll, uh . . . I'll also get rid of all your personal info."

"Now we're talking." Since I didn't fully trust him, I watched over his shoulder as he deleted the code, as well as all the documents he'd turned up as a result.

"Will you get rid of the arrest papers?" he asked.

I shook my head. "I won't share them with anybody," I said. "That's the best I can offer."

He looked at Ralph.

"I'd do what she says if I were you," Ralph said.

"Okay." He said it meekly. "It's a deal."

I wondered how easy it would be for him to get an IP address for Book Babe—and if he did, whether I'd be able to abandon my misgivings about using it. None of that mattered to me now, though. I had a possible way to help Melanie Joan, and Swinging Dick looked miserable about it. Win-win. I raised my glass of champagne and took a sip. It was delicious. "Glad we have something to toast, Terry," I said.

TWENTY-FOUR

So this is what you do when I cancel out on you," Richie said. "You go to nightclubs and drink champagne with guys named Swinging Dick."

"Don't sleep on me, sweetheart," I said. "I'm a hot commodity."

"So I've learned." Richie grinned.

"Wish I could teach you further," I said. "In person."

"Me, too," Richie said.

I smiled. I loved being around him, even if it was just over FaceTime. It was close to two a.m. He'd texted me after he'd gotten home from work, asking if I was still awake. I'd called right back. We'd been talking for a while. We were both in bed. But unfortunately, they were separate beds, 290 miles apart. It was better than nothing, though.

We'd both recounted our days, like an engaged couple living under the same roof. I'd just told him how, despite my misgivings, I'd acted on his suggestion and called his dad for tech support.

"How do you think Melanie Joan is doing now?" Richie said.

"Sleeping, I hope."

After I'd left Icon, I'd texted Tony, telling him that I had a new lead on Book Babe. I'd figured he'd be sound asleep in his own hotel room, and that he'd reply the next morning. But he'd texted right back: *Still in MJ's suite*, he'd typed. *Harold and I are sleeping in shifts.* According to Tony, Melanie Joan had tried to wrestle her phone away from Harold and escape the hotel. Twice. Each time, it had taken both of them to subdue her, and so Tony had opted to stay. I shared all of that with Richie.

"Not sure I get it," Richie said. "Why?"

"Tony said Melanie Joan wanted to clap back at Leila Donnelly."

"Video herself and post it?"

"Yes. He said she kept screaming that she wanted to use her own words, without 'policing' from Harold and him."

"Doesn't sound like a great idea."

"It most definitely was not," I said. "But she'd drunk half a bottle of wine from room service and so she was extra, as Tony put it, 'emboldened.'"

"Jesus."

"That's Melanie Joan."

Richie had been lying on his back. He rolled onto his side,

facing the screen. "I know it's been a long time," he said, "but I don't remember her being quite so . . ."

"Volatile and self-destructive?"

"I was going to say loud," Richie said. "But that works, too."

"People change," I said. "Life throws us curveballs, and sometimes they hit us and leave scars."

"Good metaphor."

"Thanks," I said. "And as you know, I don't even like baseball."

Richie smiled. "You haven't changed, though, Sunny," he said. "You never change."

I inched closer to the screen. His soft gaze on my face. I knew what he meant. In the past several years, I'd been thrown a lot of curveballs—more than one of which had been direct threats to my life. Yet I hadn't hidden away or switched jobs or become embittered or paranoid or even loud like Melanie Joan. Unwavering conviction was my superpower—or maybe my kryptonite. And it was just as true when it came to my personal life. I knew Richie had meant it as a gentle observation—a compliment, even. But it made me think of what Elizabeth had said to me at dinner. *People change, Sonya . . . you should try it sometime.*

"Richie," I said.

"Yeah?"

"When you told me you couldn't make it for dinner with my parents, I was really angry at you."

"You were?" he said. "You didn't act like it." He started to apologize, but I cut him off.

"I didn't act angry, because I knew I was being unfair. But

the thing is, that never stopped me in the past. Every time you did something that didn't fit in with my way of dealing with the world, I complained, I pouted. I was a general pain in the ass," I said. "Remember when you decided to marry Kathryn? We were divorced. You had every right. But I took it as a personal affront. Same as when you told me she was pregnant. Even last year, when we hadn't even seen each other in months and I heard you were moving to Jersey. I was furious."

"I got it, though," he said. "All those times, I understood."

"Maybe you shouldn't have."

"Why?"

"Because I shouldn't have been trying to stop you from changing."

Richie gave me a smile. "Don't beat yourself up," he said. "It all worked out."

"I know, Richie, but if it's going to keep working out, I need to . . . go with the flow a little more, I guess. Not be so selfish."

"I've been selfish, too," he said.

"Getting married and having a kid isn't selfish."

"I'm talking about now," he said. "I've been putting this job over your needs. It's because I'm new at it, but that's not an excuse."

"Richie . . ."

"Pick a night."

"Huh?"

"Any night this summer. I'll make sure I'm covered at The Room. I'll come stay with you and I'll cook dinner and you can invite your parents. Elizabeth. Anybody you want."

I smiled. "How about just my dad," I said. "And Spike."

"Deal," he said. "And I'm going to spend more time in Boston. Mondays and Tuesdays, we don't usually book bands. I'm going to work it so I don't have to be there on those nights. I'll talk to Carll Greenwald. Tell him it's a deal-breaker."

Carll Greenwald was the owner of Candy's Room. Richie and I often speculated about why he spelled his first name with two *l*'s. "You don't have to do that," I said.

"Yes, I do," he said.

"You love The Room."

"I *like* The Room. I love *you*. And you hate the Shore in the summer."

I stared at him. "How could you tell?"

"Because I know you, Sunny."

I felt a little choked up. "Thank you," I said. I wanted to touch his face. I touched the screen instead.

"Wish I could feel that," Richie said.

"Me, too." It had been a long day. An exhausting one. Already, I was starting to fall asleep.

"Soon," he said.

"I can't wait," I said.

We ended the call. I closed my eyes. Rosie twitched in her sleep and I put my arms around her. *Richie's changing. You're changing,* I told myself. *Elizabeth doesn't know everything.*

I drifted off. It was a deep sleep, velvety and dreamless—the type of sleep that spa folks like Natalie Blythe would have called restorative. I didn't toss and turn the way I usually did. I wasn't even sure I moved at all. I just stayed curled up with

Rosie, the two of us cocooned beneath the cool sheets, until my phone rang and my eyelids fluttered open.

I rolled over to answer it, rays of sunlight poking through my drawn curtains. I looked at the screen. It was Tony calling. It was also seven a.m. I answered quickly. “What’s going on?” I said.

“*Good Morning Boston*,” he said. “Turn it on. Now.”

TWENTY-FIVE

I had to hand it to Melanie Joan. You could tie her down, put her under surveillance, and lock her in a hotel room without access to the outside world—and she would still find a way to fuck up her life.

Having failed two more times to wrestle her phone away from Harold and Tony, Melanie Joan had stayed up well past dawn, waiting for both of them to nod off at the same time. And at about six a.m. by Tony's estimate, she'd seized the opportunity. Somehow she'd managed to dress, sneak out of the hotel, get a ride to the studio where *Good Morning Boston* was shot in front of a live audience, and convince the host, Sam Sharpe—who happened to be Spike's ex—to put her on the air.

I had Tony on speakerphone. He'd gotten a call from Sam's producer just as the interview was about to start, and so all either one of us had time to do was brace ourselves and watch. It was like watching a ten-car pileup in slow motion.

Melanie Joan spent two solid minutes trashing Leila Donnelly, while Sam listened, his mouth hanging open in a state of what appeared to be bemused shock. "I take pains to write strong and admirable female characters," she was telling him now. "*She* writes weak-kneed simpletons. It's as though she's a man who can't get it up and resents all women as a result."

"Oh, fuck me stupid," Tony said.

"Took the words right out of my mouth," I said.

"Melanie Joan, don't you think that's a little harsh?" Sam said, once the live audience stopped booing. "Leila Donnelly is currently the top-selling romance writer in the U.S., and one of the top three bestselling—"

"Her books are insulting to all women," Melanie Joan said.

"With all due respect," Sam said. "*My Last First Love* sold a million copies in its first week of release. And from what I hear, the vast majority of her readers are female. If her books are so insulting to women, then there must be a lot of women out there who love to be insulted."

Sam's audience cheered. He beamed at them. "Do you guys agree?" he said.

"Yes!" a group of women responded.

"Anyway, I enjoy Leila Donnelly's books," Sam said. "And I hear she just signed with your publisher." He gave Melanie Joan a sly look. "I suppose you two touring together is out of the question?"

A few guffaws erupted from the audience. Melanie Joan sat

there, stone-faced. I thought about what my dad had suggested, about getting her in front of her beloved fans to offer a public apology to Book Babe. *She'd really have to humble herself,* he'd said last night. It felt more than a little ironic now. The only one humbling Melanie Joan was Sam.

"Oh, great," Tony said. "Now Greg Scepter is calling me."

"Oh, no," I said.

"I'd say wish me luck, but what would be the point?" Tony said.

"It does feel like a foregone conclusion," I said.

As we ended our conversation, Melanie Joan was telling Sam that she was disappointed in him, in his show, and in his audience. "It was a mistake coming here," she said.

It was the one thing she'd said that was indisputable.

My phone rang. It was Spike. "Are you watching this?" he said.

"As a matter of fact, yes," I said. The positive aspect to this interview was that it seemed to be over. Sam was thanking Melanie Joan for joining him. I turned off the TV.

"I want to punch Sam in the face," Spike said. "Should I?"

"I don't think it would be helpful."

"No, but it would feel good," he said. "To me, not him."

"It would probably feel good to me, too."

Rosie was still in my bed, snoring away. I glanced at the clock on my wall. It wasn't even seven-ten a.m. yet. "Wait, what are you doing up so early?"

"You promise you won't get mad at me?" Spike said.

I frowned. "Why would I get mad at you?"

"Because," he said. "I'm here at the studio with Melanie Joan. I'm the idiot who gave her a ride."

TWENTY-SIX

Spike and Melanie Joan were at my apartment, drinking coffee in silence, when Tony showed up. "I've got some news for Melanie Joan," he said to my intercom. "It isn't good."

That wasn't surprising. I buzzed him up.

"I obviously don't know how to make good decisions anymore," Melanie Joan said.

"No argument here," said Spike. He wouldn't even look at her. Hadn't said a word to Melanie Joan since they'd arrived. I couldn't blame him. At six a.m., she'd called Spike, telling him that she needed to be at the studio for a planned public apology to Book Babe. *I know it's a big ask,* she'd said, according to Spike. *But can you take me there? Tony has an early meeting, so he can't make it, and I could use the moral support.*

If there was one thing Spike hated, it was being played for a fool. And even though Melanie Joan insisted that this had never been her intention, Spike didn't know until they arrived that 1) the appearance had not been planned, and 2) Melanie Joan had no intention of publicly apologizing to anyone. He'd stood backstage, avoiding eye contact with Sam and sinking deeper and deeper into the realization that he'd aided and abetted a staggering act of stupidity. Who could fault him for feeling betrayed?

"It was even worse in person, Sunny," Spike said.

"I'd been up all night," Melanie Joan said. "I wasn't thinking clearly."

"Yet another detail you didn't tell me about," Spike said.

"I have a copy of her latest," Melanie Joan said. "I highlighted all the misogynistic parts in yellow, the terrible clichés in green, and the parts where she's ripped off other writers—including me—in pink. I should have brought it with me as a visual."

"No, you shouldn't have," Spike said.

"It would have proved something."

"It would have proved you have too much time on your hands."

"Spike—"

"Please don't talk to me anymore, Melanie Joan."

Melanie Joan put her head down. She looked hurt.

I heard the doorbell ring, Tony outside saying, "It's me."

I opened the door. Tony was wearing his Zegna suit, with a neon-green *A Girl and Not a God* T-shirt that he'd no doubt taken from Melanie Joan's suitcase. He looked rumpled. Exhausted. There were purplish circles under his eyes.

"Melanie Joan, I don't know how to tell you this," Tony said.

"I don't want to hear it," Melanie Joan said.

Tony pressed on. "You're out. Scepter is dropping you. Greg Scepter wants no more books from you. No memoir. No fiction. Nothing."

Melanie Joan's eyes widened. "But I have two books left on my contract," she said.

"Greg claims you breached it with your, uh, recent behavior," Tony said.

Melanie Joan's eyes widened even more. "What part of the contract did I breach?"

"Morality clause," Tony said.

"You can't be serious," Melanie Joan said.

"Unfortunately, I am," Tony said. "Scepter claims your public statements have been indecent, not to mention riddled with swear words. He says it's had a direct and obvious impact not only on your sales, but on Scepter Books as a whole."

Melanie Joan gaped at him. "What does that mean?"

"It means you have to pay back your advances on the memoir and the next two novels. It means he wants nothing more to do with you." Tony said it gently, soothingly. I could tell how much it hurt him to tell her this. I knew it was a blow to Tony, professionally and personally. But he'd survive. I wasn't so sure about Melanie Joan. The hardest part of this whole ordeal was watching her learn that the one thing in life she could rely on—her writing career—had been yanked out from under her and burned to a crisp.

Who knew that one crappy review could cause so much

destruction—and that it could happen in less than forty-eight hours? I supposed that was just the way things worked these days. Quickly and brutally. No wonder I hated the Internet so much.

"I'm sorry," Tony told Melanie Joan. "I spent a long time on the phone with Greg. I offered to take a pay cut, all kinds of concessions. I even told him you'd go to rehab. But he's not changing his mind."

"You told Greg I'd go to rehab?"

"Yes."

"Do you think I need to go to rehab?"

"If it means they'll publish you again? Yes. Yes, I do."

Melanie Joan folded her arms on the table. She rested her head on them, like a child forced into naptime. "I'm done," she said quietly. "Everything I've worked for. My dreams. It's all over with."

Spike watched her. His features softened. "Screw it," he said. "You're a famous author. There are plenty of other publishers out there."

"Not many, actually," Tony said. "There are maybe three that could pay Melanie Joan in the manner she's accustomed to. And in light of what's happened, I don't expect my phone to be ringing off the hook."

Melanie Joan lifted her head. "I guess I'll just lay low for a while." She sounded strange, defeated. Not like herself at all. It could have been tiredness, but it seemed more permanent than that. "Maybe I *should* go to rehab."

"People have short attention spans, Melanie Joan," I said. "A few weeks from now, nobody will remember any of this."

Tony shook his head. "They won't remember specifics," he said. "But they will remember that Melanie Joan was canceled. And they'll probably think it was for something worse than what actually transpired."

"Jeez, Tony. Stop trying to sugarcoat things."

"I'm just telling it like it is," he said. "We all need to be realistic."

The four of us were quiet for a long time. I took a sip of my coffee. Spike cleared his throat. "What if we livestreamed an apology," I said. "A real one."

"That's a good idea," Spike said.

"My dad suggested it."

"Smart guy," Spike said.

Tony shook his head. "Too soon," he said.

"I agree with Tony," Melanie Joan said.

"So what are we going to do?" I said. "Just . . . give up?"

"I don't think I have much choice," Melanie Joan said.

My buzzer rang again. I pressed the button and asked who was there.

A deep voice replied, "Ralph."

Ralph. The vending machine.

I buzzed him in and waited for him outside my door. Moments later, my elevator opened. He filled the doorway. He had to bend and turn sideways to extricate himself.

"Hi, Ralph," I said.

He nodded. He was wearing a similar shiny suit to the one I'd seen him in last night, only this one was slightly lighter in color. He slipped a legal-size envelope out of the jacket pocket and handed it to me. "Your IP's inside," he said.

"That was fast," I said.

"That's my boss," he said. "Speedy as shit."

"I'm impressed," I said.

Ralph shrugged. "He claims he used to date the site's admin, but I'm skeptical," he said. "You scared the hell out of him, you know."

"Yeah, well."

"I don't think I've ever seen him like that before. He was spooked all night. Kept checking his phone to see if word got out about his, uh, bladder event."

I shrugged. "Sorry."

He gave me a smile. "I was thanking you," he said. "If anybody needed to get taken down a few pegs . . ."

"Oh. No problem."

"Something wrong?"

I sighed. "Did you see *Good Morning Boston*?"

He shook his head. "I do NPR. *Morning Edition*."

"Smart of you."

"I hate TV." He headed back to the elevator and pressed the button. The doors opened immediately. He squeezed inside. He waved goodbye.

I waved back.

"Hope you can do something with what's in that envelope," he said. The doors closed.

"Maybe I can," I said.

I opened the envelope. There was a map of Union, Connecticut, inside. Someone—presumably Swinging Dick—had circled an area on the outskirts of town in red ink and had written out an address beside the circle. Very old school. Swinging Dick didn't want to leave a digital trail, which was smart. Especially since the destination was only about an hour away. *Just an hour away,* I told myself. *And you've got nothing to lose.*

I slipped back into my loft and closed the door behind me. I walked into the kitchen, the envelope cool between my fingers. Spike, Melanie Joan, and Tony hadn't moved since I left. God, they were depressing. I'd seen happier faces at wakes.

"Who was that?" Melanie Joan said.

"Just . . . a business delivery." My gaze flitted from her face, to Tony's, to Spike's. Rosie trotted across the room and started lapping at her water bowl. At least someone in this house seemed rested and content.

"Do you guys think it's still worth it?" I said. "Finding Book Babe?"

Melanie Joan turned to Tony. "Do we?"

Tony shook his head.

I disagreed. But I decided to keep that to myself for now. Tony stood up. "We should head back, Melanie Joan," he said.

She started to stand, but I stopped her. "Why don't you stay here with Spike and me?" I said.

"Really?"

"You can shower, take a nap. I'll make you breakfast."

She gave Tony a beseeching look.

"I don't know . . ." Tony said.

"If you're worried about angry Leila Donnelly fans, she's probably safer here than at the hotel," I said.

"You might be right," he said.

"I think she is," Spike said. "They were all over us when we left the studio, but we managed to lose them."

"You sure you don't mind?" Tony asked me.

"Of course not. I suggested it," I said. "Anyway, you should get back to your hotel room." I looked him up and down. "Change your clothes."

Tony nodded. He wasn't going to fight me on that. "I'll give you a call later," he said.

Once he was gone, I went back into the kitchen. I refilled Spike's and Melanie Joan's coffee cups and set the envelope on the table.

"What in God's name are you smiling about?" Spike said.

I hadn't even realized I'd been smiling. "How would you two like to take a little road trip?" I said.

TWENTY-SEVEN

Spike was one of the fastest and most reckless drivers I knew, yet he'd never gotten a ticket. I asked him about that as we crossed the Connecticut border and I noticed that he was doing seventy in a thirty-five-mile-per-hour zone.

"What can I tell you?" Spike said. "I know how to sweet-talk a man in uniform."

"Me, too," said Melanie Joan. "And for what it's worth, Spike, I think you're a virtuoso behind the wheel."

I glanced in the rearview mirror. Melanie Joan was wearing her enormous sunglasses, so I couldn't read her face. But her jaw was tight, and she was clutching the armrest with both hands. Still, she refused to complain—or to say anything to Spike that wasn't excruciatingly complimentary. She'd been kissing his ass ever since he started talking to her again, which made the ride to Union more annoying than I'd anticipated.

Spike blew through a red light.

Melanie Joan let out a small yelp.

"Try not to get us killed, virtuoso," I said.

"What? It was yellow."

"Sure it was," I said.

"I believe it was yellow, Sunny," said Melanie Joan.

I sighed. "Whatever."

"Just so you know, I've never been in an accident, either," Spike said. "And I've been driving since I was fourteen."

I wanted to tell him that there was a first time for everything, but I kept quiet. I'd been the one to ask Spike to drive. I'd done it because I needed to reread Blake's profile of Book Babe on the ride and focus on my thoughts—which were basically *How can I get a hostile stranger to help me save Melanie Joan's career?*

I didn't see it as an impossible task. Like a lot of cops, ex and otherwise, I knew how to manipulate people. But that had been a lot easier in the interview room, where I'd known exactly whom I was dealing with. All I had on Book Babe was a bunch of words that she'd chosen to put out there, about books written by other people.

I went back to Blake's profile. Based on his observations, I'd constructed a mental image of Melanie Joan's nemesis—a young mother who lived in a modest home with her three-year-old child, books everywhere, a pot of tea brewing, Turner Classic Movies playing on the TV. She loved Hollywood memoirs and romances, and so I figured she was something of a romantic herself—a dreamer who, in her childhood, had practiced Oscar acceptance speeches in front of the mirror. But she also had a practical side. She read a lot of self-help books, which meant that when she looked in the mirror today, she saw room for improvement.

As diverse as her reading may have been, though, Blake had pointed out that the genres she liked all had something in common: lots of engagement on ReadAnon. He'd also cited the words she frequently chose to describe her favorite movie-star memoirs: *brave*, *revelatory*, and *aspirational*.

I searched ReadAnon for those three words, Blake had written. **The memoir reviews that included any combination of them got A LOT of likes and comments. I believe Book Babe used those words on purpose, to get eyes on her content.**

Blake knew what he was talking about. Back in the day, he explained, he used popular hashtags like **#blessed** and **#Friyay** to attract followers, and it had worked. **Just because Book Babe hasn't shown her face, it doesn't mean she doesn't want to get noticed. The only difference between her and me (the old me) is that she wants attention for her opinions, and I wanted it for my hot workout pix. JMHO!!!**

By that logic, the viciousness of her *Stronger Alone* review made a new kind of sense. "Melanie Joan," I said, "do you know what a dis track is?"

"That's patronizing," she said. "And ageist."

"Well, do you?" Spike said.

She cleared her throat. "No."

"It's a rap song that one artist releases, trashing a rival," I said. "The rival usually comes out with a dis track in response. And then maybe the instigator comes out with an even nastier one and back and forth until the feud has its own hashtag and people are picking sides and all the late-night comedians are joking about it."

"So . . . what's the point?" Melanie Joan said.

"Schadenfreude," Spike said. "And record sales."

"No," Melanie Joan said. "What's the point of telling me this?"

"Because I think Book Babe's review of *Stronger Alone* was her version of a dis track," I said.

"Meaning?"

"I think she did it to up her profile. Gain more followers. Not because she necessarily hated your book."

"Oh," Melanie Joan said.

"And when you posted that comment, you played right into it."

"Which reminds me, I've stopped taking that water pill. I've told my doctor to prescribe an alternative."

"My point is, you upped Book Babe's engagement. Her next reviews will get even more eyes on them, and she might be able to monetize it. I mean, even more than she already has. I've noticed ads on her posts, and I'm sure she gets a nice cut."

We were in Union now. According to the sign, the population was 785. Everything about it was tiny. Spike zoomed past a one-story Town Hall, a two-pump gas station, a small church, a village green that was half the size of my parents' front lawn. It seemed like a place you'd go to hide rather than to be seen. But that didn't necessarily negate Blake's profile. In a way, it supported it.

"I'm sorry," Melanie Joan was saying, "but I still don't understand what difference any of this makes."

"Sunny's looking for an angle," Spike said. We were already beyond the center of town. He was tackling the third in a series of sharp turns, as directed by the GPS. "She wants to understand what makes Book Babe tick, so you guys can get on her good side."

I gave Spike a smile. "That's right," I said.

We moved through a residential area—ranch houses, mostly. Before long, those houses began to get fewer and farther between. We hit some woods, and the GPS led us through them. "I'm keeping my eyes peeled for a gingerbread house," Melanie Joan said.

Spike snickered. The next turn landed us on an unpaved road called Robin's Way. I remembered the name from the map Swinging Dick had provided. "This is her road," I said.

"I'm a little nervous," Melanie Joan said.

"I am, too."

The road took us past a creek and up, winding around a mountain. My ears popped. Out of the passenger-side window, I could see the tops of trees.

"Nice view," Spike said.

"Your destination is on the left," the GPS said.

"It is?" I said.

"How trustworthy is this source of yours?" Melanie Joan said.

Spike drove another hundred feet or so. "GPS isn't as accurate in rural areas," he said. He drove a little bit longer until finally we saw a driveway, a mailbox out front with the same street number Swinging Dick had written. He turned in.

A two-story farmhouse with peeling yellow paint was perched at the edge of what might be politely called an English garden. Untrimmed hedges, a lawn out front that was more dandelions than grass, scraggly trees, wildflowers everywhere. A blooming wisteria was devouring a pergola that buckled under its weight. The place almost looked abandoned, save for the sleek black Porsche convertible parked on the grass beside the garage, its top down. It was as though Book Babe had completely neglected her home for the sake of this one pampered pet of a car. I could practically smell the oiled leather seats without having to open my window.

Spike pulled up behind the garage and cut the engine. I watched the house. In one of the top-floor windows, I could see a curtain moving. "Looks like she's home," I said to Melanie Joan. "You ready?"

"As I'll ever be."

We left the car. Spike stayed behind the wheel. We walked up to the door and Melanie Joan rang the bell. I heard footsteps, a female voice calling out, "Who is it?"

"My name is Sunny Randall."

"Who?"

"I'm a private investigator," I said. "I'm here with Melanie Joan Hall. We just want to talk to you. And apologize. Right, Melanie Joan?"

She didn't say anything. I nudged her.

"I do want to apologize," Melanie Joan said. It didn't sound like her heart was in it, but I gave her a thumbs-up anyway. I motioned for her to take off her sunglasses. She did.

The footsteps grew nearer, then stopped. There was a drawn-out silence. It was so warm out here, the air around us heavy with the pasty smell of wild lilies. The hum of locusts was like static in my ears. "Hello?" I said. "Are you there?"

"Wait a minute," said the voice.

We waited. And waited. Until finally, the door opened.

"Fuck," Melanie Joan said.

I had a whole speech in my head that I'd prepared in the car on the way over. It had to do with women supporting one another and how, if they agreed to publicly bury the hatchet, both Book Babe and Melanie Joan could benefit from the publicity. I was going to tell her how genuinely sorry Melanie Joan was for posting that comment—as evidenced by how quickly she took it down—and how she wanted to make it up to Book Babe by helping her add thousands of new followers.

I'd planned on saying all of this by way of introducing Melanie Joan, who had promised me in the car that, should she have a chance to speak to Book Babe, she would be contrite, cordial, and, above all, humble.

But all of that evaporated when the door opened and we found ourselves face-to-face with the homeowner—a woman in baggy shorts and a T-shirt that said I THINK, THEREFORE I READ.

That woman was Leila Donnelly.

TWENTY-EIGHT

"What are you doing here?" Leila Donnelly said to Melanie Joan. "How did you find my home? Are you stalking me?"

Melanie Joan opened her mouth, then closed it again. In all the years I'd known her, this was the first time I'd ever seen her at a loss for words.

I found that completely understandable.

"Listen, this isn't a great time." Leila Donnelly said it dismissively, like we were a pair of Jehovah's Witnesses and she had no interest in the Good News.

I thought about what Evan Woodrow had said, about Book Babe being one of Leila Donnelly's first champions, how she'd turned Donnelly into an "instant bestseller" with one five-star review. *Like it or not,* he'd said, *that's power.*

It was something, all right.

"Sock puppet," Melanie Joan said.

I had no idea what that meant.

Leila didn't seem to know, either. "I said what I said, Melanie Joan. If you want to apologize to somebody, then apologize to Book Babe."

Melanie Joan let out a mirthless laugh.

"I don't have time for this," Leila said. She started to close the door.

"Oh, I think you do." I glared at her. "Book Babe."

Leila's eyes widened. She cleared her throat. Her cheeks flushed and her gaze dropped to the floor, a tiny vein popping out just between her eyes. "I don't know what you're talking about," she said. And even though I'd always considered the reading of tells and body-language cues to be an even more unreliable science than polygraph testing, I knew a liar when I saw one. Swinging Dick's intel was correct. Leila Donnelly was Book Babe. I'd have staked my life on it.

"She's talking about you," Melanie Joan said. "How you made up an online persona and gained followers so you could hype your own books and trash your competition."

I turned to Melanie Joan. "Is that what a sock puppet is?"

"Yes," she said.

"Wow, you learn something new every day," I said.

"Well, you taught me about dis tracks, so now we're even."

Leila said, "I don't know where you get your information, but—"

"We tracked Book Babe's IP address, and it led us here," I said. "Unless maybe it's a housemate? You live alone?"

"None of your business."

"I'm taking that as a yes."

"I haven't done anything wrong."

"Your fans might not agree," I said. "I mean, from what I gather, they started reading you in the first place because Book Babe said you were awesome. And if Book Babe is *you*, well . . ."

Somewhere within her house, a young child started to scream.

"Don't forget how she put a target on my back by posting a video in support of her own sock puppet," Melanie Joan said.

"Yeah, I don't think the readers will like that, either."

The screams grew louder. Leila whirled around. "Tommy, *be quiet*!"

The screaming stopped.

"Terrible threes, am I right?" I glanced at her feet. "I see you got over those swollen ankles you wrote about."

Leila's shoulders straightened. Her gaze moved from my face to Melanie Joan's. Slowly, her expression changed, her eyes hardening, her chin inching forward. A plan formulating in her mind. "Go for it," Leila said.

Melanie Joan gaped at her. "What?"

"Go ahead and out me." She turned to me. "If you think Leila Donnelly fans are going to take the word of that washed-up, fossilized hack over me—especially after that fiasco of a TV interview," she said, "you're even dumber than you look."

Melanie Joan's cheeks flushed. Quickly, she put her sunglasses back on.

"The truth hurts, I know," Leila said.

"You're hardly an authority on the truth," I said.

"Fuck you, Leila," Melanie Joan said. Her voice cracked. "If anyone's a hack, it's you."

Leila ignored her. She kept talking to me. "Old, bitter, desperate. All her best days behind her. Nobody wants to read her romances anymore, so she decides to write the least relatable memoir ever—and naturally, no one wants to read that, either! You almost can't blame her for making up such a crazy story about me. I mean . . . *anything to be relevant again.*"

Melanie Joan seemed frail and unsteady on her feet, as though all the energy had been yanked out of her. Without saying a word, she turned around and headed back to the car.

I stayed where I was. I wasn't sure I'd ever hated another person as much as I hated Leila Donnelly. And considering some of the people I'd come in contact with, that was saying a lot.

"They'll believe *me*," I said. Leila started to close the door, but I blocked it with my foot. "When you get a chance, google me. Sunny Randall. You'll see that I'm pretty trustworthy."

"I've never heard of you."

"I never heard of you, either, until today," I said. "And now you're just . . . everywhere. Like a really shitty song that I can't get out of my head."

"That's adorable."

"It's accurate," I said. "Anyway, I can't wait to contact my friends in the press. Let 'em tell the world about the *real you*, so to speak."

"I don't . . . I don't talk to the press."

"*I* do. And like I said, I'm trustworthy."

"Don't you fucking dare."

I smiled sweetly at her. "Is that a threat or a challenge?" I said. "Because I react the same to both."

Leila stared at me, her face growing paler.

"You're right about one thing," I said. "The truth *does* hurt. You'll see."

The child started screaming again.

"Shut the hell up!"

The scream grew louder, then erupted into sobs.

"You really ought to check on Tommy," I said. "He doesn't sound happy."

TWENTY-NINE

Back in the car, I told Spike that Book Babe and Leila Donnelly were one and the same.

"That's nuts!" he said. "Call your editor, Melanie Joan. Tell him to stop the presses. Or start the presses. What's the right terminology?"

Melanie Joan shrugged. She said nothing. She didn't pick up her phone.

"How about Tony?" I said. "He's going to be thrilled."

"Not right now," she said. "I don't want to tell anybody at the moment."

"But . . . that review she posted is worthless," Spike said. "Your editor and agent should know."

She shook her head.

"Maybe we should keep it to ourselves and make her sweat?"

I tried. "Is that your line of thinking? You want to see if she posts a positive review and an apology on her own? That might carry more weight with Evan. But I still think we should tell Tony."

Melanie Joan stayed silent.

Spike and I looked at each other.

I pulled down my visor and glanced in the mirror. Melanie Joan sat in the backseat, arms and legs crossed tight, half her face shielded by her sunglasses. Unreadable.

"Melanie Joan?" I said. "Are you okay?"

"I hate her," she said. "I hate Leila Donnelly."

"Me, too," I said. "We all do."

"She called me washed-up," Melanie Joan said. "And fossilized. And . . . old."

"Sticks and stones," Spike said. "And anyway, you know that's bullshit. You're fabulous."

Melanie Joan said nothing for a long while. She smoothed her hair and crossed her hands demurely in her lap.

"Spike's right, you know," I said. "You really shouldn't let anything she said back there—"

"You know what? I think I need a nice long nap," Melanie Joan said. And then she was through talking.

Two hours later, when I was in my office and Spike was at his restaurant and Melanie Joan was back at her hotel, presumably taking that nap, Blake came in from reception and told me that someone named ForeverLove@hotmail.com had emailed my website. He wouldn't have bothered me, he said, but the subject line was URGENT in all caps.

I was amazed that anybody still used Hotmail, but I opened it anyway. I had a feeling I knew who the sender was.

The email consisted of one line: *It's LD. Can we please meet?* Plus a phone number. I found the "please" part interesting. I called the number. A woman picked up. I recognized that whispery voice immediately.

"Hello, Leila," I said.

"I need to talk to you."

"What about?"

"Nothing I can say over the phone."

I took my time responding. "Can Melanie Joan come?"

"Just you."

"Why?"

"Because what I have to say is very . . . sensitive. Plus, she hates me."

"Do you blame her?"

She breathed, in and out. "No."

I didn't say anything.

"Sunny, listen. What you guys think about me is true. But only partly."

"Which part?"

"The part I can't say over the phone."

I took a moment. Thought about it. "I don't know."

"Please," she said. "I'll come to you. Banners Kitchen & Tap. Five p.m."

I'd been to Banners. It was a sports bar. Burgers. Beer.

Enormous screens. Very public, yet at the same time, the perfect place for a famous romance writer to go unnoticed. I looked at the clock on my desktop. It was three-fifty p.m. "You're leaving now?"

"Yes."

"What about Tommy?"

"He's at my mom's."

I was curious about what she had to say to me, but I didn't want to seem too eager. I looked at the clock on my computer screen, waited for the minute to pass. When it seemed like enough time had elapsed, I responded. "Okay."

"Thank you," she said. "And thank you . . . for not telling Melanie Joan."

She hung up.

At six p.m., I was nursing a beer at a high-top near the bar at Banners. The Red Sox were playing the Padres on the forty-foot screen. Everyone at the bar was shouting, and everyone on the screen was going wild. Home run for the Sox. The sound system was far too excellent for its own good. Banners annoyed me nearly as much as baseball did.

Leila Donnelly still hadn't shown. I was starting to wonder if this wasn't some kind of ill-advised prank. For the third time, I called the number she'd emailed me. Again, the call went straight to voicemail and the mailbox was full. "Okay, Hotmail," I said. "You had your chance." I couldn't even hear my own voice in this place. Fenway was probably quieter.

I took a few more swallows of my beer. Then I started scrolling through my contacts.

I knew more journalists than I'd thought. I figured I'd call my friend Tom Gorman at *The Globe* first—keep things Boston Strong. Then I'd go wide with the story. And what a story it would be: how the Taylor Swift of romance had duped her loyal fans.

The bar crowd quieted down a bit. I prayed nobody would hit another home run, at least until I could pay my tab. I got out my wallet and my phone vibrated. I thought maybe it might be Leila, but no such luck. Tony's name was on my screen. I'd called him shortly after we returned from Connecticut to tell him about Book Babe's true identity. He'd been thrilled, of course. *Let's keep this close to the vest for now,* he'd said. *See how much public groveling we can get out of her.*

It was the last I'd spoken with him. I wondered if Leila had decided to talk to Tony rather than to me. If that was the case, I wished she'd told me before I'd wasted a full hour at a sports bar.

As I accepted the call, Bregman stepped up to the plate. Everyone around me started cheering. I'd forgotten my earbuds as usual, so I plugged my left ear in order to hear Tony. "You'll never guess what I'm watching on the world's biggest TV right now," I said. "Seriously. You will not guess."

"Is she with you?" Tony said.

"Who?" I said.

"Who else?"

I sighed. "We dropped her off at the hotel at about one," I

said. "She was planning on sleeping all day, which seemed like a good idea."

"Yeah, well, it would have been."

"What?"

"We've lost her again," Tony said.

"Oh, no."

"She told Harold that she was hitting the sack. He ran out to do a few errands, and when he checked in on her, she was gone. She'd shoved pillows under the covers like a goddamn middle-schooler sneaking out past curfew."

"Maybe she's at the hotel gym?" I said. "Or out for a walk."

"We checked the gym," he said. "And it would be a long walk, even for Melanie Joan. She's been gone for at least three hours."

I exhaled. "I don't understand her sometimes."

"Sometimes?"

Bregman hit a home run. The place exploded in cheers. I needed to pay my bill and get out of this hellhole. "Have you tried Spike's?" I said. "She sort of has a thing for him."

"I know," he said. "I tried. She's not there."

Just as he said it, I thought I heard the sound of my own name ringing out from the din. "Wait a minute," I said. I listened. There was no mistaking it. Melanie Joan's voice was strange like that. It occupied its own special register. "She's here," I said.

THIRTY

I told Tony I'd call him later. Then I stood up and set about scanning the crowd for Melanie Joan, who was much less imposing physically than she was vocally.

When I spotted her, she was elbowing her way past two college-aged guys in Red Sox T-shirts, nearly upending their beers in the process.

"Melanie Joan!"

"Sunny, thank God." Melanie Joan rushed at me and threw her arms around my shoulders. She smelled of Bottega Veneta perfume and gin.

She took a step back and smiled. "You look wonderful," she said, as though she hadn't just seen me a few hours ago.

"Thanks," I said. "You, too."

Melanie Joan had changed into jeans and a black silk blouse

and slicked her hair into a chignon. Chic as ever. But her cheeks were flushed, her eyes a bit wild. I wondered how much gin she'd had, and where she'd been drinking it.

"Where have you been?"

"Terrorizing your poor assistant again," she said. "Good thing he's never been trusted with any state secrets. He gave up your location very easily."

"Did Blake tell you *why* I'm here?"

She shook her head.

"I was going to meet Leila Donnelly. She said she had some important information for me, and to keep it to myself."

"She contacted you?"

"Yes."

"When?"

"Couple hours ago," I said. "Anyway, I've obviously been stood up, so all bets are off."

"Wait," Melanie Joan said. "You haven't talked to the press about her yet, have you?"

I shook my head.

"Have you told anyone else?"

"Just Tony. He said we should keep it to ourselves."

"Thank God."

"Why?"

A huge group of patrons started chanting Bregman's name so loudly, you'd have thought he'd just been chosen as Pope.

"Can we go somewhere quieter?" Melanie Joan asked.

"Absolutely," I said.

She waited for me to settle my tab, and we walked out onto

Causeway Street. It was well past six, but the air was as warm and thick and bright as it had been at noontime. These endless summer days were starting to feel oppressive. We moved to the side so a cluster of twentysomethings could get past us and into Banners. It was hard to believe they were going in there willingly, but obviously I was in the minority as far as mass baseball viewings were concerned.

"It's good to be out of there," I said.

Melanie Joan nodded. "Let's walk," she said.

We walked in silence for a little while. As always, I found myself racing to keep up with her. I wondered how many steps she got in on an average day. The number was probably staggering.

Once we'd cleared a few blocks, I touched her arm. "What is going on with you?" I asked.

She let out a breath. "Sunny, I've been doing a lot of thinking," she said. "And I've made a decision."

"Yeah?"

"We should just let this whole Leila Donnelly thing go."

I stopped walking and stared at her. "What? Why?"

"I've been replaying everything I've done over the past few days over and over in my mind. I pretended all of those things had been done by someone else—an acquaintance I was hearing about. And it hit me, Sunny."

"What?"

She started walking again. "I don't like the person I've become."

I took off after her. "What are you talking about? You were

trolled by an arrogant bitch and her sock puppet," I said. "She tanked your memoir before it could even be released. Who could blame you for acting out a little?"

"You're being too charitable."

"No, I'm not," I said. "I want you to get your fans back. And I want to get even with Leila Donnelly. Don't you?"

She shrugged.

"Who are you, and what have you done with Melanie Joan Hall?"

"I don't know, Sunny. Maybe Leila Donnelly was right. Maybe I really am washed-up and out of touch. And old."

"Stop it."

"Maybe I've been privileged for so long that my memoir is unrelatable. Maybe Leila Donnelly's books are better than I think they are, and this was the universe's way of showing me that I should . . . I don't know. Stop writing. Travel. Live a different kind of life. Maybe go back to Utica."

"That's ridiculous."

"It's not."

She stopped walking. I was grateful.

Melanie Joan turned and faced me. Her mascara was smudged. Her eyes glistened. "For the last thirty years, I've put every ounce of my energy into being a bestselling author. I've worked so damn hard on the books and even harder on this . . . this persona I've created. And look where it's gotten me. The entire world hates me now."

"We can change that."

"I don't think I want to," she said. "I know that might sound weird."

"Might?"

"Everything happens for a reason, Sunny."

"No, it doesn't."

"Yes, it does. And you know what else? I should thank Leila Donnelly."

I stared at her. "Are you drunk?"

"No. I'm just seeing myself. Realistically, for once. And what I truly am . . . is too old for this shit."

I took her by both shoulders and stared into her eyes. "Listen to me," I said. "I'm going to get us an Uber. We're going back to your hotel, and you're going to eat a nice meal and get a good night's sleep. And then tomorrow morning, I'll come by and you can tell me whether or not you still feel the same about yourself, your life, and Leila fucking Donnelly."

She sighed.

"Please."

"I don't know."

"I've put in a lot of hard and dangerous work *for you*, Melanie Joan Hall. It's the least you could do for me in return."

She took a long, deep breath, in and out. It reminded me of the yogic breathing Natalie Blythe had done the previous afternoon.

"I'll do it," she said, "if you join me for dinner."

"Of course," I said.

We Ubered back to the Ritz-Carlton and I went up to Melanie

Joan's suite with her. Together, we called Tony, and Melanie Joan promised him, with Harold and me as her witnesses, that she would not attempt to escape again.

We ordered up steaks and Caesar salad and champagne from room service, and the three of us talked about our favorite TV series and the brutal summer weather and the best restaurants in Boston and L.A. and London and New York. Melanie Joan and I reminisced about the case that first brought us together—that deranged, homicidal ex of hers—and how our lives had changed since then. We talked about Richie and Rosie and Spike and my parents and Harold's grandson and cooking and music and politics and Broadway shows. We talked about anything and everything in the world and in our lives—except for where Melanie Joan had been during the past few hours.

I was aware of that omission, but it didn't seem to matter. Not until the next morning, when I was back at my loft and in bed with Rosie and I was awakened yet again by a phone call from Tony Gault. "Can you and Spike come to Connecticut with me?" he said as I struggled to open my eyes.

"Why?" I said.

"State Police want to question us."

I said it again. *"Why?"*

"Leila Donnelly has been murdered. And as far as I can tell, Melanie Joan is a suspect."

THIRTY-ONE

"Explain to me why you and Melanie Joan Hall decided to drive to Ms. Donnelly's house," said the detective. I was in the State Police barracks in Westbrook, which was about an hour away from Union. The detective's name was Gleason, and he'd been questioning me for a while. He looked like a younger Larry David, but he had a rich baritone voice and he wasn't at all funny, which made for a sort of cognitive dissonance. I wasn't enjoying our interaction. I couldn't remember the last time I'd talked to a police officer when I was the one answering the questions, and I much preferred it the other way around.

I'd yet to see Melanie Joan, who'd come to Westbrook separately from Tony, Spike, and me. She'd driven in with her chauffeur, Charles. From what I'd been able to gather from Gleason, both Charles and Melanie Joan were persons of interest in the murder of Leila, who had been found shot to death yesterday, in her own home, with her own gun, not long after I'd spoken to her on the phone.

"We wanted to talk to Book Babe," I told Detective Gleason.

"And who is that?"

It was the third time he'd asked me this. I was starting to get annoyed. "The screen name of a reviewer on a website called ReadAnon," I said. "Book Babe had trashed Melanie Joan's memoir, and Melanie Joan wanted to apologize, in person, for retaliating with a nasty comment."

"I saw a screenshot of that comment. It was more than nasty."

I sighed heavily. "Anyway, as I've already explained, we didn't know that Book Babe and Leila Donnelly were the same person until she answered the door."

"How did you get the address?"

"Source of mine."

"Name of the source?"

"Prefer not to say."

"Fair enough." Gleason cleared his throat. "Can you tell me about Ms. Hall's state of mind when you left the interview?"

"Quiet."

"Can you elaborate?"

"Not until you explain to me why you think Melanie Joan had anything to do with Leila Donnelly's death."

Gleason folded his hands on the table and watched me intently. "Prefer not to say," he said.

I let out an exasperated groan. "Listen, Detective, I can tell you with certainty that Leila Donnelly was alive when we went to her house, and alive when we left. She was alive when I spoke to her at approximately three p.m. and made plans to meet with her in Boston. Beyond that, there is nothing I know."

"That's consistent with our timeline," he said. "And when we went through Ms. Donnelly's phone, we could see the call you placed to her. It was two-fifty-six."

"See? I'm being honest."

"Apparently," he said.

"So . . . I guess we're through, then."

"Sure," he said. "But there's just one more thing."

"Who are you, Columbo?"

His brows knotted, as though he didn't get the reference.

"Old TV show? Peter Falk?"

He lifted his briefcase from the floor and set it on the table.

"Columbo always used to say, 'Just one more—'"

"I know the show." He removed two pairs of latex gloves from his jacket pocket and handed one of the pairs to me. "Do you mind?" he said.

"Not at all," I said.

He went to work putting on his gloves. I did the same. He opened the briefcase and removed an item—something in an evidence bag. He put it down on the table. There was a hardcover book inside. Gloves safely on, he slipped it from the bag. "We found this next to the body," he said. "It's a copy of *My Last First Love* by Leila Donnelly."

"That's not really surprising, is it? The crime scene was her house. I imagine she owned a lot of copies of her own books."

"Actually, no," he said.

"Hmph. Well, what do you know?"

"I'd like you to take a look at it," he said. "Tell me if you notice anything familiar." He stood up and gave the book to me, asking me to be very careful while handling it. I wanted to tell him that this was a waste of time—that I'd never even seen a Leila Donnelly book, let alone looked through one. What exactly was I supposed to find familiar?

But I didn't. The faster I could get through this interview, the sooner I could leave, talk to Melanie Joan, and find out what was going on. Carefully, I took the book and opened it.

I turned to a random page. My mouth went dry. I started flipping through it, Melanie Joan's voice in my mind. *I highlighted all the misogynistic parts in yellow, the terrible clichés in green, and the parts where she's ripped off other writers—including me—in pink.* I turned more pages. I could feel Gleason watching me closely. I said nothing, hoping my expression stayed the same, that my cheeks didn't flush, that nothing on the surface of my skin betrayed what was going on beneath it.

The book looked like an Easter egg.

"Ever see Melanie Joan Hall with this particular book?"

"No." I was telling the truth. I'd never seen her with it.

"You sure?" he said.

"I'm sure," I said.

"You know that Leila Donnelly didn't have surveillance cameras at her house," he said. "Her only protection was the gun she was ultimately killed with."

"I didn't see cameras there," I said. "But I didn't look for them. We wanted to talk to her, and we did. We left. End of story."

He nodded. "What would you say if I told you that a witness called local police yesterday, at around three-forty-five p.m.?" he said. "Said they were jogging by and heard screams coming from Ms. Donnelly's house. On their return route, the jogger saw a limo in the driveway that had not been there before, and a woman fitting Ms. Hall's description getting inside."

I stared at him. My head felt light.

"What would you say, Ms. Randall?"

"I'd say . . ." I cleared my throat. "That's a pretty steep road to jog on."

He said nothing. His gaze drilled into me.

"This is the first time I'm hearing this information," I said.

"That's fairly obvious," he said. "Anything else you want to say about this book?"

"No."

He nodded and slipped it back into the briefcase. He removed his gloves. I did the same. If there was one thing I was sure of, it was that I needed to get out of there quickly. "You have any more questions for me?"

"None at the moment." He gave me a business card. I looked at it. His first name was George. Usually, when cops introduced themselves to me, they gave me their first and last names. Not humorless Larry David, though. He'd been Detective Gleason from the start. "If you remember anything that might be of help, I'd appreciate a call," he said.

"All right."

"Do you have a card as well?"

I grabbed my purse and fished out a business card, willing my hands not to tremble. "I hope you're looking at other people," I said. "Melanie Joan Hall is not a murderer. I can assure you of that."

"I'll be in touch," he said. I couldn't have imagined a more disheartening response.

THIRTY-TWO

When I was through with my interview, Gleason called Tony into the room. Spike was still waiting. "How did it go?" Spike said.

"It went," I said.

"That good, huh?"

"I'll tell you about it later," I said. "Where's Melanie Joan?"

"She and Charles left to get something to eat," Spike said, explaining that, since the two of them hadn't been charged with a crime, yet, they took full advantage and cut their interviews short. I was pretty sure that by *get something to eat*, Spike meant *find the best defense attorney money could buy*. At least, I hoped so.

I texted Melanie Joan: *I need to talk to you two ASAP.*

She replied: *Driving back to Boston.*

I typed: *Turn around!*

For several seconds, there was no reply. Then those three dots, which pulsed for much too long a time. And then: *OK.*

I asked when they'd be back and Melanie Joan replied: *About 15 mins*. Which was good. That gave me just enough time to use the ladies' room, grab a much-needed cup of coffee from the vending machine (Mr. Personality hadn't even thought to offer me one), and get my gun back from security.

"You mind heading back with just Tony?" I said to Spike.

"I'll miss your backseat driving," he said, "but I'll survive."

I smiled. We said goodbye.

"Never a dull moment for us," Spike said.

"We should be so lucky," I said.

Somebody must have alerted the press or posted about Leila Donnelly's murder on social media. Because by the time I left the police barracks, there were three news vans setting up in the parking lot, plus dozens of amateur sleuths and/or fans milling around, some commiserating with one another, others trying to capture the moment—any moment—their phones up and recording. I searched the lot for Melanie Joan's limo. I checked the parameters in particular, assuming that with this type of crowd forming, she'd want to keep her distance.

No sign yet.

I felt a tap on my shoulder. I half-expected Melanie Joan, but instead I found myself inches away from a young woman with flushed cheeks and wild eyes, her hair done up in a messy bun with a tiara shoved into it. I took a step back. She wore cargo shorts and a stained T-shirt that said HAPPILY EVER AFTER. Oh, and she was also sporting angel wings. If the look she was striving for was "fairy princess after a weeklong bender," she'd nailed it.

"Do you know anything about what happened to Leila?" the young woman said.

"I don't," I said. "Sorry."

"I heard it was whatshername. Melissa Joan Hart. She killed Leila."

For some reason, I felt the need to correct her. "Melanie Joan Hall."

"Whatever," she said. "Did you see her on that TV show? The morning thingy?"

"Yes."

"I saw a clip online. She's psycho."

"I watched the whole thing and I didn't think so."

"You didn't?"

"Nope. A little tired, maybe. Upset. But otherwise, sane." *You, on the other hand* . . . I gave her what I hoped was a polite smile and took a step away.

She didn't take the hint. "You want to know what I heard?"

"Not really."

"I heard that Hart shaved Leila's head after she killed her, and wove her hair into a shawl. That's how they caught her. She was *wearing the shawl*."

I stared at her for a few seconds. "Yeah, that doesn't sound like a real thing that happened," I said.

"Why not?"

"Um . . . It isn't shawl weather?"

"You just don't understand psychos," she said.

"I suppose I don't."

"I'll tell you something," she said. "Leila's books saved me. *Mr. Forever* got me through the worst breakup of my life. It taught me that there's a special plan for everybody. That there's a Mr. Forever out there for *me*, and to trust my feelings and never settle and my Mr. Forever just might be Timothée Chalamet. Leila showed me this, with her beautiful, beautiful words."

I glanced around the lot again. What was taking them so long?

"Now there won't be any more Leila books," she said. "No books, no messages. Do you even get how fucked-up that is? *Do you?*"

She was starting to genuinely scare me. I inched away some more, wondering if it was fair to judge an author by her fans. "I'm sorry for your loss," I tried.

"If Melissa doesn't get the death penalty, then someone else will do the job."

I shuddered. *Would it help to explain due process? Probably not.*

My phone pinged with a text. Saved by the bell. Literally.

It was from Melanie Joan: *We're across the street.*

I looked up. Melanie Joan's limo was parked against the curb, the hood shielded by a maple tree. "My ride's here," I told the fairy princess. Then I took off.

Charles hit the button, unlocking the doors. I slid in back, next to Melanie Joan, and slammed the door behind me.

"Who was that you were talking to?" she said.

"A lunatic," I said.

"I guessed that from how fast you got away from her."

"And maybe her outfit gave you a clue?" I said. "It's a police station. Not Comic Con."

Melanie Joan narrowed her eyes. "What was she saying?"

"Nothing important," I said. "But promise me you will keep a low profile until they clear you."

"Why?"

"Listen to her, Ms. Hall," said Charles.

"Hire a bodyguard, too," I said.

Melanie Joan peered out the window. The deranged fairy princess stared after us with her big, unhinged eyes.

"Thank God for tinted glass," I said.

"Amen," said Charles.

"I'm starting to get scared," said Melanie Joan. "You're scaring me, Sunny."

"Better scared than dead," Charles said. He pulled away from the curb slowly, his shoulders tensed, his face serious. "There's a lot of fuckin' weirdos out there. Pardon my French."

I waited until we were away from the station and on the road to ask why the hell they drove back to Leila Donnelly's house yesterday afternoon.

THIRTY-THREE

Melanie Joan believed the Connecticut State Police were trying to pin a false narrative on her. She told me so. "I'd never kill anyone," she said. "Not even *her*."

"I hope you didn't phrase it like that with Gleason."

"I'm not stupid, Sunny."

"I didn't think so."

I took a good look at Melanie Joan. She was wearing an oversized black T-shirt, black leggings, her hair tucked into a baseball cap, her eyes hidden behind her ever-present sunglasses. Every part of her was shielded from view, save for her arms, which were noticeably bonier. She looked thinner as a whole, those usually cultivated muscles suffering from neglect. I wasn't sure whether the change had been rapid or it had been going on for a while now and Melanie Joan had been dressing to hide it. Either way, it was startling.

"Are you getting a lawyer?" I asked.

She nodded. "I called my attorney in L.A. and he set up a meeting for me with Rita Fiore. Have you heard of her?"

I tried not to smirk. "I have."

"She any good?"

"In my opinion, she's the best criminal lawyer in New England." That was true. I didn't mention that Rita also happened to be dating my ex, Jesse Stone. At least she had been dating him the last time I'd asked around, which had been before my pre-engagement to Richie. Back then, I used to have other opinions on Rita Fiore that were purely personal, probably unfair, and definitely irrelevant. "You're in excellent hands," I said.

"That's good to know," she said. "I'm hoping this will all just go away soon and I won't even have to make use of her services."

I frowned. The way things were looking, I doubted that. "Melanie Joan?" I said.

"Yes?"

"I need you to be honest with me."

"I'm always honest with you."

Charles cleared his throat.

"In this instance," I said, "I consider an omission to be a lie."

"What did I omit?"

Charles cleared his throat again.

"Are you all right, Charles?" Melanie Joan said. "Do you need a lozenge?"

Charles kept his eyes on the road. "Ms. Randall can't help us if you keep things from her," he said.

"That's right," I said.

Melanie Joan removed her sunglasses and put her head down. She pulled off her baseball cap and ran her hands through her hair and replaced it. I had the feeling she wanted to come clean with me and that she was just trying to work up the nerve.

I decided to give her a little push. "Why did you go back to Leila Donnelly's?"

"How do you know I—"

"Please," Charles said. "Just tell her."

Melanie Joan's gaze flitted to the front seat, then back to me.

"You're among friends," I said. "You're not in the interview room."

"Okay," she said. "Okay."

I waited.

"Okay," she said again. "After you dropped me back at the hotel, I told Harold I was going to sleep. And I wanted to. Truly. But I couldn't stop thinking about what Leila had said. Not the awful things she'd called me. I've got a thicker skin than that. It was more about how . . . dismissive she was of me. My books. My career. My life. It tore at me, just like Book Babe's review. Which makes sense now, seeing as they were the same person."

"If it wasn't for Melanie Joan Hall," Charles said, "there'd be no Leila Donnelly."

“Thank you, Charles,” Melanie Joan said.

“It’s the truth,” he said.

“Anyway, I . . . I suppose I wanted to make her feel the way she’d made me feel.”

“Disrespected,” Charles said.

“Yes. And I knew Charles would understand, so I called him. I asked him to go back to my town house and bring me that copy of *My Last First Love* I told you about. I looked through it again, and it was even worse than I remembered. I mean, the green highlighted parts alone . . . God, I should have brought that to *Good Morning Boston*.”

“It wouldn’t have made a difference,” Charles said. “That audience wouldn’t know true talent if it socked them in the jaw.”

“You’re probably right,” Melanie Joan said.

“So you decided to bring it to Leila Donnelly,” I said.

“It was my idea,” Charles said.

My eyes widened. “Really?”

“I thought it might make Ms. Hall feel better to have the last word.”

“Charles gets me,” Melanie Joan said.

I looked at Charles. His gloved hands resting on the wheel. A possible conspiracy-to-commit-murder charge was looming over him, all because he’d been outraged at the way his boss had been treated. And yet here he was, still concerned for Melanie Joan, still trying to build her up.

Charles *did* get her. He believed in her, just like Harold and Tony and Spike and I did. Melanie Joan Hall had a way of inspiring loyalty in people. It was why I’d found it surprising—and a little disgusting—that her publisher had been willing to dump her so easily.

"So you convinced Harold to leave his post, and then you escaped from the Ritz-Carlton," I said. "Charles was waiting for you outside. You took the book with you, and you both drove back to Leila's house in Union."

"I had the address from our trip there," Melanie Joan said. "Charles plugged it into his GPS."

"We made good time," Charles said. "Didn't hit a lot of traffic."

"You get to the house," I said.

"Could use a good reno, that place," Charles said.

"I thought so, too," I said.

"Sweet ride, though. Porsche 911 Carrera. You see that?"

"I did," I said.

"What a honey. A nineties model, if I'm not mistaken."

"Anyway," I said. "You both walk to the door. You have the book with you."

"No," Melanie Joan said.

"No?"

"I went alone. I felt bad enough the last time we were at her house, with you fighting my battle for me, Sunny. I wasn't going to return accompanied by a big, imposing man in a uniform."

"So Charles dropped you off," I said. "What time?"

"Maybe three-thirty? Four at the latest," Charles said.

"I asked him to come back in twenty minutes," Melanie Joan said.

"Then what did you do?"

"I rang the bell," she said. "There was no answer. I rang it again. Still no answer."

"Did you hear anybody in there? Voices?"

"Not voices," she said. "I thought . . . maybe I heard some movement in there."

"What type of movement?"

"Like someone was dragging something across the floor."

"Interesting."

"It's interesting now," Melanie Joan said. "But I didn't think so then. Anyway, it stopped when I rang the bell."

"What did you do?"

"I was so frustrated and angry, I just started yelling at Leila Donnelly through the door," she said. "I told her I didn't appreciate what she'd said to me, and that at least I put effort into my books. At least they didn't read like a million other pieces of trash out there, filled with sexist tropes. I told her that she's the hack. Not me. And I told her I had proof."

"Proof?" I said.

"The *book*," Melanie Joan said. "All the highlights. On the way there, I'd written a key on the title page—the meaning behind each color."

It was more of a visual aid than proof. But that wasn't the part I was concerned about. "So your handwriting was in that book."

"Yes."

"And you left it at her house."

"Yes," she said. "Leila Donnelly wouldn't answer, so I put it on her doorstep. Another stupid, impulsive thing to do."

"Melanie Joan," I said. "Were you ever inside the house?"

"No."

"You swear you are telling me the truth?"

"I swear on everything and everyone that's ever been important to me," she said.

"When I came back twenty minutes later, she was still on the front porch," Charles said.

"What did you do next?"

Charles said he'd taken Melanie Joan to the Whiskey Rocks Bar and Rodeo steakhouse in Dudley, Massachusetts. She drank. He ordered a Coke and kept her company.

"I had a couple gin and tonics," Melanie Joan said. "I was very, very depressed."

"Why?"

"I just kept repeating the whole scene in my mind. Yelling at her through her door. Screaming, really. The desperation in my voice. The fact that she didn't respond, even to tell me to leave. I just felt so . . . inconsequential. I talked to Charles about it. I told him that instead of going to Leila's with that book, I should have started planning a new life for myself. Leave the writing to the Leila Donnellys of the world, you know? He had a clearer head than me since he was the designated driver, but he seemed to understand what was bothering me so much. He thought, too, that maybe it was time for me to hang it up."

"That isn't true," Charles said.

"You even said—"

"Sleep it off. That's what I said. Not *hang it up*. That's two different things."

"So you weren't inside the house," I said.

Melanie Joan looked at me. "Why do you keep asking that?"

"Because the book was inside the house, Melanie Joan. The police found it next to Leila's body."

Melanie Joan gawked at me.

"Jesus," Charles said.

"So . . . at some point, someone must have opened that door and taken the book inside," Melanie Joan said.

"Somebody did," I said. "Yes."

"And it's got my handwriting on it."

"Yes," I said.

Melanie Joan's phone dinged at the same time as mine did. We both looked at our screens. It was a text from Tony—a link to an article on a website called *Real Crime Daily*. I clicked on the link and read it.

"Oh my God," Melanie Joan whispered.

"What's going on now?" Charles said.

I couldn't say anything. Not right away. The article was about Leila's murder. There was no mention of the highlighted book. The police were probably keeping that under wraps for now. But there was another detail—one that Gleason had never bothered to mention when he was questioning me. There had been a message scrawled on Leila Donnelly's wall in what appeared to be her own blood.

It read: JUSTICE FOR MJH

"My God," Melanie Joan said.

"What's going on?" Charles said again.

"We're fucked, Charles, that's what's going on," Melanie Joan said. "We are utterly, thoroughly *fucked out loud*."

Our phones pinged again. It was another text from Tony, telling us that he just heard from Evan. In twenty minutes, he said, Greg Scepter would be holding a press conference.

THIRTY-FOUR

We were about five minutes away from the scheduled start of the press conference when Charles spotted a service plaza and pulled off I-90. He parked the limo in one of the spaces. Melanie Joan took her iPad out of her Birkin and found Scepter Books' Instagram, which was broadcasting it live.

The presser was apparently being held in the large conference room at Scepter Books' home offices in New York. A podium had been set up at the rear of the room, and the table had been moved out to make way for the dozens of reporters milling around, but even on the small iPad screen, Melanie Joan recognized the Art Deco light fixtures. "The last time I was in that room, it was because Gloria Scepter had thrown a surprise party for me, celebrating the millionth sale of *Cassandra Reborn*," she said. "They wheeled out the most beautiful cake I've ever seen. White buttercream, hundreds of edible flowers. You know what it said on it?"

"We love you, Melanie Joan," Charles said.

"That's right, Charles," Melanie Joan said. "Different times . . ."

"We'll get through this," I said.

"I'm sorry, Sunny, but even if we do, it won't be the same," Melanie Joan said. "Gloria Scepter was so thoughtful, so wise. The complete opposite of her son."

"Did he have a job before he inherited the company?" I said.

"Some tech thing," she said. "Cryptocurrency, maybe? Something as soulless as he is."

On-screen, Greg Scepter approached the podium. He looked to be in his early thirties, and he was tall and pale, with short, curly hair. He wore a black T-shirt under a black suit that looked expensive but purposefully ill-fitting, as though he'd gone to Murat's in Beverly Hills and requested "extra-baggy." He accessorized the ensemble with a chunky gold necklace that would have looked a lot better on Rosie.

"He has Mark Zuckerberg's fashion sense," I said.

"But not his charm," Melanie Joan said.

As if to illustrate that statement, Greg pulled an iPhone out of his jacket pocket and read from the screen in a monotone voice. "It is with great sorrow that we announce the passing of the immensely talented Leila Donnelly, who had signed a five-book deal with Scepter Books and was scheduled to release her first book with us, titled *The Prince and the Peach*, in the fall," he said.

"*The Prince and the Peach*?" I said.

"The heir to the British throne falls for a Georgia farm girl," Melanie Joan said.

"You've read it?" Charles said.

She shook her head. "I don't need to. I could probably summarize the whole plot for you, too, just from that title. That's how by-the-numbers Leila Donnelly's books are."

On-screen, Greg Scepter was detailing Leila's "rags-to-riches story" for reporters. "Struggling, single, and pregnant with her little son, Leila cleaned out her life savings to self-publish her first book, *The Heartbeat Chronicles*," Greg said. "It turned out to be a wise investment. Championed by a slew of online critics, *The Heartbeat Chronicles* became a runaway hit—and changed the lives of romance readers everywhere."

"I wouldn't call it a slew," Melanie Joan said.

"Right?" I said. "It was Book Babe. It was *her own self.* Leila Donnelly was the slew."

"She's since gone on to publish six more blockbuster books," Greg said. "Leila Donnelly lived out a real-life 'happily ever after' that was tragically cut short yesterday when she was murdered in her own home. Leila is survived by her mother, Marianne Donnelly; her son, Tommy; and, of course, her many, many fans."

"Marianne," I whispered.

"What?" said Melanie Joan.

"Nothing."

As Greg Scepter opened it up to questions, I angled my body away from hers and searched Instagram for Marianne Donnelly. I found a few accounts, but none really caught my eye. I tried "Mary Anne" and was equally unimpressed. I gave "Mary Ann" a try. Same thing.

On-screen, Scepter was telling a reporter that if he wanted details on Leila's murder, he should ask the State Police. "I don't want to misspeak," he said. "I do that sometimes."

"He does that all the time," Melanie Joan said. "Because he never pays attention to people." It made me think.

I tried "Marion Donnelly." One of them stood out. The profile pic was of a thin sixtysomething woman, posing with a little boy around Tommy's age. Her bio simply said "Mimi," and she'd posted only a few pictures—a cat, scenery that may or may not have been the Connecticut countryside, and that same little boy as a baby. She had a total of fifty-nine followers. I took a closer look at the one picture of Marion. She wore a sleeveless blouse and had delicate features and short salt-and-pepper hair. There could have been a family resemblance (that was always hard to tell). But what made me hopeful was the tattoo on this Marion Donnelly's left arm—a pink-and-white flower. It was identical to Leila's.

I sent her a direct message from my account, sharing my full name and phone number and the fact that I was investigating Leila Donnelly's murder. **If this is the correct Marion Donnelly, I offer you my deepest condolences,** I wrote. **There is nothing in the world more difficult than losing a child, and I'm sure you share my desire to see Leila's REAL killer brought to justice.** I wondered if Marion would take me seriously. My Instagram account was called RosieRandall and featured pictures of my dog wearing various jackets and hats. But since it was my only social media, it would have to suffice.

On the screen, an overly enthusiastic podcaster type was

asking Greg Scepter if *The Prince and the Peach* would still be released.

"Yes, right on schedule," he said. "And fortunately, Leila has left us with three additional manuscripts, which we intend to publish over the next three years."

Greg then asked if anyone had any more questions. I felt like I knew what was coming. I hoped I was wrong.

A reporter from CNN asked, "Any truth to the rumor that Melanie Joan Hall is suspected of Leila Donnelly's murder?"

And there it is.

Greg nodded thoughtfully, taking his time before he spoke. "I believe in our judicial system, and I believe that the truth will come out," he said. "But I can state now that Melanie Joan Hall is no longer with Scepter. Publication of her memoir, *Stronger Alone*, has been canceled indefinitely. We wish her peace. And we are hopeful she will listen to her conscience."

I stole a glance at Melanie Joan. She looked as though someone had punched her in the gut. *No wonder she hates Greg Scepter so much,* I thought. It was bad enough he'd dumped her without even so much as a discussion first. Tacitly accusing her of murder in front of a roomful of reporters was a whole new low. I checked my Instagram for a reply from Marion Donnelly. Nothing.

"Canceled indefinitely," I said. "I can't figure out whether that's an oxymoron or just redundant."

"I'd say redundant," Charles said.

"But aren't cancellations definite? How do you cancel something indefinitely?"

"That's true," Charles said. "I'm going to have to think on this."

Melanie Joan said nothing. I put a hand on her shoulder. She shrugged it away.

Another reporter asked about the plot of *The Prince and the Peach*, and Greg replied with more or less the same description Melanie Joan had given. "It'll be a real treat for her fans," he said, segueing into more praise for Leila's readership. "Scepter has been tagged in so many heartfelt posts about Leila, and we've received flowers, condolence cards, and countless phone calls," he said. "As shy and reclusive as I knew her to be, I fully believe that Leila is somewhere out there, smiling over this tremendous outpouring of love."

More reporters shouted questions. Greg Scepter thanked everyone and told them he needed to get back to work. The livestream ended. None of us said a word. Leila powered down her iPad and carefully returned it to her bag. I checked my DMs again. Still nothing. I turned my notifications on.

Charles moved into the front seat, put on his seatbelt, and pulled out of the parking space. As he made his way back onto the turnpike, the three of us stayed silent. Our silence continued for most of the ride. I did a lot of thinking.

Once we were entering Boston, I spoke. "When is your meeting with Rita Fiore?" I said.

"Tomorrow morning at ten," Melanie Joan said.

"Make it sooner," I told her. "Make it today."

THIRTY-FIVE

Charles called Rita Fiore on the limo's Bluetooth, and she said she'd meet with Melanie Joan and him at four p.m., which was approximately our arrival time back in Boston. "I can't go to a lawyer's office dressed like this," Melanie Joan said, sounding like herself for the first time in ages. It gave me the tiniest shred of hope.

"How about we make it four-fifteen, and I come up to your room at the Ritz-Carlton?" Rita said. "You can freshen up a little, but you don't have to force yourself into heels."

"Sounds perfect," Melanie Joan said, before mouthing to me, *I like her.*

I smiled and gave her the thumbs-up.

"Hey, is Sunny Randall in there with you?"

"Hi, Rita," I said.

"Listen, I'm representing an associate of your once and future father-in-law," she said. "His name is Connor McMurtry. Nice guy. I mean, for a so-called hit man. You know him?"

"I think so," I said. Truth was, I found most of Desmond's associates to be sort of interchangeable—a recent exception being Swinging Dick.

"Small world, right?" she said.

"Especially when it concerns Desmond Burke."

"Yeah, it is," she said. "Anyway, Connor told me about your and Richie's re-engagement. Congrats."

"It's a pre-re-engagement, but thanks," I said.

She chuckled. "And here I thought attorneys were the biggest sticklers for language."

"Sunny's only a stickler for language when it comes to her commitment status," Melanie Joan said.

"Hey, who asked you?" I said.

The three of us laughed. Charles laughed, too. For a moment, "things going back to normal" felt like a very real possibility. You could say whatever you wanted to say about her courtroom theatrics, but a major part of Rita's skill set was putting anxiety-ridden clients at ease.

Rita told Melanie Joan and Charles she'd see them soon.

"Any instructions we should follow?" Melanie Joan said.

"Be honest with me," Rita said. "Don't leave anything out."

"Okay," Melanie Joan said.

"Also, please don't talk to anyone else about the case. Stay in your hotel room as much as possible."

"Okay."

"And for the love of God, do not go on TV anymore."

Melanie Joan cringed. "Got it."

"All righty, then, see you both soon," Rita said. "Give my best to Richie, Sunny."

"Sure thing." I nearly told her to say hi to Jesse for me, but sadly I still wasn't quite that evolved.

Once we ended the call, Melanie Joan sat back in the leather seat. She stretched out her legs and gazed up at the dome light. For the first time since this morning, she seemed semi-relaxed. Or maybe she was just exhausted.

We drove for a long time in silence. At one point, Melanie Joan asked Charles to turn on the radio, and he said no. "I don't want to risk whatever's on the news," he said.

Melanie Joan just nodded, her face serious and deathly pale. Where was Rita Fiore's chipper voice when you needed it? I thought, *Jesse's lucky to have her around,* and surprised myself yet again.

When we arrived at my office, it was about a quarter to four. Charles pulled up in front of the building. "I hope the rest of your day goes smooth and easy," he said.

"I doubt it will, but thanks."

I said goodbye to them both.

I was about to get out of the car when Melanie Joan stopped me. "Sunny?"

"Yeah?"

"I'm going to ask you something, and I want you to be honest with me."

"Okay."

"Do you think I killed Leila Donnelly?"

I looked her right in the eye and told the truth. "Absolutely not."

"Thank you," she said.

I got out of the car. The whole way up to my office, I kept thinking about Melanie Joan's eyes, how shattered they looked.

When I walked in, Blake greeted me. "Saw the news, and . . . What the fuck?" he said.

"That seems to be the question of the day."

"How were the Connecticut police? Did they seem understanding?"

"Um. No."

"That sucks," he said. "Anyway, there's a guy here to see you."

He didn't say this until I was opening my office door. This was Blake's sole problem, as far as I could see—his habit of delaying important information until it was too late.

"What's his name?" In order to drive home this teaching moment, I said it with my door wide open, when I was staring into the rheumy eyes of my visitor.

"Evan Woodrow," Blake said. He was a smart kid, but some things he just didn't get.

THIRTY-SIX

Ms. Randall, I need to talk to you," Evan Woodrow said.

"You can just call me Sunny," I said. "It's one less syllable, so this will go faster."

"I get it," he said. "You hate me."

I winced. "*Hate*'s a strong word," I said.

The fact was, I felt kind of sorry for Evan Woodrow at the moment. He looked more of a mess than he usually did. His comb-over was mussed, his thick glasses scuffed and foggy. He wore a different suit than he'd worn the last time I'd seen him, and somehow this one looked even more frayed. Could it have been he was so upset about what was happening to Melanie Joan that he'd done away with what little attention he paid to his appearance?

At any rate, I felt bad enough for him that I closed the door and offered him a seat. But not bad enough to ask Blake to bring in coffee.

"What brings you here, Evan?" I said.

"Melanie Joan."

"I figured," I said.

"I'm worried about her."

"We all are."

"No, Sunny," he said. "What I'm saying is, I've been worried about her for a while."

"What do you mean?"

He cleared his throat. "When was the last time you were around Melanie Joan for an extended period of time?"

I thought about it. "She hired me when she had that stalker situation," I said.

"Which stalker?"

"Well, both, actually," I said. "But I was talking about the most recent one."

"That was around the same time they were shooting *Girl and Not a God* for Netflix," he said.

"Right."

"She hadn't started writing her memoir."

"If she had, she didn't mention it."

"No, she hadn't," he said. "I know this. She didn't start writing it until two years ago. She wrote it in three sleepless months. It was an agonizing process, for her and for me."

"Okay," I said. I was starting to get a little frustrated. "Is there a point here?"

Evan grasped his hands together. Two clenched fists in

his lap, the knuckles pressing against his skin. "Writing that memoir . . . Reliving the abuse she suffered with John Melvin in such a concentrated way," he said. "I think it loosened something in her brain."

I squinted at him. "What?"

"I think it made her . . . emotional."

I staved off the inevitable eye roll. "You don't think Melanie Joan Hall was emotional before? Seriously?"

"Not like this," he said. "She's become reckless lately. Drinking more. Flying off the handle all the time. She harangued the copyeditor on *Stronger Alone* to the point where the poor woman had to take a weeklong mental health break."

The eye roll could be contained no longer. "The book meant a lot to her," I said. "If she were a man, you'd probably be calling her a tortured genius."

Evan leaned forward in his chair. "I've been Melanie Joan's editor for going on twenty-five years, Sunny," he said. "I've always been her biggest supporter. But I have to tell you . . . She's become more and more erratic since writing that book. You saw that comment she posted on Book Babe's review. Never in my wildest dreams would I have imagined her even thinking those things."

I grimaced. He had me there. "It was the water pill talking," I said. "It doesn't mix with alcohol and she had a few too many tequilas."

Evan sighed. "Come on," he said. "I've seen her drunk plenty of times. And when I first heard that a nasty comment she posted and deleted was making the rounds and that Greg was furious about it, I was sure he was overreacting. He didn't know her the way I did. It was just Melanie Joan being Melanie Joan."

I nodded. "Right. That's what it—"

"But then I saw it in its entirety," he said. "The way it was worded. I almost thought that it was some kind of joke. That someone had . . . had hacked her or something, because the Melanie Joan I know would not say those things about another woman."

"She wouldn't," I said. "It was the pill and booze. She doesn't even remember writing it."

"Well," he said, "what does that say about her?"

"What are you getting at, Evan?"

"Look, nobody wants Melanie Joan to go to jail," he said. "I don't want her to have killed Leila Donnelly. But at this point, I honestly don't know what she's capable of. Especially if, as you just said, she's been experiencing blackouts."

I stared at him. *This was what he'd come here to tell me?*

"Do you understand what I'm saying?"

I did understand. I considered telling him that Leila Donnelly had been Book Babe—and had been far crueler online to Melanie Joan than she'd been in response. But then I realized that 1) he probably knew that by now and 2) even if he didn't, it would only bolster the case he was trying to make.

"I don't want to believe Melanie Joan committed murder," Evan said. "I don't want you to believe it, either. But from what I've seen of her, it's possible. And I'm just asking you to keep your eyes open."

I stood up. "They are open," I said. "Thanks for dropping by."

He stood up, too. He had terrible posture. "This isn't something I enjoy."

"When we find out who really killed Leila Donnelly," I said, "I'll make sure and let you know. In the most humiliating way possible."

I showed him to the front door. When we passed Blake's desk, he started to apologize for not bringing in coffee, but I held a hand up.

"Mr. Woodrow is in a hurry to leave," I said.

"Okay, bye!" Blake said.

"You hate me more than ever now, don't you?" Evan said, once I'd walked him into the hallway.

"You're perceptive about some things," I said. I stepped back into my office space and closed the door.

"What was that about?" Blake said.

"Nothing worth discussing."

I returned to my desk, thinking about what Evan Woodrow had said—how quickly he could believe the worst of a woman whom he'd known for a quarter of a century, and who had made his entire career.

If Evan believed Melanie Joan was capable of murdering someone, I didn't even want to imagine what was running through Greg Scepter's mind. Or, for that matter, Gleason's . . .

"Sunny, did you see this?" Blake said.

I got up and walked to his desk.

"This came up on my Google Alerts," he said. He had a CelebrityScandals.com article pulled up on his screen. The title was: ROM-CRIME: DID MELANIE JOAN HALL KILL LEILA DONNELLY? After a brief paragraph detailing what I already knew, the article consisted of a series of captioned pictures—author photos of Melanie Joan and Leila, a press conference pic of Greg Scepter, a Getty image of mourning Leila fans taken in front of the Connecticut State Police barracks, separate, side-by-side shots of Tony and me, taken in nearly the same spot, with a caption that read **Team Melanie Joan** beneath them, along with our names and job descriptions.

To my horror, they'd also included a screenshot of Melanie Joan's infamous comment, with all the offensive words blacked out. It hit me that even if the world *had* found out that Book Babe had been a fake account created by Leila Donnelly, it probably wouldn't have mattered much. The comment had that type of staying power. And if Melanie Joan was eventually tried for Leila's murder, it would be shown to the jury. Even with Rita Fiore on her side, she didn't stand a chance.

Another photo captured Leila Donnelly's house, the front door bound with crime scene tape. I stared at it. A couple cops stood on the front porch, their backs to the camera. In the driveway, I could make out part of a medical examiner's van. The picture had been taken at sunrise, just after Leila's body had been found. I'd been to a lot of crime scenes. They evolved very rapidly. By now, I imagined, the tape was still there, but Leila's body had been removed, along with the murder weapon, Melanie Joan's highlighted book, and other items the police thought were relevant to the case, including furniture. But there might still be something there worth looking at, or maybe a cop more amenable than Gleason.

Union was only an hour away. I handed Blake the key to my loft and asked if he could feed and walk Rosie on his way home.

Then I grabbed my purse, made sure I had my gun, wallet, and car keys, and hurried out of the office. I hoped there wasn't too much traffic heading toward the Connecticut border.

THIRTY-SEVEN

Driving to Connecticut three times in less than twenty-four hours was something I never thought myself capable of doing willingly. But here I was, on my way back to Union again, talking to Richie on my Bluetooth and feeling like a commuter.

Interestingly, if you added three round trips from Boston to Union, Connecticut, the mileage was less than that of one round trip to Asbury Park. But as I was telling Richie, that didn't stop this latest journey from feeling especially long.

"What's Union like?" Richie asked.

"Reminds me of that town in the movie *Groundhog Day*," I said. "But that could just be because Melanie Joan and I keep seeing it again and again and again."

“Makes sense,” he said. He was quiet for a little while.

“What are you thinking?” I said.

“Nothing, really,” Richie said. “I just can’t believe how much has happened since you met with Swinging Dick.”

“Jeez, you’re right,” I said. “I feel like he should be about forty by now.”

Richie laughed. “Your life moves fast,” he said.

“Too fast for my liking,” I said. “And not enough Richie Burke in it.”

“Agreed,” he said.

I looked out the window. It was past seven-thirty and still bright as ever, which annoyed me. It made this overly long day feel endless. The exit sign for Union loomed ahead of me. Just about a mile to go and I’d be there. Again.

“So, I talked to Carll,” Richie said. “He’s out of town, but he’s back Wednesday. I arranged to meet with him. I suggested we have lunch, and he agreed. He offered to buy.”

“Lunch?” I said. “I’m impressed.”

“Don’t be.”

“But it could have been an email.”

“No, it couldn’t,” he said. “You tell your boss you want to meet face-to-face, they take you more seriously. And this is serious.”

I smiled. “It is.”

“I wouldn’t even tell him what the meeting was about,” he said. “I said I just had something that I wanted to discuss with him. I think I scared him.”

"Anybody would be scared of losing you," I said. I blushed a little hearing myself say this. Richie and I were embarrassing sometimes.

"You're slightly biased there."

"Nope. I'm speaking objectively," I said.

"Why I love you," he said. "Your objectivity."

I glanced in the rearview. I was still blushing. "Anyway," I said. "I kind of wish you were here for all this."

"Kind of?"

"Just slightly."

We were quiet again. Richie and I often did this—spending time in each other's company without saying a word. I found it comforting, even over the phone. And I was pretty sure he did, too.

I passed the sign letting me know Union was the next two exits. I remembered driving here with Melanie Joan for the first time, Spike behind the wheel. At one point, Melanie Joan had looked Union up on her phone. She talked about the town's small population and wondered aloud if it was anything like Utica. She'd been hopeful then. We'd all been hopeful—or at least we'd believed that there was a tiny chance that we might be able to right the sinking ship that was Melanie Joan's career. Now I was just trying to keep her from getting jailed for murder.

"What are you thinking?" Richie asked.

"I'm thinking about how much has happened since I met with Swinging Dick," I said.

"Great minds," Richie said. He asked how close I was to Union.

“I’m in it,” I said. I was passing the town square again, heading toward the woods where Melanie Joan had joked about looking for a gingerbread house. I said goodbye to Richie because I was about to make that series of turns—same as Spike had done the previous day—and I needed to pay attention.

I gazed out the window and focused on the road and tried to feel hopeful again.

THIRTY-EIGHT

Despite all the press Leila Donnelly had been getting, her former home felt just as isolated as ever. I was relieved. After my experience in the parking lot at the Westbrook police barracks, I'd feared I'd have to push my way around news vans and gangs of cosplaying readers.

But as I drove past, I saw that the house on Robin's Way wasn't even crawling with cops, let alone fans and media. If it weren't for the one squad car parked in the driveway and the yellow tape across the door, you'd have thought the worst crime committed at this dilapidated old house had been the paint job.

I parked about twenty feet up the road and checked myself in the visor mirror. My makeup was okay, my hair combed. I had been wearing the same Ashley Williams T-shirt dress since this morning, but the jersey material didn't crease and my white Chucks were still miraculously spotless. After I glossed my lips and pinched color into my cheeks, I was satisfied that I looked less exhausted than I felt. That was all I could ask for on a day like today. "You're a professional," I told my reflection. "Time to act like one."

I slipped my PI's license out of my wallet, grabbed my bag, and headed toward the house.

By the time I reached it, two uniformed cops had left the squad car and were standing in the driveway in front of the rear bumper, hands hovering over their holsters like this was *High Noon*.

"Easy there, cowboys," I said.

One of the cops was about Blake's age, wide-eyed and scrawny. The other was older and meatier, with a deeply ruddy face that was either his natural complexion or the heat getting to him. I couldn't tell.

"Hi, there, Officers!" I waved at them.

They didn't wave back.

"This is a crime scene, ma'am," said the ruddy-faced one. "I'm sorry your favorite author's passed and all. But I'm going to have to ask you to leave."

I winced. *So much for looking professional.* I took a few steps closer and held up my PI's license. "I'm actually working this case," I said. "I'm a private investigator."

Ruddy took it from me. He read it closely, his partner glancing over his shoulder. He handed it back. "State Police is working the case," he said.

"I'm working it from a different angle," I said.

"What angle?"

"I was hired by someone who is being questioned as a suspect."

The two of them looked at each other. "Detective Gleason can talk to you, ma'am," said the scrawny one.

"He already did."

"Then there you go," Ruddy said. "Have a pleasant evening."

There was something different about the driveway. I tried to catch a glimpse around the squad car, but it was blocking my view, and I felt like if I tried to pass these two to get a closer look, one of them—probably Ruddy—might go Marshal Kane on me. So instead I slapped on my brightest smile. "Look, the murder happened inside the house, right?"

Scrawny glanced at his partner nervously, like he'd forgotten his most important line in the middle of a live performance.

"It did," Ruddy said.

"So how about if I just look around the grounds."

"I dunno . . ."

"I won't cross the tape. I won't attempt to go into the house. You can accompany me."

"I need to guard the driveway."

"Then how about your partner, Officer . . ."

"Clam," said Ruddy.

"Officer *Clam*?"

Ruddy burst out laughing. "That's his real name," he said. "Weird, right?"

"It's German," the other cop said. "It starts with a *K* and has two *m*'s at the end."

I looked at Klamm, whose face was now redder than that of his partner. You could tell he got teased about his name a lot. A kid trying to prove himself on a small local police force, with a name that sounds like one of SpongeBob's friends. I couldn't help but feel sorry for him. "Nice to meet you, Officer Klamm," I said. I moved a little closer and stuck out my hand.

Klamm shook it tentatively.

"When he gets mad, we call him Steamed Klamm," Ruddy said.

"No, you don't," said Klamm.

"Not to your face," Ruddy said. He turned to me. "Are his hands . . . Klammy?" He laughed some more. He cracked himself up.

I gave Ruddy flat eyes. He just kept chortling away. He seemed about fifty years too old for this. "What's your name?" I asked him.

"Hanson."

"That's interesting."

"Why?"

"I once dated a guy with that last name."

He grinned. "Oh, yeah?"

"Yeah, I did." I looked him up and down. "He had a really small . . . appetite."

Klamm snorted.

"Can't hear the name Hanson without thinking of it," I said. "I mean, it was tiny. Like a bird." I looked him up and down again. "Or a kitten."

Hanson crossed his arms over his chest. He wasn't laughing anymore. But Klamm was.

"Can you show me around the grounds, Officer Klamm?"

Hanson started to say something, but Klamm interrupted. "I don't see why not," he said.

THIRTY-NINE

You shouldn't let him get to you," I said to Klamm as we trudged through weeds around the back of the house. "I mean, the whole thing is stupid anyway. It's not like you came up with your last name yourself."

"I know, right?" he said.

"Honestly? I know a guy named Carll and he spells it with two *l*'s. He chooses to do that. Corrects people when they spell it the way it's supposed to be spelled. To me, that's a hell of a lot weirder than a last name you were born with."

Klamm nodded. "Hanson can be kind of a jerk."

"Don't need to convince me."

The weeds were tall. I reminded myself to do a tick check at the first opportunity. Gnats hovered around our faces. The sun was just starting to set, but it was still so hot and humid that the air around us felt like breath. "So, Officer Klamm," I said, "were you here for the initial response?"

"Yeah," Klamm said. "I was here when the ME came. I helped bag evidence."

"Anything strike you as unusual?"

"That's hard to say," he said. "I mean, I'd never been at a murder scene before."

"First one's rough."

He nodded. "I gotta tell you, I don't think I was prepared."

"No one is ever prepared," I said. "The blood . . ."

"It wasn't just that . . ." Klamm stopped walking. "The killer shot her in the back of the head with a .45. The back of the head. She wasn't even facing him, and he blew her skull apart." He cleared his throat.

A warm breeze ruffled my hair, bringing with it a pasty scent. Wild lilies. Just like yesterday, when Melanie Joan and I had stood at the front door of this house, waiting to meet Book Babe face-to-face.

"Or her," Klamm said. "I didn't mean to say 'him.' The killer could have been a woman, I don't know. But who does that? Who shoots a lady in the back of the head?"

I remembered Leila standing there facing us, her slim frame and her hard eyes and her I THINK, THEREFORE I READ T-shirt. Leila Donnelly, alive and breathing.

It was the first time I'd really given thought to what had been done to Leila. My dislike for her aside, I wouldn't have wished it on anyone, a death like Klamm had just described. A violent explosion that had come out of nowhere, one she hadn't even been able to brace for. Her skull blowing apart, not in the midst of a confrontation, but at a time when she'd been comfortable enough to put her back to her killer. I tried to imagine Melanie Joan shooting Leila Donnelly in the back of the head. I couldn't.

"And with her own gun, in her own house," Klamm said. "Who does *that*?"

"Someone who knows where she keeps the gun," I said.

He nodded slowly.

At the back of the house there was a big sliding glass door. The curtains were drawn, but only partially. I walked up to it and peered inside. From where I was standing, I could make out the far wall, the bloody, scrawled message: JUSTICE FOR MJH. I shuddered. "Is this the room where the body was found?"

"Yeah," Klamm said.

The room was empty, save for a battered old couch and a plastic bin full of kids' toys. At the center of the dusty floor was a big, clean square where a throw rug used to be. "Did there used to be more furniture in that room?"

"Uh huh," he said. "There was a desk over there with some papers on it. Couple folding chairs. Nothing fancy."

"Seems like she lived pretty simply for a famous author," I said.

"That's what I thought when I first saw it," he said. "I figured maybe she had another place somewhere else and this was like her writing retreat or whatever. But from what I hear, nope. This was it."

"Anything else that was collected?" I said. "I know there was a highlighted book."

"The murder weapon."

"Yeah, besides the gun."

"A bookcase," he said. "It was filled with books, and we took those, too. Because of the blood spatter, I think. It was everywhere."

I stepped back from the house and started toward the garage. "I imagine you took her computer, too."

"There was no computer."

I stopped walking. "What?"

"No desktop. No laptop. Nada. We searched the whole house."

"There was a computer," I said.

"Wait, what?"

"That's how I knew where she lived," I said. "My client and I were able to get an IP address from something she posted on the Internet, and it led us here."

I started walking again.

"So, either she, like . . . left it somewhere," Klamm said.

"Or the murderer took it," I said.

"Yep," he said. I kept walking. "Did it seem like anything else was stolen?"

He shrugged. "She had a flat-screen upstairs, some jewelry. A big wad of cash in her dresser drawer. None of that was taken."

He followed me until I reached my destination. The place I'd wanted to take a closer look at in the first place. The side of the garage, where that sleek, spoiled brat of a convertible

Porsche had been parked the previous day. I stared at the spot. The Porsche wasn't there. And there was no evidence that it had ever been. No tire marks on the grass. No dribbles of oil or air conditioner fluid.

"Did you guys impound her convertible?" I asked Klamm.

He stopped walking and squinted at me. "What convertible?" he said.

FORTY

According to Klamm, there had been only one car registered to Leila Donnelly—a navy-blue Ford Taurus. And at the time the body was found, it was in her garage with a full tank. "We would have noticed a convertible Porsche," he told me.

He walked me back around the garage. I asked for his phone number and he gave me a card. I gave him mine. I said goodbye to Klamm and Hanson. Hanson just glared at me. He must have been very sensitive about his appetite size. I didn't bother getting his phone number.

When I got back to my car, I slipped Gleason's card out of my wallet and called him. He picked up right away. "Detective Gleason," he said. No first name.

"Hi, George, it's Sunny Randall."

"Yes, I knew that from the caller ID."

Jokingly, I complimented him on his detecting skills. Unsurprisingly, he didn't laugh.

I decided to cut to the chase. "I'm wondering if anyone in your investigation has mentioned a black Porsche 911 Carrera convertible."

"No," he said.

"Okay, well, I think there's a possibility that the person who killed Leila may have driven that type of car."

"Why do you think so?"

"I saw one parked outside Leila Donnelly's house yesterday, when Melanie Joan and I spoke to her. I assumed it was her car, but apparently it's not."

"So, when you stopped by," he said, "there may have been someone else in the house besides the child you said you heard."

"I would assume there was."

"That's really interesting."

"Why?"

"I've been trying to find friends of hers, an agent, a nanny, even. Anybody who might have visited her house around the time of her murder. She didn't seem to associate with anyone. Closest we've been able to find is a DoorDash driver who goes up there pretty frequently. Not in a Porsche, though. And anyway, he was delivering in a different town that day."

"What about her mom?"

"The only people to visit her house that day were you and Melanie Joan Hall."

"And the killer."

He said nothing.

"What I'm trying to get at is, maybe her mother knows of someone else. Maybe she's worth talking to about that."

"She doesn't know anything," he said.

"You're sure of this?"

"She doesn't want to talk."

"Doesn't want to talk at all? Or doesn't want to talk to you?"

He didn't answer the question. "Did you get the Porsche's license plate?"

"No," I said. "It was parked next to the garage, on the grass. The license plate wasn't fully visible, and anyway, like I said—"

"You assumed it belonged to the homeowner."

"Yes."

"Thanks for the information," Gleason said. He didn't sound thankful.

"George?"

"Detective Gleason."

I ignored the correction. "Do you have an ID on the so-called jogger/witness?"

"No."

"Maybe that was his car, then. Think about it. Maybe he wasn't jogging. Maybe he was in the house when Melanie Joan supposedly dropped by. Maybe he had just killed Leila and was looking for someone to pin the murder on."

Gleason didn't say anything for what felt like a long time.

"Are you still there?" I said.

"How do you know the jogger was male?" he said.

I rolled my eyes. "It was a lazy assumption," I said. "But that isn't my point."

"I know what your point is," he said.

"How much would it hurt to check a few surveillance cameras in the town of Union? Or E-ZPass records?" I said. "How many resources would it drain to look into the possibility of a killer who drives a very distinctive car and doesn't happen to be Melanie Joan Hall?"

He sighed. "I'll look into it," he said. "Thank you for calling."

He ended the call. I wanted to throw my phone at the window. "You will not look into it," I said. "Obviously." I was starting to get a headache—a mixture of nerves and poor hydration and this heavily pollinated country air.

The nerves were the worst part, though. I was genuinely nervous for Melanie Joan.

I called Rita Fiore and got her voicemail. I left a message about the Porsche and told her that Charles had seen it, too. "He said it was a sweet ride," I said. "I doubt he recalls the license plate, but who knows? I just wanted to pass along the info, and you can do with it what you will."

I started up my car and began driving down the mountain. I figured I'd go into Union, get a bottle of water at the one convenience store I'd noticed. I could ask around about Leila, see if random strangers had opinions on any Porsche-driving secret enemies this hermit of a woman might have had. Hell, maybe I could track down that DoorDash guy. Thinking about it made my head hurt even more. On a good day, I hated this type of meandering investigation. *Fishing with a gill net,* as my dad would have said. And this wasn't a good day. Fishing with a gill net required time and patience, and right now I was short on both.

My phone pinged with a text. I cringed, thinking about what it might say. I hadn't been getting the best news lately. I waited for another ping, but none came, and so I figured maybe it wasn't an emergency. Just more lousy news. I waited until I was safely down the mountain and through the woods and on the edge of town. When I saw the convenience store I'd planned on visiting, I pulled into the parking lot and read the text.

"Well, how about that?" I said.

The text was from a number with a Connecticut area code: *It's Mimi*, it read. *I got your DM. Can you meet?*

FORTY-ONE

I wasn't about to play hard to get. I texted Leila Donnelly's mother that I happened to be in Union and could meet her anywhere, at any time, and that I hoped that time was soon.

I waited. When I didn't hear back right away, I grabbed a bottle of water in the convenience store and brought it up to the counter, figuring that as long as I was here, I may as well set up my gill net. "You mind if I ask you a weird question?" I said to the clerk after she rang me up.

"I get weird questions all day long," the clerk said. She was probably in her early twenties, with pin-straight black hair, an ornate neck tattoo, bright blue eyes, and no-nonsense glasses that made her seem approachable. I had no doubt she got weird questions, and that many were far more intrusive than anything I'd ever dream of asking. "What's up?" she said.

I cleared my throat. "Did Leila Donnelly ever come into this place?"

"Who?"

"Famous romance writer. Just died?"

She gave me a blank look.

"I'm guessing you've never heard anybody talking about her, either. She lives relatively close by."

The clerk shook her head. "I'm more of a horror fan."

"Okay, fair enough. One more?"

"I got time."

"You ever see a black Porsche 911 Carrera around here?"

"Is that like . . . a convertible?"

"Yeah."

"Okay, now, that definitely is a weird question."

I looked at her. "Why?"

"Because I literally saw a car just like that in the parking lot today. It was at the beginning of my shift. I went out for a smoke. There it was. We don't get too many cars like that around here."

"When was that?"

"Half an hour ago."

"Really?"

"The driver pulls in. I noticed the car, obviously. It's a wicked-hot car. I wanted to see who was driving it. I stayed out there for a while. Smoked a second cigarette. But I never got to see the driver because the top was up and they never opened the door."

“Is that unusual?” I said. “People just hanging out in your parking lot?”

“Yes and no,” she said. “I figured maybe they were texting. A lot of people pull into our lot to text. But it seemed like a long time to be sitting in a convenience store parking lot. I decided they were probably meeting somebody, and I started feeling like a stalker. So I went back inside. Refilled the soda machine. Then I went outside again to smoke another cig and, guess what, the Porsche still hadn’t moved.”

“When did they leave?”

“Recently.”

“Meaning?”

“About five minutes before you showed up,” she said.

I frowned. “That’s weird,” I said.

“Hey, are you a cop or something?” the clerk said. “Was that, like, a criminal in the Porsche?”

“No to the first question. Maybe to the second.”

“Why are you asking questions if you’re not a cop?”

“I’m a private investigator,” I said.

“That sounds exciting.”

“Do you really think so?”

“You’d be surprised at what passes for exciting around here.”

I smiled. “Thanks for talking to me.”

“Anytime,” she said. “I’m Violet, by the way.”

“Sunny.”

I gave her my card. She read it.

"Can you do me a favor?" I said. "Call me if you see the Porsche again?"

She said she would and I thanked her. My phone dinged—another text from Mimi Donnelly: *Come anytime*, it said. She also sent a location pin.

Fishing with a gill net wasn't as bad as I'd thought.

FORTY-TWO

I texted Mimi that I was on my way and then took off, obediently following the GPS's directions till I reached my destination, which, as it turned out, was twenty miles away.

It was in a high-end condo complex called Maple Village that boasted a pool with a clubhouse, tennis courts, a small golf course, and really nice landscaping. I drove through it slowly. Judging by the residents I saw, some sitting on porches overlooking manicured lawns, others walking little dogs or going on assisted walks themselves, uniformed health aides at their sides, Maple Village catered to senior citizens. As far as quality of life went, it felt light-years beyond Leila Donnelly's broken-down farmhouse.

It made me think, *This is where her publishing earnings have been going.* Because I knew how pricey these places could be.

My parents had been looking into a few of them, just after Dad's retirement. But they decided to hold off until they could better afford the HOA fees—and this was just for the independent-living section. Once you moved on to assisted living, memory care, and the nursing units, these regular charges went up exponentially.

I stopped my car in front of the pinned address—a ranch house with a neat row of pink roses in the front. There was one car in the driveway—a silver RAV4. I parked behind it and jogged up the steps and rang the bell.

The door opened quickly. Mimi Donnelly poked her head out. She looked similar to the way she did in her Instagram picture, but her hair had grown out a bit. She wore it in a ponytail. "Sunny?" she said.

I told her I was sorry for her loss.

"I'm just glad you wrote me," she said. "The detective on Leila's case seems to have tunnel vision."

"He said you wouldn't talk to him."

"I just won't say what he wants me to."

"Join the club," I said. "Full disclosure. I'm a private eye."

"I know. I looked you up online."

"And my client is Melanie Joan Hall."

"The romance writer. The one Detective Droopy Dog is ready to arrest."

"He reminded me more of Larry David," I said. "But yes."

She rolled her eyes. "I mean, I don't know her personally," Mimi said. "But I've seen enough of Melanie Joan Hall to know she probably can't shoot a Glock .45."

"I do know her personally," I said. "She can't shoot anything."

Mimi managed a smile. She seemed calm, but her eyes were bloodshot and her face had a drawn look to it, as though she was using all her energy to keep from bursting into tears. She took a few steps back and opened the door wider and asked if I wanted to come in.

I could hear jingly music and hyperenthusiastic voices coming from the other room—some kids' show playing. "Thank you," I said.

Mimi wore white cotton slacks and pink Crocs and a pale blue T-shirt that said WORLD'S GREATEST GRANDMA on it. Despite the getup, she seemed a little young for this complex—and for the house, which, if the living room/dining room was any indication, was all cream-colored carpets and heavy wood furniture and oil paintings of big-eyed children with overly complicated frames. The sofa was beige, with a green pineapple print. It was covered in thick plastic, the likes of which I hadn't seen since Richie and I were newlyweds and we visited his ninety-five-year-old aunt in Dorchester. *Try not to say anything about the couch condom,* Richie had said as we walked in.

It all looked clean and orderly, though—which was a lot more than I could say for Leila's farmhouse. I thought of little Tommy, shuttling back and forth between these two vastly different homes. Then I thought of the farmhouse again. The Porsche parked outside.

"That RAV4 out front," I said. "Is it yours?"

"Just finished paying off the loan," Mimi said.

"Nice."

"Thanks."

"You own any other cars?"

"No."

"Happen to know anybody who drives a Porsche 911 Carrera?"

She frowned. "No," she said. "Why?"

I looked at Mimi. She seemed trustworthy enough. But then again, we'd just met. And I made it my business not to reveal important information to witnesses before getting to know them. "Just a potential lead," I said. "No big deal." Mimi offered me a seat on the plastic wrap. I noticed two baby monitors on the coffee table, one pink and one blue. The kids' show piped out of the blue one.

"Nice place," I said.

"It isn't mine," she said. As if on cue, an elderly woman's voice rasped out of the pink monitor. "Mimi!"

"Yes, Mrs. Dorsey!"

"I need my bed changed."

"Excuse me for a minute," Mimi Donnelly said.

She stood up. A little boy came galloping into the room and started tugging furiously on Mimi's arm. "Who's here?" he said. "Who's this?"

"A visitor for Grandma," she said. "Tommy, would you like to keep Grandma's visitor company while I go help Mrs. Dorsey?"

I smiled at the little boy. He had dark, serious eyes and fine features—a ringer for his grandmother, and his mother, too. Mimi ruffled his hair and I noticed the flower tattoo on her arm, identical to Leila's.

"Hi, Tommy," I said. "I'm Sunny."

Tommy's eyes widened in terror. He wrapped both arms around Mimi's leg and hid behind her.

I wondered if he recognized my voice from when I'd told off his mother. I felt a tinge of guilt.

Mimi sighed. "Don't take it personally. Tommy's just a little shy, aren't you, buddy?"

"I go with Grandma! *Grandma!*" he shouted.

"Please, keep that child quiet!" said the pink monitor.

"Yes, ma'am!" Mimi called out. "Tommy, you settle down now," she said quietly.

He did, almost immediately. This was a kid who listened to his grandma, if not his mother.

"You work here," I said.

Mimi nodded. "Mrs. Dorsey has late-stage emphysema and limited mobility due to severe osteoporosis," she said. "She needs twenty-four-hour care, and I'm a skilled nurse who needs a place to live, so we're a match made in heaven." She gave me a weak smile, then turned to Tommy. "You want to go back to Grandma's room and watch TV?"

He nodded, his dark eyes fixed on my face. Slowly, he disengaged himself from Mimi's leg and backed away from me, as though I were a dangerous animal.

"That's a good boy," Mimi said. "You want ice cream later?"

He nodded more vigorously, then retreated down the hall.

"I assumed this place was yours," I said. "And that Leila bought it for you."

She shook her head. "I wouldn't take Leila's money," she said.

"Why not?" I said. "She makes a lot."

"Yeah," Mimi said. "But I don't know how much she owes or who she owes it to. It scares me. And I don't want Tommy involved with that kind of money."

My eyes widened. "What?" I said.

The pink monitor called out her name again. "I'll be right back," Mimi said. "Make yourself comfortable."

Talk about an impossible request.

FORTY-THREE

"What kind of money?" I said, once Mimi had left Mrs. Dorsey's room and I'd taken a few swallows of the tea she'd insisted on serving me, and we were both seated side by side on the plastic-covered couch.

"Excuse me?" she said.

"You said 'that kind of money' when we were talking about your daughter's income," I said. "As far as I know, it came from writing romance novels."

She sipped her tea and set it back down on the flowery china saucer. "Not always," she said.

"What do you mean by that?"

Mimi shook her head. "I'm just speculating. What do I know?" She squeezed her eyes shut and swallowed hard. Keeping herself together. "Nothing," she said. "That's what I know."

I decided to take a few steps back from the topic. I took another sip of tea and gave her what I hoped was an encouraging smile. "It seems to me like you know a lot," I said.

"Like what? You've just met me."

"I know," I said. "And since I met you, I've seen you calm down a three-year-old in seconds. There are entire books written about what you just did."

"Tommy? He's easy."

"He didn't seem easy when he was with Leila yesterday," I said.

She said nothing for several moments.

"We went to see Leila yesterday. My client and I. We had an IP address for someone who had posted a terrible review of Melanie Joan's memoir. It turned out to be Leila."

"And that's why that cop believes your client shot my daughter?"

"Yes," I said.

"Well . . . that's a theory, I suppose."

"Anyway, Tommy was acting up. And Leila was having trouble getting him to settle down."

"She's normally pretty good with him," Mimi said. "Was, I mean. Was. My daughter *was* pretty good with her son. When she was alive." She closed her eyes again.

I put a hand on hers. "I'm sure she was," I said. "And I'm not saying this out of disrespect for Leila. I'm just saying that in order for a kid to trust you the way Tommy does, you need to understand him." I took a breath. "I think you understand people."

She opened her mouth as if to say something, then reconsidered. "Thank you," she said.

We sat quietly for a few moments, the kids' show chirping out of the blue monitor, the pink monitor silent, save the hum of an air conditioner.

At last, Mimi spoke. "Leila and I were never close."

I hadn't expected that.

"I loved her, of course, but we didn't have much to talk about. Ever. She was a real daddy's girl."

"I get that."

"You have one of those?"

I smiled. "I am one of those."

"Yeah, well. Give your mom some grace. She's trying."

"She's trying, all right," I said.

Mimi made herself laugh.

"Tell me about Leila," I said.

Mimi took a deep breath, her bloodshot eyes fixed on some far-off spot. "She was an unusual kid. She had strange interests for a girl." She coughed. "God, that sounded sexist. I think I've been hanging around Mrs. Dorsey for too long."

"How was Leila unusual?"

"She was kind of a nerd, I guess. She and her father were both Trekkies. Serious Trekkies. They watched the shows, of course. They both collected memorabilia. They went to conventions together. They even talked about getting jobs as extras on one of the spin-offs. I think Bill was just saying that to humor her, but still."

"That's hardcore."

"Very," Mimi said. "Her sister. She lives in Hawaii, but she's on her way out here. When the two of them were growing up, Carolyn was more like me—sporty, social. No cultlike obsessions. But Leila wanted more than anything to be a crew member on the *Enterprise.* It's what made her decide to start writing."

"*Star Trek* made her want to write?"

"Yes," Mimi said. "First it was *Star Trek* fan fiction. Then she started writing novels of her own. Sci-fi. Her dad loved these novels. He read them all. I couldn't get through a single chapter."

I took another sip of my tea. I wanted to ask her what all this had to do with where Leila's money came from. I was hoping I'd find out. If there was one thing I'd learned from questioning the parents of murder victims, it was that this type of overwhelming grief could take strange turns. Parents often went through their children's entire histories in order to get to the point, if there even was a point. A lot of times, it was just a way to keep them alive for a few moments longer. "Did Leila ever publish any of the sci-fi books?" I asked.

She shook her head. "They had a very small audience. Her friends and her father. She was happy with that." Over the blue monitor, a character with a high-pitched British accent was talking about a new baby sister. Tommy started to laugh. Mimi smiled. Her eyes sparkled. A tear trickled down her cheek. She wiped it away.

"Where is Leila's dad now?" I said.

"Bill passed away ten years ago. Heart attack. Leila was just twenty-one. She took it very, very hard. Her sister was no longer living at home, so it was the two of us for a little while. I tried to bond with her. I even suggested these damn matching tattoos." She rubbed the flower on her arm.

"I noticed. It's pretty."

"It's a sweet william. For my Bill. Our Bill."

"That's nice," I said.

"I thought so," she said.

"Must have made Leila feel better."

"Maybe for a day," she said. "She just wasn't the same. She dropped out of community college, and she moved to New York. She had it in her head that she was going to publish those sci-fi books to honor her dad's memory, and that New York was the place for her to *get seen* as an author. I told her she needed more of a game plan than that. She said she had her mind made up and she was an adult and could do whatever she chose. She didn't want to hear anything I had to say."

"That must have been frustrating."

"It was." She sighed. "You know that Instagram of mine that you found?"

"Yes?"

"I made it when Leila moved out to New York, so I could follow her on social media. She didn't post very often, but at least I could see her face."

I winced. I was sure I'd tortured my mother over the years, but not like that. "New York is so expensive," I said. "How was she surviving?"

"I heard through mutual friends that she was staying with

some rich boy she'd met at one of those conventions. But she had a falling-out with him."

"What about?"

"He ran with a rough crowd. Bragged about burglarizing a mansion in Southampton when he was seventeen and spending the money on drugs. He scared Leila, I think."

"Boy, Trekkies have changed."

"I thought the same thing," she said. "Anyway, I guess I should have been grateful to this rich kid, because she got disgusted enough with him to move out of his place, and that's when she called me. I helped her find a new apartment. A studio in Queens. She managed to get a job waiting tables. It paid her rent. Barely."

"Was she happy?"

"At first, I think? Once she was settled, she stopped wanting to talk to me again."

"Ugh. Why?"

"I don't know. I felt like she had secrets she didn't want me to find out. But maybe I'm just flattering myself and she just plain didn't like me."

"Mimi . . ."

She waved me off. "Anyway, what could I do? She was a grown woman. She even deleted her Instagram. I started sending her money every month, just so I could know from the cashed checks that she was alive."

"But wait," I said. "At some point, she became *the* Leila Donnelly."

"Yep," she said. "The reclusive, mysterious Leila Donnelly."

"Did she call you when that first book became a hit? Is that how you got back in touch again?"

She shook her head. "I found out she was a bestselling romance writer when my friends started asking me if I could get them autographed first editions."

I gaped at her. "Seriously?"

She nodded. "I downloaded her first book and I read it," she said. "It didn't sound like Leila at all."

"How?"

"It was so . . . gushy. Leila was never gushy. It was like the book had been written by a stranger."

"So," I said, "what made her want to talk to you again?"

"Tommy."

"That makes sense."

"When he was born, he gave Leila a reason to move back home," she said. "There was no father in the picture. I got that he was a fling—someone who'd never even given Leila his phone number. Leila said, 'Mom, I'm afraid I'm going to mess up with my son.' And I said, 'Don't worry. I'll help you take care of him.' I expected a snide response, but she was so grateful, and it's been . . . It was . . . Well, Leila just keeps surprising me. And Tommy's a love."

"He adores you," I said.

"The feeling's mutual."

"Is your visitor still here?" said the pink baby monitor.

"She'll be leaving soon, Mrs. Dorsey!"

"Did you offer her tea?"

"Yes, I did, Mrs. Dorsey!" Mimi waited. When it was clear

that Mrs. Dorsey had no more questions, she turned to me and leaned in. "The day Leila died, she called me. She asked me to watch Tommy, and I said of course. She wanted me to meet her down at the convenience store in Union. She handed Tommy off to me in the parking lot. It was the first time in a while that I'd had a good, long look at her and she was so . . ."

"What?"

"Scared."

"Did she say why?"

"No, but she was adamant about meeting in a public place. This is a young woman who rarely leaves her house."

"That must have seemed strange."

"She said, 'I'm finally about to do the right thing, Mom, so wish me luck.'"

A thought came to me: When I'd talked to Leila on the phone, she'd told me that Tommy was with her mother. Looking specifically at the timeline, she'd probably just come back from the convenience store parking lot. I remembered the way her voice had sounded—that hushed, anxious tone. I'd thought she was being manipulative—trying to gain my sympathy in order to keep me from going to the press. But looking back on it, I realized she'd sounded genuinely frightened. *Sunny, listen. What you guys think about me is true. But only partly.*

Which part?

The part I can't say over the phone.

Why had she returned to her house after dropping off Tommy? Was she picking something up? Her gun, for protection? Or was there something else she'd wanted to show me? I thought of the computer. The one she'd used to write her Book Babe reviews. The one the police had never found.

The British voice on Tommy's TV show was talking about jumping in muddy puddles. Tommy called for his grandma softly, as though he'd fallen half-asleep and this was an involuntary action. Calling for Grandma. Like the beating of a heart. "It's that word *finally* that haunts me," Mimi was saying. "I'm *finally* doing the right thing. So Leila had been doing the wrong thing for a very long time. Right? Doesn't that make sense?"

"Yes," I said.

"I wish it didn't."

Mimi took both of my hands in hers. Her face was flushed, her eyes thick with tears. "Sunny," she said, "I don't know if I can survive this."

"You can," I said. "I know you can. Because I know you love Tommy and Tommy needs you and—"

The blue monitor shrieked. Mimi jumped from the couch.

"What's happening?" yelled Mrs. Dorsey. "What on earth is going on?"

Mimi didn't respond. Tommy was screaming. *"Grandma, help! Help!"*

Mimi pushed away from the wall and hurled herself down the hallway.

I followed. She threw open the door to her room. There was a neatly made bed with an old-fashioned bedspread—white, with pink roses and ruffles. A chest full of toys at its foot. A pile of stuffed animals atop a toddler bed against the wall. A crudely drawn pig with a British accent was on the TV, telling her mommy how much she loved her.

I didn't see Tommy at first. But then I did. He was on the floor, sobbing, his face pressed to the window. "It's okay, baby," Mimi said. She crouched down and took him in her arms and rocked him back and forth. "What's wrong?" she said. "What's wrong, honey? You can tell Grandma. Why are you crying?"

I moved to the window and peered out. A black Porsche convertible was parked at the curb in front of the house. It was the same 911 Carrera that I'd seen at Leila's. The top was up, though. In the purplish twilight, I could see the silhouette of the driver inside. A big, hulking man with cropped, curly hair. I couldn't make out the details of his face, but I knew he was angled toward the window. He was watching us.

"I'll be right back," I told Mimi.

"What's going on out there?" Mrs. Dorsey hollered from the end of the hall.

I grabbed my purse and hurried out of the room, then threw open the front door and ran straight at the Porsche, just as it pulled away from the curb.

"Stop!" I yelled. To no one.

The sound from the tires echoed, like a scream.

FORTY-FOUR

By the time I was able to get into my car and start it up, the Porsche was long gone. Fortunately, I'd managed to get a good look at the license plate. I remembered the number long enough to text it to myself. Then I found Klamm's card and called him.

"Hey, Sunny." He said it as though we were old pals. I liked this kid.

"Still at the crime scene?"

"Yep."

"Any news?"

"None. We had three more sobbing ladies drop by to pay their respects. But they left when we asked them to."

"How's Hanson? Throwing any more hissy fits?"

He chuckled. “He’s out back, taking a whiz,” he said. “What’s up?”

“Remember that Porsche 911 Carrera I told you about?”

“The one that disappeared?”

“Yeah,” I said. “Well, I got the plate number.”

“Wow. Really? How?”

“I’ve got my ways.”

“Do you want me to tell Detective Gleason?”

“No, I’m not telling him about it,” I said. “Not now, at least. At the moment, I only trust you.”

“Hey . . . um. Thanks.”

“I’m just wondering if you could do me a huge favor and run it for me?”

“Sure.”

I heard the squad car door opening, the scuff of Klamm’s shoes as he got inside. “What’s the plate?” he asked.

I opened the text to myself and read it to him over speakerphone.

“Got it. One sec . . .”

“Take your time,” I said.

As I waited, the violet sky deepened. An elderly woman passed my car on a motorized scooter with an American flag affixed to the back. A man trailed behind her, walking a small, sprightly beagle. The lights went on in the house next door. Then in another, farther down. In a strange way, it all felt magical—one of those rare moments I wanted to re-create on a canvas, just so I could keep it. That’s what painting was to me, really. A way of trapping time and making it stand still.

Klamm returned to the phone. "The car is registered to somebody named Edward Piro," he said. He gave me an address in New York City, an apartment on Park Avenue.

"Park Avenue. Nice," I said.

"Goes with the car," Klamm said.

"Yep."

"No outstanding warrants," he said.

"A respectable citizen," I said.

"According to his license plate."

"And I'm assuming the car wasn't reported stolen."

"You assume correctly."

"Thank you, Officer Klamm," I said.

"Good luck," he said. "Let me know if you need anything else."

I thanked Klamm again and ended the call.

"Mr. Edward Piro of Park Avenue," I whispered.

I pulled out my phone and googled the name. I found several Edward Piros, but most were obituaries. I tried Edward Piro and Park Avenue and found the same Edward Piros, with "Park Avenue" crossed out. For a guy with such a flashy car, Edward Piro kept a very low profile.

I thought about going back into Mrs. Dorsey's house, but decided against it. It was pretty clear that Tommy wasn't a fan of mine, and I didn't want to traumatize him any more than he already was. I found Mimi's text on my phone and called the number. She picked up. I could hear the cartoon pig in the background.

"Tommy okay?" I said.

"Yeah, he feels better now. Don't you, baby?"

I heard a tiny "Yeah."

"I think I'd better head out," I said. "Tommy deserves a break."

"Thanks, Sunny," Mimi said. "We're going to have ice cream and then bedtime. It's been a long, difficult day."

"It has."

She lowered her voice. "You asked me about a Porsche, when you first came by."

"Yes."

"Why?"

I decided to be honest. I knew her now. "When Melanie Joan and I went by your daughter's house, I saw it parked outside."

"That same car."

"Yes."

"My God . . ."

"Did Tommy . . . Has he said anything about the car? Did he tell you why he was crying?"

"Just 'bad,'" she said. "He kept repeating it. 'Bad, bad, bad.'" Her voice cracked. I could tell she was trying to tamp down more tears. "Poor little boy."

"He loves you very much," I said. "Take good care of him, Mimi."

"I will," she said. "And if I see that car again, I'll call you and nine-one-one. In that order."

"Call nine-one-one first," I said.

"All right."

"Can I just ask one more question?" I said. "Did Leila ever mention somebody named Edward Piro?"

"No," she said. "Never."

"Do me a favor. If you happen to be going through your daughter's things, let me know if that name turns up?"

"Edward Piro."

"Yes."

Mimi told me she would. "I should have gotten more involved in Leila's life than I did," she said. "Maybe if I had, she wouldn't have—"

"Stop," I said. "You've done great. You've done the best you can. We only have so much control over the people we love. And unfortunately, that's not a lot."

Mimi drew a long, shaky breath. In the background I could hear Tommy's small voice, asking for ice cream. "Stay safe, Sunny," she said quietly.

"You, too," I said.

After I was driving for a little while, I called Blake's cell phone. Not surprisingly, he was still at my loft, playing with Rosie. He'd always found it difficult to say goodbye to her, and who could blame him? I missed her already.

"I hope you don't mind, but I made myself dinner here," he said. "I bought my own keto-friendly food. I'm eating dinner super-early these days because I'm doing intermittent fasting and I like to eat after my morning gym run. Tomorrow morning is leg day, and I'm extra-starving after leg day, so I knew I couldn't eat a late dinner, because that would mean skipping breakfast, am I right?"

I exhaled. It was exhausting, sometimes, the amount of information Blake divulged on a regular basis. "That's fine," I said.

Blake told me that he'd cleaned up afterward and that he was leaving "some awesome food" in my fridge—homemade green juice, half a dozen eggs, frozen bison patties. "You can have as much as you want," he said. "The eggs are cage-free and organic. The bison is an excellent source of protein."

"I'm getting hungry just thinking about it," I said. "Listen, though, can you do me a favor and research somebody for me? I googled him, but I got nothing."

"Sure."

"His name is Edward Piro and he lives in New York, on Park Avenue." I glanced down at my phone and read him Piro's address.

"What kind of info do you need?" Blake said.

"Anything. Everything. What he does for a living, who his friends and family are, where he went to school. If he's been married, divorced. Pet peeves, favorite breakfast cereal and prestige TV series, whether he'd choose Kylie, Kim, or Kendall . . . Everything. His rap sheet, too. I'm serious about that one. I want to hear about every parking ticket."

"Dude. I'm on it."

"Most important," I said, "find out what his connection is to Leila Donnelly."

"Oh, ho," he said. "This should be interesting."

I smiled. Working for me had taken its toll on Blake James's speech patterns. "It had better be interesting, am I right, dude?"

"Spot on," he said.

Blake asked me if I wanted him to hang out at my place till I got home. "Rosie might need another walk," he said, and I realized he was right.

I thanked him. We said goodbye and ended the call. My stomach growled. I realized I'd been running on caffeine all day, with no actual food since the egg-and-cheese sandwich I'd scarfed down during the morning drive to Connecticut. I wasn't sure I could make it back to Boston without grabbing a bite first. Since Union was on the way home, I opted to drive back to the convenience store. The sandwiches had looked pretty good, and I knew how to get there. That was enough to sell me on the place.

It took just about ten minutes from where I was at this point. On my way, I called Tony and let him know what I'd learned so far. He told me he thought I should call Gleason and share my info about Edward Piro.

"But Gleason wasn't interested when I told him about the car in the first place. I don't think he believes I'm telling him the truth about this stuff."

"Because he's got such a hard-on for Melanie Joan."

"Yeah, there's that," I said. "I also don't think he likes me very much."

"How could anybody not like you?" Tony said.

"It could be because I'm a PI, or because I'm a woman," I said. "Or because I'm a woman PI."

"Or because you're a wiseass," Tony said.

"That, too," I said. "The man has literally zero sense of humor."

"How about if I tell him? I got along with him okay."

"You did?"

Tony sighed. "He's been working on a screenplay. It's about—get this—a State Police detective." I could practically see the eye roll.

"Ah."

"Anyway, I can tell him that I heard something about this Edward Piro guy hanging around with Leila around the time she was killed."

"But you can't mention me."

"Don't worry, I won't," he said. "I'll play the dumb Hollywood guy and tell him that some Park Avenue friend of mine told me. Somebody who knows somebody who knows Ed. I'll get him to buy it."

"You're good at that," I said.

"Getting people to buy things?"

"Playing the dumb Hollywood guy."

"Wiseass."

I smiled. "I try."

"Can I tell you something?" he said. "Just as an aside?"

"Yeah?"

"These past few days are the most time I've ever spent with you, clothes on. Just talking."

"I'm aware of that."

"But you know what?"

"What?"

"You're actually, like . . . really fun to talk to."

"Thanks," I said. "I feel the same."

"I mean, not that it wouldn't be more fun naked."

"Understood."

"But since that isn't a possibility. Unless, I don't know. Is it?"

"You're good, Tony. Quit while you're ahead."

He laughed. I laughed, too.

"You know I'm just kidding," he said. "Unless—"

"Bye, Tony."

I ended the call smiling. Tony Gault wasn't that bad to work with.

FORTY-FIVE

The lights in the convenience store were exceptionally bright, even by convenience-store standards. I hadn't noticed it earlier because I'd been here in the daytime. But now that it was dark out, I felt like this place could have doubled as a surgical theater, only with cigarettes and lotto tickets.

It was busier in the store than it had been when I bought the water, and Violet was no longer here. The new clerk was a teenage boy with half-closed eyes and a hairstyle that added four inches to his height. He was probably stoned. And so I had a feeling I wouldn't have been able to talk to him the way I'd talked to Violet, but that was okay. A gill net can catch only so many fish in one day.

I grabbed a bottle of iced tea and a ham-and-cheese sandwich and got in the back of a lengthy cash register line. I was still waiting when Mimi called.

"Can you tell me that name again?" she said after I answered. "You asked if I thought it sounded familiar?"

The person in front of me finished paying. I walked up to the register and set my purchases in front of the clerk. "Edward Piro," I said.

"That's what I thought," Mimi said. "Edward."

I noticed some large, homemade dog biscuits in a box at the counter and took one out to buy. It was the least I could do for Rosie after abandoning her for an entire day. "Why do you ask?"

"It might be nothing," Mimi said. "But remember that rich boy I told you about? The one Leila stayed with when she first moved to New York?"

"Yes," I said as I gave the clerk my credit card. "The Trekkie, right?"

"Well, she did meet him at a *Star Trek* convention, so I would assume," Mimi said. "But I don't know anything about him—not even his last name."

The clerk pointed to a stack of brown paper bags. I nodded yes. He put my things in and handed it to me. I thanked him. He said nothing. I headed for the door.

Mimi was saying, "I did just remember his first name, though. Leila told me during the one phone conversation we had around that time. I think she just wanted to give me something. A little piece of information so I'd . . . you know . . . hang up."

"What was his first name?" I asked.

"Teddy," Mimi said. "That's short for Edward, isn't it?"

"It can be," I said.

"Yeah, well, it's been in my mind," she said. "Figured I'd pass it along."

"Thank you," I said. "How's Tommy?"

"He's okay," she said. "I think he might be starting to miss his mommy."

"I'm sorry, Mimi."

"I know," she said. "One day at a time."

After we hung up, I texted Blake, asking him to research Teddy Piro, too.

I was already out of the store and in the parking lot when I sent the text. I looked up from my phone and my arms went slack. The bag I was holding fell from my hand. The black Porsche 911 Carrera was parked at the edge of the lot, just under the lone streetlamp. I picked up the bag with one hand and slipped the other into my purse, my fingers finding my gun, my palm resting on the frame. I didn't take it out, but I kept my hand on it as I walked toward the sleek car, the light reflecting off it in rainbows, like an oil slick.

"Edward?" I said.

I peered inside the car. There was nobody behind the wheel. I glanced at the floor. Front and back. Nobody was hiding. I saw a coil of rope on the rear seat, alongside a rectangular metal box that looked like a tool kit. I slipped my phone out of my purse and snapped a picture of the box, another of the rope. I took a few steps back, photographed the length of the Porsche, then moved to the rear of the Porsche and took one of the license plate. *How long has his car been parked here? And where is he now?*

I looked at the pictures as I walked back to my own car. I wasn't sure what they proved. A toolbox and a rope could be in the rear seat of a fancy sports car for any number of benign reasons. But at least I had something.

Why is Piro here? Where is he?

I had just reached my car when I felt the answer to my second question—footsteps behind me, something pressed to the back of my neck. It was the barrel of a gun. I froze. My phone dropped out of my hand and clattered to the pavement.

"Edward Piro?" I said.

He breathed into my hair. The barrel jammed against the top of my spine. I felt a whisper in my ear—a voice that was all breath, no tone behind it. "Sunny Randall."

I froze.

I heard the click of the gun's safety releasing. I wanted to step on his foot or elbow him in the gut, then reach into my purse again and grab my .38. But I didn't. I couldn't. I was paralyzed. I hated myself for that. Hated my body for betraying me. *Move. If you're going to die, at least die fighting back.*

"It can happen anytime," he whispered. "Anyplace. Whether you expect it or not. We're everywhere."

We? I said nothing. I couldn't move my lips to talk.

"We know everything about you. Mind your own business or it will happen. I'm watching. We're watching."

The barrel lifted from my neck. My body finally got unstuck.

My right hand dove into my purse and grabbed my .38. I yanked it out and took it in both hands and whirled around to face him.

Nobody was there.

The Porsche's lights switched on. It tore out of the parking lot. I thought about how long I'd been standing there, unable to move. Enough time for a big guy like the one I'd seen in that car to get all the way across a decent-sized parking lot. *Never again,* I told myself. *You are never going to freeze up like that again.*

I got back into my car and started it up. I opened the iced tea and took a bite of the sandwich and turned on the AM news to get the voices out of my head. *You were weak. You were afraid. You're a woman, not a child. There's no excuse. Never again.*

I ate my sandwich as I drove, listening to commercial after commercial until I managed to stop berating myself and think of nothing but driving.

The last commercial ended, and the announcer came back on—the same exceedingly animated guy that my dad used to listen to when I was a kid and he'd take me to Saturday soccer practice in his shiny Audi. This announcer had to be close to one hundred by now, yet that cheesy radio voice hadn't changed a bit. He still hung on to every *r* like a long-lost love. "Our top story tonight," he said. "Queen of Romance Melanie Joan Hall has been arrested for the murder of Leila Donnelly."

I nearly drove off the road.

FORTY-SIX

It was the laptop. Connecticut State Police had obtained a warrant to search Charles's Town Car, and in the trunk they'd found Leila Donnelly's missing laptop, which contained drafts of her most recent manuscripts, her signed contract with Scepter Books—and the hundreds of reviews she'd written as Book Babe.

Someone had leaked that information to the press, which I found ironic. After all this time, Leila Donnelly had been outed for having a sock puppet that she'd weaponized against Melanie Joan. But it had happened posthumously, and instead of destroying Leila's career the way I'd assumed it would, it had given romance fans even more reason to hate my old friend.

"Police sources allege that Melanie Joan Hall had discovered that her rival had been behind the one-star review," the syrupy-voiced announcer was saying. "They see that as a potential motive for the shooting. An overreaction? Certainly. But for the Queen of Romance, melodrama has been known to reign supreme."

I groaned. This guy should have retired about forty years ago.

My phone rang. It was Spike. "Where are you?" he said.

"Connecticut border," I said.

"Did you hear?" Spike said.

"Just," I said. "It was on the radio."

"I just heard, too. Tony told me. He's here with me now, at the restaurant." Spike told me they were in his office and that I was on speakerphone.

"Did Melanie Joan call you, Tony?" I asked.

"No, Rita did," Tony said. "MJ had one phone call, so of course she chose her attorney."

"Of course," I said.

"She's getting booked right now. She'll most likely be held overnight at the Hartford Correctional Center."

"I'll turn around," I said.

"No," Tony said. "She specifically said she didn't want any visitors there except Rita."

"Why not?"

"Rita didn't say."

"I'm sure she wants as few people as possible to see her in institutional attire," Spike said. "They also confiscate makeup, so . . ."

"Right."

Spike could have taught a Ph.D.-level course in Melanie Joan. I tried to picture her getting cuffed and fingerprinted, her makeup and jewelry thrown into plastic bags, along with her sunglasses, her red-bottoms. It felt like psychological torture. I hoped Rita could calm her down. "What about Charles?" I said.

"Both of their bail hearings are tomorrow morning. Rita thinks he has a much better chance than she does of getting released."

I had to agree. The charges against him weren't as serious. Plus, he wasn't famous enough to be made an example of.

"Rita said she wasn't sure she should be representing both of them, because Charles might want to turn on Melanie Joan and cop a plea."

"She obviously doesn't know Charles," I said. "I think he'd sooner do a fifty-year sentence than turn on Melanie Joan."

"Agreed," Spike said.

"Yeah, what is it about her?" Tony said.

"What is it about *us*?" Spike said.

I suggested we all meet at my apartment later tonight to share information. We set a time—nine p.m. This was turning out to be the longest workday of my life. Or at least the most eventful. I swallowed hard, remembering the convenience store parking lot again, Edward Piro's gun jammed into my neck.

"By the way, Sunny," Tony said. "I was able to get hold of Detective Gleason, and I let him know about that name you gave me."

"What did he say?"

"He told me that he'd look into it," he said. "But I think he was bullshitting me."

"Why?"

"Well, for one thing, he started talking about his screenplay," he said. "And for another, Melanie Joan was arrested an hour after we talked."

I exhaled. "So it's not just that he doesn't trust *me*."

"Nope. He's also a dick."

"It's just as well," I said, Piro's words in my head. *I'm watching. We're watching.*

"Why?" Tony asked.

"I feel like there are already too many dicks involved in this thing."

"Am I supposed to take that personally?" Tony said.

I laughed a little. "I didn't mean you."

After the call ended, I found myself thinking of that car again. Of Piro showing up at Mimi's house. And then at the convenience store. Both times, it had been between ten and twenty minutes after I'd arrived. And what had his purpose been, parking outside Mimi's so obviously, peeling away from the curb as soon as I ran out? Holding a gun to the back of my neck and releasing the safety, just so he could remove it? And then there was that repeated use of the word *we*.

We're everywhere . . . We know everything about you . . . We're watching.

Piro wanted to scare me off. He wanted to stop me from investigating Leila Donnelly's murder by making me feel hunted, surrounded.

It was a campaign. And it had started after I told Gleason about the Porsche convertible. Not that Gleason was involved.

Not necessarily. He was probably just someone who couldn't fathom being wrong about something. Not a great trait in a cop, but it didn't make him part of a criminal conspiracy. Did it?

I shook my head. Already, Piro was accomplishing what he'd set out to do, which was to make me paranoid and confused. I wasn't going to let him.

To my mind, the first thing that needed to be addressed was how Piro kept finding me. And as far as that went, I had a pretty good idea. I was on the turnpike now, the next service plaza three miles away, according to the sign I'd just passed. I glanced into the rearview mirror. Checked the whole area behind me for headlights that appeared to be driving a little too close. I didn't see anyone, but that didn't mean anything. I'd never seen him. Not until he wanted me to.

I saw the exit for the service plaza. I pulled off at the last possible minute, without using my blinker. There were a few cars in the lot, but no Porsche. I drove up to the pumps and filled up my tank. After I was done, I scanned the area one more time. Then I grabbed my phone and gun from my purse.

I clicked the phone's flashlight on and then I crouched down and checked the undercarriage of my car, the gun clasped in my right hand in case someone came up behind me. I saw nothing unusual, and so I checked the front and rear bumpers. Nothing. I tried the wheel wells next, one by one, running my fingertips around their circumference. It was nerve-racking. I had to act thoroughly, but I had to be fast. Finally, I found it, affixed to the left rear wheel well. A small, round tracker. *Knew it.*

I removed it quickly and dropped it in the trash can between the pumps. Then I slipped back into my car and got back on the turnpike. "Fuck you, Edward Piro," I said.

FORTY-SEVEN

By the time I got back to my loft, Tony and Spike were already there. Blake had let them in. They were sitting at my kitchen table with my assistant, who was toiling away on his laptop as Rosie slept at his feet.

"What's up?" I said.

Rosie jumped up and greeted me. I don't know that I was ever happier to see anybody.

"A lot's up," Blake said. "And it's literally just happened within the past ten minutes."

"Talk to me," I said. I reached into my purse and pulled out the homemade dog biscuit I'd bought at the convenience store. Rosie sat back on her haunches and put her paws up—a trick I hadn't seen her do in so long, I'd thought she'd grown out of it. I gave her the biscuit.

"Good girl," I said as she scurried over to the dog bed with her new treat. "Good girl."

"Blake found Edward Piro," Tony said.

It was the only thing he could have said that could have torn me away from my dog. "What?"

"Yo, spoiler alert," Blake said.

I looked at Blake. "You really found Piro?"

"Took, like, forever," he said. "I had to use that search engine we pay for. I hope that's okay."

"Of course it's okay," I said. "Who is he?"

"I mean . . . I didn't find out that much, yet. But it's something."

Spike said, "Does anybody want coffee? Or whiskey? Whiskey and coffee?" All of us took the third option, except for Blake, who, because of his dietary restrictions, could drink only water after eight p.m.

Spike went into the kitchen.

"You sure it's the same Edward Piro?" I asked.

"Yes," Blake said. "He's on Park Avenue. Same address. I got a phone number for him, too. A landline."

Spike returned from the kitchen with whiskey and coffees for himself, Tony, and me, as well as a glass of water, without ice, for Blake. He carried them like the food service professional he was, not spilling a drop. I was impressed. When I got mine, I took an enormous swallow. Whiskey and coffee was one of those things you didn't realize how much you needed until you had it.

"Does he have an arrest record?" I said.

"No," Blake said.

"That's surprising," I said.

"Why?" Spike said.

I explained to the three of them why I wanted information on him in the first place, starting with my first sighting of the Porsche—and how it had disappeared after the murder.

"I remember that car," Spike said. "When you and Melanie Joan were talking to Leila, I kept thinking about how out of place it was next to that house. What type of person Book Babe had to be to lavish all her money on that one showy car."

"Yeah, well, it wasn't hers," I said. "And once I was able to find out who the car was registered to, things took a turn . . ."

"Meaning?"

"Meaning somehow Piro learned that I'd found him out, put a tracker on my car, and started harassing me."

"God," Tony said. "And I thought my job was stressful."

"Did you see him?" Blake said.

"That's a tricky question."

"What do you mean?" Tony said.

"I saw him once in silhouette, and then a second time, he came up behind me and held a gun on me, but I never got a look at his face."

"Jesus," Spike said.

"I know," I said. "It's been quite a day."

"Okay, well, in that case, I don't think the guy who stalked you was Edward Piro from Park Avenue," Blake said.

"Why not?" I asked.

"Because Edward Piro from Park Avenue is ninety-two years old."

I stared at him. "Really?"

"Teddy Piro, on the other hand . . ."

"Wait, what? There's a Teddy *and* an Edward?"

"You gave me the name Teddy to look up after I'd found Edward." Blake tapped at the laptop. "I couldn't find much on him. Just a really shitty LinkedIn profile. But just now, I decided to look up both names together, and this came up." He turned the laptop to me. On the screen was an obituary in the archives of the Albany *Times Union* for Sergio Piro—a local banker who had died at the age of eighty-five in 1995. "That's Edward's dad," Blake said. "Look at the last paragraph."

I read it. **He is survived by his son, financier Edward Piro; former daughters-in-law Beatrice, Linda, and Rayanne; and grandchildren, Donna Withers (and husband, Troy), Samantha Smythe (and husband, Bradley), Danielle Piro (and husband, Brian Langford), and Edward "Teddy" Piro Jr.**

"Teddy is Edward's only son," I said. "And his youngest."

"Yeah," Blake said. "Probably spoiled. Classic bad apple."

"And what do we think his connection is to Leila Donnelly?" Tony said.

"Well, for one thing, Leila's mother told me that when Leila was in her early twenties, she moved out of her house and stayed with some rich friend of hers in New York that she met at a *Star Trek* convention," I said. "His name was Teddy."

"Aha," Tony said. "He's an incel. He was probably stalking Leila because she rejected him. Maybe he saw how famous she'd gotten and decided they belonged together."

"We probably shouldn't jump to conclusions," I said. "It could be a coincidence that the Trekkie's name was Teddy."

"That's right," Blake said. "We never assume."

"Is there a way to figure out if *Star Trek* Teddy is Teddy Piro?" Tony asked.

I thought about what Mimi had said about him. The burglary in the Hamptons. "Did you look for arrest records?" I asked Blake.

"I couldn't find any."

"You looked up Edward and Teddy both?" Spike said.

"Yep."

I nodded. "But juvenile records are sealed."

"Huh?"

"Can I borrow your laptop?"

"Sure."

I took the laptop from Blake and went to the website of *The Southampton Press*. I clicked on the archives. If Teddy Piro was around Leila Donnelly's age, he would have been seventeen in 2012, but I needed to account for the possibility that he was a few years older or younger than her. As Blake, Tony, and Spike discussed the best way to look for more info on Teddy, I searched the terms "burglary," "juvenile," and, just for the hell of it, "Piro."

Several articles popped up, most all of them with "Piro" missing. But when I got to the year 2010, I hit paydirt—a whole series of articles about a burglary that took place in July of that year, in which more than $35,000 in jewelry, cash, and electronics had been stolen:

> The seventeen-year-old suspect–whose name is being withheld due to his age–is the son of prominent financier Edward Piro, who maintains a summer home down the road from the burglarized residence.

"Maybe we should just contact Edward Piro and ask if his son knew Leila," Tony was saying.

"Parents don't always know everything about their kids," Blake said.

"And they don't always tell the truth, either," Spike said.

Tony conceded that it might not be a great idea to call Edward Piro, and they moved on to Melanie Joan's bail hearing, which was slated to take place the following morning.

"We should go. She needs supporters there," Spike said. "What do you think, Sunny?"

I couldn't respond. Couldn't open my mouth to speak. I'd just gotten to the final article in the series about the Piro robbery, in which several residents expressed dismay over the fact that the seventeen-year-old had gotten off with just probation. *It's all about privilege,* said one of these Southampton residents, who was no doubt extremely privileged. But that wasn't the part of the story that was making my heart pound. It was the final quote in the piece: *I think [the boy] has learned his lesson,* it read. *Money isn't everything. The Piros are good neighbors, and it's time we all moved on.* It had come from the owner of the burglarized home, famed publisher Gloria Scepter.

FORTY-EIGHT

At nine-forty-five p.m., Rita Fiore called. She told us that Melanie Joan had been fully processed and was now at the Hartford Correctional Facility, with the bail hearing to take place tomorrow at eleven a.m. Charles had already been released on his own recognizance. "She changed her mind about you guys coming to the hearing," Rita said. "She'd like to have Spike there. And maybe Tony."

"Not me?" I said.

"She wants you free so you can catch the real killer," Rita said. "Not that you should feel pressured or anything."

"Actually, Rita," I said, "I think I'm getting close." I told her everything that had happened since this morning, with Tony, Spike, and Blake filling in most of the details I forgot to mention. I still felt like we were leaving things out, but at least she got the gist. When I got to the part about a teenage Teddy Piro robbing the house of Melanie Joan's late publisher, she said, "No fucking way." And I replied, "Everything's connected. I just need to figure out *why*."

"If you can figure it out before jury selection, I'll buy you a bottle of scotch."

"Macallan 18?"

"Macallan 12."

"Good enough. I'm on it."

We decided that while Spike went to Melanie Joan's bail hearing, I would try to figure out the link between Teddy Piro, Leila Donnelly, and the Scepters—if there was one. Meanwhile, Tony would put some feelers out with the press, pitching a story about how sexism and ageism had fueled this rush to judgment and how certain members of the Connecticut State Police were unwilling to consider any other suspects besides Melanie Joan.

By the time we were done talking, I felt like we had something that may have felt like a plan.

"Sunny, can I ask you something?" Rita said, just before we ended the call.

"Sure." I braced myself.

"Would you be amenable to my hiring you sometime?"

My eyebrows went up. I wasn't sure what question I'd been expecting from Jesse Stone's girlfriend, but it hadn't been that one.

"I often need a PI," she said. "And you are really, really good."

"Thanks, Rita," I said. "Blake makes me look a lot better than I am."

Blake beamed at me.

"Duly noted," she said.

"I'd be honored if you hired me," I said. "But maybe not for Desmond's hit man."

"Alleged hit man," she said.

"Right," I said. "I can only handle so many conflicts of interest."

She laughed. "You got it," she said. We ended the call.

Blake forwarded all his information to my email address before closing his laptop and returning it to his satchel. Everybody started collecting their things and leaving my place, wishing one another luck tomorrow and talking about what a big day it was going to be.

The whole time, I kept thinking about how strange this case had been—how a one-star review had somehow resulted in Melanie Joan Hall getting arrested for murder, and in my becoming friends with both Rita Fiore and Tony Gault. *You wake up in the morning, and from that point on, there are no rules, no guarantees. You can't predict a damn thing that's going to happen to you.* I tried to remember who had said that to me. And then I did. Felix Burke. Desmond's brother. A murderer. My kindred spirit. Felix had been dead going on five years. I missed him every day.

Spike was the last to leave. On his way out, he stopped and turned to me. "What was that you told Rita about only being able to handle so many conflicts of interest?"

“I know,” I said. “I lied. I live for conflicts of interest.”

“Me, too. They’re like potato chips. You can never have just one.”

I laughed. We hugged goodbye. I hoped I’d never spend a single day in a world that didn’t have Spike in it.

Once I was alone, I stood in my apartment for a few moments, enjoying the silence and the safety, which, like everything else in life, were temporary and only relative. I walked back to the kitchen table and picked up my phone, clicked on my email icon. I looked at the information Blake had found and forwarded to me, thinking of all the paths that had crossed to get us to this point—Blake’s and mine, mine and Melanie Joan’s, Melanie Joan’s and Leila Donnelly’s, Leila Donnelly’s and Teddy Piro’s, Teddy Piro’s and Gloria Scepter’s. I glanced at the clock on my phone’s screen. Was ten p.m. too late to call a ninety-two-year-old man?

I went back to my home page. The top news story glared out at me: **“At this point, I don’t know what she’s capable of”: Melanie Joan Hall’s longtime editor reveals the “year from hell” that led to her unraveling.**

That answered the question. No, it was not too late. Nothing was too late when it came to Melanie Joan, because she was getting massacred so relentlessly, by people she’d thought were her friends. First I went to my contacts and blocked Evan Woodrow. Then I called Edward Piro’s landline.

FORTY-NINE

Edward Piro picked up after two rings. And while he cleared his throat extensively before saying hello, he sounded neither sleepy nor confused.

"Mr. Piro," I said as he continued to cough. "My name is Sunny Randall. I hope you don't mind my calling so late. I need to speak to you about your son."

He didn't reply right away. He coughed some more. A barking that faded to a wheeze. It hurt me just listening to it. "Are you okay?" I said.

"Sorry," he said. "Touch of bronchitis. Happens to me every summer. That damn pollen."

I exhaled. "Okay."

"What the hell did Teddy do now?"

"I'm hoping you might be able to give me some insight."

"Has he been driving my car again?"

"What?"

He said it again very loudly, as though we had a bad connection. *"My car. The black Porsche convertible. Has Teddy been driving it?"*

"Yes," I said. "He's been driving it."

He coughed some more. "I'm aware of the speeding tickets, ma'am. And the lapsed insurance. He was supposed to pay that. I put him in charge. Was he driving intoxicated again? Do I need to pick him up?"

I swallowed.

"Officer? You still there?"

"I'm . . . I'm not a police officer," I said. "I'm a private investigator. And I'm not calling about speeding tickets."

"Oh, thank God," he said. "You have no idea the gray hairs that kid has given me. The expense. The embarrassment. You'd think he'd cool his jets once he hit thirty, but no. Three years past the big three-oh, and he's worse than ever . . ." He started to cough again. I waited for it to subside. "I had him too late," Piro said. "You know his mother is the same age as my next youngest kid? I don't know what I was thinking. Rayanne and I were married just long enough to bring Edward Jr. into the world. Then she skipped town and left me, a man in my sixties, with a colicky, moody, pain-in-the-ass baby. I don't know how many nannies I went through with that kid. I should have quit the whole parenting business when I was ahead."

I wasn't sure what to say. I hadn't expected Mr. Piro to be awake, let alone this talkative. He had to be very lonely, I decided. I pressed on. "Sir, your son, Teddy, may have something to do with the murder of Leila Donnelly."

"Oh . . ."

"I don't know if you've seen anything about it in the news, but—"

"Yes," he said. "Yes, I've seen it."

"His car," I said. "*Your* car was seen at the crime scene at the time of the killing."

"It . . . It was?" he said. "Oh, God. Teddy wouldn't . . . But . . . I don't know him. Not the way a father should. He gets crazy sometimes."

"What do you mean by that?"

"I should have gotten help for him . . . A shrink. I didn't . . . It's my fault he's so messed up. I was a terrible father."

"Don't feel bad, Mr. Piro. Please."

"Did he kill her?"

"I don't know," I said. "He could have lent the car to someone. He could have been pressured into taking part in something he didn't want to do. I don't know Teddy. All I know is that a woman is dead, and my dear friend is in jail for this murder. I just want to help her clear her name. Okay?"

He didn't respond for a very long time. I waited, listening to his soft, persistent coughing. Hoping he would speak. "I . . . I have some papers. They might be helpful. Also some things that I found in the car this morning. I think they may have been Lee's."

"Leila," I said quietly. "That was her name."

"I know," he said. "But Teddy called her Lee."

My mouth dropped open.

"My son needs help. I'm too old to keep him under control. I don't know . . ." He started coughing again. "He may have to be locked up. For his own good. You know?"

"Can you help me, Mr. Piro?"

"I can send you the things I have."

"Can I come to your place tomorrow morning? I can pick them up. We can talk a bit if you're up to it. I just have a few questions."

He cleared his throat and launched into another coughing fit. I waited for it to subside. "Sure," he said. "Come tomorrow. I'll give the doorman your name."

FIFTY

Edward Piro had asked if I could get to his apartment by ten a.m. I'd said I could, even though it meant I had to leave Boston by six a.m. at the latest. After driving all over Connecticut the previous day, I couldn't imagine pressing an accelerator for four hours. So I'd asked Blake to drive me to New York. I'd promised him overtime. He'd said no to the overtime, but I insisted. *You're missing leg day,* I'd said. *It's the least I can do.*

So now the two of us were in my car, driving along Park Avenue at nine-forty-five. We'd made good time, despite my insistence on checking the entire car for trackers every time we left a rest stop, and Blake's lengthy search for a keto-friendly breakfast sandwich.

Until today, I'd never fully realized how much Blake's life revolved around food. It was like a religion with him, the whole keto thing. Right now, he was eating a venison sausage, which he'd informed me was "low in energy-draining carbs and high in essential nutrients," like a contestant on one of those survive-in-the-wild shows. I hadn't asked.

He'd bought the sausage at a rest stop farmers' market along the New England Thruway. As he drove, he was cutting off slices of venison with his pearl-handled pocketknife—an incredibly inappropriate gift from his lowlife father. "He gave it to me when I was, like, three," Blake was saying now. "If my sister hadn't taken it away from me and hid it till I turned fifteen, I probably would have cut my lips off."

"Jesus," I said.

"I know, right?" He sliced off two more slices of sausage, popped one into his mouth, and offered me the other. I took it. It wasn't half bad. Blake was steering the car with his knees, but I managed not to backseat-drive about it. Spike would have been shocked. "At least the knife comes in handy now," Blake said.

"How do you live with somebody like that?" I said. "Especially when you're small and vulnerable?" I was thinking about Teddy Piro's Porsche parked in Leila Donnelly's driveway, of the way Tommy had screamed when he'd seen that same Porsche outside his grandmother's house. *He kept repeating it. "Bad, bad, bad."*

"You must have been in a constant state of terror," I said.

"You want to know the truth?" Blake said. "I don't remember him at all."

"You don't?"

"Not from when I was little." Blake sliced off another hunk

of sausage and shoved it into his mouth. Then he put the rest back into the bag, dropped it on the backseat, and returned his hands to the steering wheel as he finished chewing. "It's funny," Blake said. "People always say little kids are resilient, but it's just that their brains aren't fully formed. They can't remember shit, which is a blessing."

I looked at him. "I bet you're right," I said.

"I'm pretty sure I am." Gently, he placed the knife on the dashboard. The sun glinted off the blade. "Resilient," he said. "That's just a word to make bad parents feel better."

Piro's apartment building was a creamy wedding cake of a prewar structure, on Park and 74th. "Nice," I said.

Blake nodded politely. I knew it wasn't his taste. He liked brand-new buildings—the kind with giant signs out front, advertising for customers. "I like to be the first person to live in a place," he'd once explained. Blake had a lot of peccadilloes, I was discovering. One of them was that he believed older buildings were unsanitary.

Blake dropped me off in front of Piro's building. He put the hazard lights on, jumped out of the car, and wished me luck. I thanked him. "I guess I'll explore the city while you're up there," he said.

"Don't explore too far," I said. "We can't stay here all day."

"I won't. Don't worry."

Just as he was about to open the car door, I got a call from Spike. I put him on speaker.

"Melanie Joan was denied bail," he said.

"What?" Blake said.

"Oh, no," I said.

Blake shook his head. "Crap."

"On the plus side, she's made some friends in prison. For instance, her cellmate thinks her Book Babe comment was iconic." I could hear the cringe in Spike's voice.

"We're getting her out of there," Blake said.

"We are," I said. "And Edward Piro Senior is going to help us."

"Good luck," Spike said. "It would be nice for a change."

We both thanked him. After we hung up, Blake threw open the car door and grabbed the pocketknife off the dashboard. He dropped it into my purse. I smiled at him. "What's that for?"

"Luck."

"The pocketknife your father gave you? Before he went to prison?"

"That's not the knife's fault."

"True." I told him I'd text him when I was done with Piro.

"Should we do, like, a code? So I know right away whether you've got answers or not?"

"Sure," I said. "If I've got answers, I'll say something literary."

"Cool," he said. "And if not?"

"I'll say something about food."

"Awesome," Blake said. "We should do codes more often."

"We should." As I watched him get back into my car and drive away, I hoped for something literary.

FIFTY-ONE

The lobby of Edward Piro's apartment building was all pink marble, including and most notably the doorman's station. It reminded me of a Greek palace, or a mausoleum, or a combination of the two.

The doorman was a slim, efficient-looking guy with close-cropped hair and wire-framed glasses. He wore a spotless navy-blue uniform with shiny gold buttons that looked better suited to winter. It might have been wool, though it could have been a heavy cotton. But either way, he was lucky the lobby was air-conditioned. I was wearing a featherlight Elie Saab T-shirt and a satin skirt, and I was still recovering from the two minutes I'd spent outside. I gave him my name, and he said Mr. Piro was expecting me. "Take the far elevator," he said. "Floor twelve."

I walked through the lobby, my heels tapping on the marble. I was the only one in the elevator, and so it took me straight up—an express trip.

When I reached the twelfth floor, the doors opened, and I was inside Piro's apartment. The living room, to be exact. It was very mid-century modern. Or maybe just mid-century. There was a long wooden coffee table in front of a watermelon-colored couch that didn't look very comfortable, matching chairs on either side. Wall-to-wall carpeting with a Frank Lloyd Wright–style pattern and a sleek credenza that housed a turntable, shelves of vinyl records, and, anachronistically, a flat-screen TV. There was another flat-screen against the left-facing wall—this one enormous, over a fully stocked wet bar with a tiki motif. If I didn't know who lived here, I'd figure Edward Piro for either an especially pretentious young hipster or a meticulous old man who never got around to redecorating. Either way, he liked watching TV.

To my right there were swinging doors that probably led to a kitchen. A few windows, looking out on Park Avenue. A long hallway that stretched out from the far end of the room. "Hello?" I said. "Mr. Piro?"

There was no answer. I heard coughing coming from somewhere down the hallway. I wasn't sure whether to follow the sound or wait. I spotted a manila folder on the coffee table, the name *Teddy* handwritten on the cover. Was that there to keep me busy while I waited, like a magazine in a doctor's office? I walked over to the table and opened the folder and saw a mug shot of Teddy Piro from when he was seventeen. Under that, there was a small article about the Hamptons burglary in the *New York Post*. I skimmed it. It didn't name him, but it did include a quote from his father: *As a family, we are devastated. We'd appreciate being left alone at this difficult time.* Next was a stack of high school report cards, bound by a rubber band. I flipped through them. They were riddled with D's and F's, with a few C's thrown in, in classes like woodworking and fire safety. I also saw a letter from the dean of a boarding school. At the top, it said: *RE: The expulsion of Edward Piro Jr.* I kept flipping through the pile—another mug shot, from when Teddy was a few years past high school, a full rap sheet that included arrests for DWI, reckless driving, operating a boat without a license, and assault. It was like a scrapbook of bad behavior. A typewritten note from Edward to his son that had been dated last year, detailing how deeply he'd disappointed him. It almost made me feel bad for Teddy Piro—having a father who kept a folder like this.

"Mr. Piro!" I called out.

There was more coughing.

"Are you okay?" I stood up and moved toward the hallway, following the sound.

"Mr. Piro?" I said again.

No response. I walked past an empty bathroom, a guest bedroom. Framed pictures adorned the walls—Edward Piro Sr. and his children, his wives. Mr. Piro was slim and straight-backed, with thick silver hair and a tight smile. His wives and daughters all looked like they belonged in shampoo commercials. I saw a few of a chubby young boy with a grim face. He stood out in this picture-perfect, smiley family. I assumed he was Teddy. He had the same build as the man I'd seen parked outside Mimi Donnelly's, and in most of the pictures, he looked miserable. There was one, though, that stood out. I stopped in front of it. It was of the same boy, but as a teenager. And he was actually smiling. He wore a red *Star Trek* uniform, and he was standing next to another, skinnier boy who wore the same uniform, in blue. They were at a convention, posing like their favorite characters, plastic phasers aimed at the camera. The skinnier boy looked sort of familiar, but I couldn't quite place him.

Then I noticed the last picture. It wasn't framed. It was printed out on computer paper and taped to a closed door at the end of the hall. Teddy looked to be in his twenties. He and that same, skinny friend flanked a girl in a halter top and jeans. She had dark hair and frightened eyes. I stared at the tattoo on her arm—that pink-and-white flower. I swallowed hard. The girl was Leila Donnelly. The skinny friend, as I now saw, was Greg Scepter. I knocked on the door. "Mr. Piro? Are you in there?"

There was no answer. I slipped one hand into my purse. I felt Blake's knife before I found my gun, so I dropped it into the pocket of my satin skirt, just to get it out of the way. Then I returned my hand to my bag and found my gun. It was so quiet in this hallway, as though someone had drained all the energy out of the place, all the air.

I placed my other hand on the doorknob and turned it slowly.

I didn't hear the sound until I'd pushed open the door. It showed how thick these walls were, because once I was in the room, it filled my ears: The beeping of monitors. The sucking sound of a ventilator. The lights were dimmed, the shades drawn. It took a few moments for my eyes to adjust enough to see the man on the hospital bed. A frail, silver-haired man on life support, his chest rising and falling again and again, that unnatural rhythm, as though someone was blowing him up and deflating him. "Mr. Piro," I said quietly.

I heard movement behind me. My pulse sped up, but I stayed calm on the outside. In control. *You're not freezing this time.* I grabbed my gun out of my purse with two steady hands and spun around, holding it in front of me.

A man filled the doorway. He was at least a foot taller than me, broad-shouldered and big-boned. His face was the same as in all the pictures. "Teddy," I said. In one meaty hand, he held a gun of his own.

"I see you've met my dad," Teddy Piro said.

It was the same voice I'd heard on the phone last night, when I thought I'd been talking to Edward.

FIFTY-TWO

Drop your gun," I said.

Teddy Piro stared at me, his lips pursed, his cheeks flushed. He looked like an angry Botticelli cupid.

I held my own gun straight out in front of me. "Drop it," I said again.

Piro's cupid mouth twitched into a smile. I hated him. I'd always hated people who smiled when nothing was funny.

"Lower your fucking gun," I said.

He lowered his gun. Then he fired it. The bullet grazed my thigh. My flesh seared. Tears sprung into my eyes. I glanced down. Blood bloomed on my leg. My white satin skirt was thick with it, the knife dragging at my pocket. I gritted my teeth and fired my own gun. But my aim wasn't good. I was in too much pain. My knee buckled and I fell to the ground, my .38 dropping from my hand.

"That's a good girl," Teddy Piro said. His eyes were tiny and pale blue, like two chips of ice. He knelt down and picked me up, kicking my gun across the floor. He brought me to another room and kicked open the door, carrying me over the threshold. I bit his arm. He didn't even flinch. He was solid. It made me think of Leila Donnelly, who was smaller than me and probably weaker physically. It made me think of her little son, Tommy.

"I told you to mind your business," he said. "But you wouldn't listen. You wanted to know what happened. You . . . You called my dad. What the fuck is wrong with you?"

He dropped me onto a hard chair and turned around for a moment, the gun shoved into the belt of his jeans. I glanced around. It was a small guest room with two neatly made twin beds. The chair where he'd dumped me was part of an old-fashioned desk set. The desk was tall and narrow, with shelves stacked with *Star Trek* figurines. He turned around for a moment and opened the desk drawer. My wounded leg shrieked, but I managed to slip my hand into the pocket of my bloody satin skirt. "You killed Leila Donnelly," I said. "Why?"

He didn't answer.

"Why?" I said again as I palmed Blake's knife.

"I'm not here to answer your fucking questions."

I struggled to my feet, my leg throbbing. I was dizzy, my vision clouded. I braced myself and stood up just as he turned around, a stack of zip-ties in his hand.

Oh, no you don't.

I thought of Natalie Blythe's yogic breathing. *In on ten, out on ten . . .* I tried it as he lunged at me, heavy hands on my shoulders. *In on ten . . .* It didn't help. I was still in pain. But at least it gave me something to think about besides the blood pouring out of me, the way my brain was swimming. He pushed. I resisted. "Sit the fuck down," he said. "Or I'll have to shoot you again." I kicked the chair away. He stumbled. He went for his gun. I slammed myself into the desk and pushed the figurines off the shelves. Grabbed one of them in my bloody hands. It was an old one. Spock. Probably rare. At any rate, it was made of something breakable. "Give it back!" he yelled. I threw it across the room and heard it smash to bits.

For the briefest of moments, Teddy Piro was suspended. Torn. *Shoot me again or check the status of his precious figurines.* I could feel it. I took advantage.

I plunged Blake's knife into Teddy's gut. He roared at me. The gun dropped to the floor. As I knelt down and grabbed it, I saw spots in front of my eyes. *Keep going.* I pushed the door open and fell into the hall, the gun slick in my hand.

I heard something. It was coming from the living room—a male voice shouting, "Hello!"

"Help!" I shrieked, with Teddy behind me, his footsteps on the carpeted floors.

"Hello?" said the male voice again. "Where are you? What's going on?"

The voice was muffled. It could have been a neighbor. The

doorman. The police. Blake. *Please, please . . .* "Help!" I shrieked again. "Help me!"

Teddy grew closer. The gun was heavy in my hand, my head light. I shot at him and missed. Shot again and connected. He grasped his shoulder but kept moving. He was indestructible, like a tank. He was moving faster now, his shoulder bleeding, the knife sticking out of his side a minor hindrance. A trifle.

I shot at him again. The gun clicked. *Seriously?* I pulled the trigger again. Clicked. Pulled the trigger. Clicked. "Unbelievable," I whispered. Was it confidence that had made Teddy Piro come at me with an almost-empty chamber? Or stupidity? I was leaning toward the latter. I'd seen his report cards.

I made my way to the end of the hall with Piro close behind, twinkling dots of light all around me, a ringing in my ears like chimes. Church chimes. He must have hit an artery or something. I was starting to get delirious.

"Help." I said it again in a faint, small voice as I made it into the living room. Blackness flooded my field of vision. I fell to the carpeted floor, at the feet of the man in Piro's apartment. Not a cop. Not Blake. For a second, I thought I might be hallucinating, but I was not. It was Greg Scepter. "What the actual fuck, Teddy?" he said.

Scepter was still talking as the room went black.

FIFTY-THREE

The first thing I was aware of was the stiffness in my leg. The next was Teddy Piro's voice, muffled and insistent. ". . . sick of being the only one getting my hands dirty," he was saying. "It's your turn, asshole."

Scepter's voice countered: "I didn't ask for what you did."

"Oh, fuck you, buddy. I helped you. Now it's your . . ."

My eyelids fluttered open. I was on a metal folding chair in a bright room with no windows, my hands zip-tied behind my back. I was still wearing my bloody skirt, but the blood had dried—a huge, rust-colored stain. I looked closer at my leg. The tightness around my thigh. My wound had been bandaged. I was alone, Scepter and Piro arguing just outside the door. What did they want from me? Why hadn't they killed me? What was going on?

"I am so unbelievably sick of you," Scepter was saying. "Twenty-five years. We're like your dad in the other room. We just keep going, Teddy. It's time to pull the plug."

"I'm sick of you, too," said Piro.

"Then why do you keep calling me?"

"Why do you keep coming?"

"You're ruining everything. Do you not fucking get it? Are you stupider than you look? Is that even possible? *People are going to come looking for her.*"

There were metal shelves in this room. Blinking lights. My eyes adjusted. The blinking was coming from computers. Laptops. Dozens of them lined the shelves, their screens alive with activity.

"That's why you've got to do it," Piro said.

"Jesus Christ, Teddy."

The computers were all active, text scrolling on their screens. At the top of each screen was an embossed label. From where I was sitting, I couldn't read the text, but I could read the labels. They were all different names. ROBERTA ADAMS, one said. GRAHAM WILSON, said another. One of the others read LEILA DONNELLY.

I scooched my chair closer. I still couldn't make out Leila Donnelly's text. Graham Wilson's was legible, though. It looked like an action scene, being written in hyperdrive.

. . . knew I'd never come back to Logan County unarmed . . . the screen read. Two seconds and probably fifty paragraphs later, I saw the words *THE END.*

What was this room? What was going on?

Scepter and Piro were still arguing, but they'd moved. I could hear them clearly now. They were just outside the door.

"I took the fall for the burglary. My dad never forgave me for that. You robbed from your mom and I took the fall."

"Dude, let it go. We split the fuckin' money. And we were seventeen!"

"Okay, well, what about Lee, then? I didn't want to kill her."

"I didn't ask you to."

"She was going to tell. She was going to the press. Your whole life. Everything you've worked for. Your dream would have been destroyed—"

"You honestly think I *wanted* you to do that, Teddy?"

"Of course you did, choad. You told the press you've got three more of her books. But the truth is, AI could write a hundred of them, and the bots could go nuts for them all. You could say you discovered a secret cache of Leila Donnelly content and you wouldn't have to worry about the real Lee getting all squeamish about it."

"Teddy," Scepter said. "She was the mother of my child!"

I actually gasped.

"Go fuck yourself," Teddy Piro said.

"She *was*."

"No more talking, Greg. Do it, and we'll be even. Clean slate. I'll help you with the body."

The door opened. Greg Scepter stumbled into the room, and then the door slammed shut behind him. He was wearing a white linen suit with a white T-shirt underneath, blood spatter across the front. He had on the same chunky necklace he'd worn for the press conference. It was even cheesier in person. And he was carrying my gun. "I'm sorry about this, but Teddy's such a dickhead," Scepter said. "He won't let me out of here until I kill you."

FIFTY-FOUR

You don't want to do this," I said.

"You're right. I don't." Greg Scepter said it loudly, as though he wanted Teddy to hear. "But my friend out there is insane. There's no reasoning with him."

I yanked at the zip-ties. They bit into my wrists. I closed my eyes. Made myself think. "You're not a killer. I can tell."

"I know I'm not. But as you can see, I'm in a tough situation."

I took a breath. Let it out slowly. "Did your mom ever meet Tommy?" I asked.

"What?" he said.

"Gloria died two years ago. Did she know that she was a grandmother?"

He shook his head.

"That's sad, don't you think?"

"Sort of," he said. "You know, I've only seen the boy once myself. I went to Lee's house so she could sign the contract and there he was. He didn't know me. He hid from me."

"How about making things right?" I said. "For Tommy and for your mom? And for Leila."

Greg crouched down beside me and gazed at my face. His eyes were cold and beady, but I saw something behind them. The hint of tears. "I offered her a nice buyout," he said quietly. "This never had to happen."

"Leila?"

He shook his head. "Melanie Joan."

"Oh . . ."

"I knew my mom loved her, but the fact was, she was a money drain. Never made back her advances. Didn't even come close."

"Isn't that true of most bestselling authors?"

"Yeah, but that doesn't make it any less of a shit business model," he said. "And that memoir . . ."

"What about it?"

"It was going to tank even worse than her romances. I wanted a much smaller print run, but Tony Gault and my mother had it engraved into her contract. No print run smaller than five hundred K. It was ridiculous. She was about to bankrupt my company."

"She put your company on the map," I said.

"That's ancient history."

"She still has tons of fans."

"Yeah, right," he said. "Anyway, I offered her a sweet buyout, but her ego was too big." He moved closer to me. Put a hand on my shoulder. "Don't you see?"

"Don't I see what?"

He sighed. "I didn't have any other choice but to post that review."

I stared at him for a very long time. My eyes felt dry and itchy. I realized it was because I hadn't blinked. "Leila Donnelly wasn't Book Babe," I said. "You were."

Greg shook his head. "Book Babe is AI."

"Wait. What?"

"It's a program I invented back in college," he said, "and it's the future of book marketing. My mom wanted nothing to do with it. She never understood algorithms and she was wrong, wrong, wrong. You should see what a five-star Book Babe review can do for sales. And the engagement is off the charts. It now has more real followers than bots."

I knew it was a mistake to keep asking Greg questions. The fact that he was answering me so honestly gave him all the more reason to kill me. But I couldn't help it. I needed to know. "How did Leila fit in?"

"She was Teddy's friend. He met her at a convention. She wanted to be a novelist, but she couldn't write for shit, and so we used my technology to make her dream come true. To make *our* dream come true. It was an experiment, and it worked. She was almost a partner. Until, you know . . . she wasn't."

I looked around the room. "These laptops."

"My stable of authors."

"Jesus . . ."

"They're here for now, but I can move them anywhere," he said.

"This isn't right."

"Why isn't it?" he said. "They don't go on tours and make you pay for them. They don't demand huge advances. They write bestsellers in five minutes. They don't ask for extensions or bigger cuts of the royalties. They don't have skeletons buried in their closets that can get them canceled at the most inopportune moment. Hell, they don't even have closets."

"They don't have souls."

"With all due respect, Sunny. Who the fuck cares?"

"People care. People want to connect with other people. It's why they go to book signings."

He shrugged. "Deepfakes are so easy to make now. My authors can talk to readers over Zoom, do virtual chats with book clubs—nobody will know the difference."

"Smart readers will know."

"Oh, really? You seem pretty smart, Sunny. And I bet you thought Leila Donnelly's video was real."

I stared at him, speechless. I honestly couldn't say a word.

"Anyway, Melanie Joan should have known when to quit." He knelt down behind me. "Teddy should have known when to quit, too."

I heard a click and a gunshot. It rang in my ears. I held my breath. I wasn't hit. It dawned on me that Greg Scepter hadn't intended to shoot me. I could feel him loosening the zip-ties on my wrists, his hands wrapped around mine, the familiar weight of my own gun in my palm.

"You done?" Teddy said from outside the door.

"Yep!" Greg called out.

The door opened and Greg yanked my right arm so that it was straight in front of me, the gun in my hand. He squeezed it. Pressed his fingers over mine to pull the trigger. It was my gun. My .38. I heard the explosion of it, felt the familiar kickback. Teddy Piro fell to the ground, a red stain spreading quickly through the front of his shirt.

"There we go," Greg said. With my gun in his hand, he moved over to Teddy and listened to his chest. "Gone," he said. "You're a good shot, Sunny."

He didn't have to say it. I knew what he thought was going to happen. Teddy's gun was on the floor outside the open door. Greg set my gun down in order to pick it up. And then he put it in Teddy's lifeless hand and aimed it at me. "I'm sorry it has to end this way," he said.

"And I'm sorry your friend can't properly load a gun."

I pushed up from the chair as he pulled the trigger, the empty chamber clicking. He pulled it again and I rushed at him, making him lose his balance. He reached for my .38. I grabbed it before he did—and shot Graham Wilson. The laptop screen exploded.

"No!" Greg shouted.

I shot Roberta Adams, Maddy Price, Ashley Delacroix, Leila Donnelly. Keyboards shattered. Computer innards turned to smoke. The air stank of melted plastic. Greg lurched toward me. "I'm going to kill you!" he screamed. I shot him in the foot. He writhed on the floor. “You ruined them! You ruined everything!”

He started to cry. I watched Greg Scepter, moaning and sobbing beside the body of the friend he’d just killed. Weeping his heart out over a bunch of dead laptops. I’d never known his mother, but I was sure she’d have been ashamed.

I shot Lindsey St. James and Peter Salsbury and every other soulless, bloodless electronic author until there were no more of them to shoot. And then I limped into the other room, past their bleeding, sobbing creator, and called 911.

While I was waiting for the police and paramedics, I remembered that I needed to text Blake. “Something literary,” I said to myself. “What’s something literary?”

The End, I typed. It was a no-brainer.

EPILOGUE

Two months later

It wasn't the water pill. It wasn't the booze. It wasn't the mixture of those two elements, either, that made Melanie Joan post that horrifying comment on Book Babe's review, because, as it turned out, she'd never posted it. Like every other terrible thing that had happened to her back in July, the comment that had gotten her into so much hot water had been Greg Scepter's doing.

But at least he let her know.

After copping a plea deal (twenty-five years in prison, no

parole), Scepter took out a full-page ad in *The New York Times*—an apology to Melanie Joan Hall that he claimed to be writing in memory of his mother:

> Ms. Hall posted a few juvenile insults that might have offended some. But I used my program to take them into the stratosphere. I asked my AI, "What are the worst things one woman can say to another?" and it obliged. I added those hateful words to a screenshot of her original comment and spread it all over the Web. For that I am truly sorry.

The apology ad had come out in this morning's *Times*, and Melanie Joan had happily devoured every single word. Right now, she was doing a dramatic reading of it at my kitchen table in front of Spike and Flynn, Richie and myself, Blake and Rosie—a sort of impromptu dinner party we'd thrown to celebrate Scepter's sentencing.

The timing couldn't have been better, the sentencing having taken place today, a Monday. Richie was in Boston Mondays and Tuesdays all summer and fall, and on this particular Monday, Melanie Joan was in town to promote *Stronger Alone.* Though the book wouldn't be out for another six months, her new publisher was sending her on an extensive publicity tour to promote her backlist, rev up interest in the memoir, and spark preorders. She'd be at the Harvard Coop tomorrow night. She'd turned down multiple requests from *Good Morning Boston*—including one that came with two dozen red roses from Sam Sharpe. *Thank God you dumped him,* Melanie Joan had told Spike during our monthly Zoom cocktail hour, before theatrically tossing the roses into the garbage.

She kept reading. "'I know now that Melanie Joan Hall is one of the greats,'" she said, her voice a pretty good approximation of Greg's. "'And I intend to spend many years reading her books and escaping into the glorious worlds she has created.'" She put the newspaper down. "I am satisfied with that piece of writing," she said. "I can only hope it wasn't created by AI."

"I don't know. 'Escaping' may not be the best choice of words," Spike said.

"Good point," Melanie Joan said.

"Speaking of good points," I said. "Remember that not-so-good one you made in July, about how the world has changed and readers want different things and so it might be time to retire?"

Melanie Joan sighed. "Sunny Randall, who can never resist an I-told-you-so."

"Guilty as charged. But that's not what I'm saying."

"What *are* you saying?" Richie said.

I thought about everything that had happened within the past two months—from Melanie Joan's massive comeback, to Specter Books' fall from grace, to Mimi Donnelly's formal adoption of her grandson, Tommy, to the decision of Edward Piro's three surviving children to take him off life support, give him a proper burial, and execute his will (from which his only son had been notoriously absent) as he had wished. "I guess I'm saying that not everything has to change," I said. "Some things have evolved to the point where they shouldn't be messed with. At least . . . not for a while."

"Books, for instance," Melanie Joan said.

"Food," Flynn said. "I mean, this beef stroganoff you cooked . . ."

My face flushed. Beef stroganoff was one of three dishes I could make adequately—a truth that had existed for my entire adult life. "It's very old-fashioned, I know," I said.

"But, Sunny," Flynn said, "it's *good*."

I looked at Richie, who had served the beef stroganoff to everyone and poured the wine and greeted our guests, and who would later be alone with me, enjoying our time together after five days apart. "Are *we* good?" I said quietly.

He took my hand in his. "We are," he said.

Flynn stood up and raised his glass. "To good friends, good food, good reading," he said, "and to all those other things that don't need to change in order to thrive."

I smiled and clinked glasses with everyone, my throat catching a little as I swallowed my wine.

I had to say, it was the best toast I'd ever heard.

ACKNOWLEDGMENTS

Much thanks to my wonderful agent, Deborah Schneider, and to everyone at Penguin Random House—especially this book's editor, Tom Colgan, for his patience, positivity, and insight. I am also grateful to Esther Newberg and to the estate of Robert B. Parker for allowing me the enormous privilege of spending time with Sunny and her friends.